Am I the Killer?

Am I the Killer?

A Luca Mystery Book 1

Dan Petrosini

ISBN: 978-1-515004622

Other Books by Dan

Luca Mystery Series

Am I the Killer—Book 1

Vanished—Book 2

The Serenity Murder—Book 3

Third Chances—Book 4

A Cold, Hard Case—Book 5

Cop or Killer?—Book 6

Silencing Salter—Book 7

A Killer Missteps—Book 8

Uncertain Stakes—Book 9

The Grandpa Killer—Book 10

Dangerous Revenge—Book 11

Where Are They—Book 12

Burried at the Lake—Book 13

Suspenseful Secrets

Cory's Dilemma—Book 1

Cory's Flight—Book 2\

Cory's Shift—Book 3

Other works by Dan Petrosini

The Final Enemy

Complicit Witness

Push Back

Ambition Cliff

Acknowledgments

Special thanks to Julie, Stephanie and Jennifer for their love and support, and thanks to Squad Sergeant Craig Perrilli for his counsel on the real world of law enforcement. He helps me keep it real.

Preface

I'd been charged with murder. The cops say I beat someone I knew to death. I absolutely didn't like the guy. Fact is, I hated him. We had a history, and none of it was good. But did I really kill him? Sure, I fantasized about him being dead and had dreams, many of them vivid, of me knocking off the bastard. I mean, after all the crap he did to me, who could fault me for feeling that way? On the other hand, I'm really a good guy and just can't believe I could beat someone to death, no matter what they did. It's just not who I am.

So, did I do it? It's a simple question you'd think I'd know the answer to. The problem is, I've got memory issues from a head injury I got serving in Afghanistan. It's really frustrating. For me, trying to remember something is tough. Sometimes there's just nothing there.

I don't know why, but my life's been a struggle, even though I've always tried to do the right thing. People say doing the right thing makes life easier. But with me, I'm still waiting for the payoff.

Growing up, I was a good kid, never complaining, even when my brother, Vinny, mistreated me. Then, I stood by Mom, taking care of her when she got sick after my father and brother took off. Shit, I even enlisted in the Marines, where I got dicked around by the government, and where'd all this get me? Right frigging here, accused of murder.

Most people think I can't remember the events that led to the murder charge, but others, including the prosecutors, believe I won't say what happened to save my tail. That I'm faking it.

I do what needs to be done. But . . . you know what? Jeez, I forgot what the point was.

Anyway, maybe you can sort things out. I sure can't, or is it I won't?

My name's Peter. It's one of the only things I'm definitely sure of these days. So, here's my story—parts of which, I'm sure are true:

Day of Arrest

Fumbling, I reached to shut off the blaring alarm clock. I succeeded, cutting the noise down to a constant ringing in my ears and popped out of bed. Ugh, moving too fast brought on a wave of disorientation that made me slow down. I sat on the edge of the bed, and before rising swallowed a mouthful of queasiness.

Rubbing my ears, I lurched into the bathroom to take a leak. It was one of the few things I didn't need a reminder of. As the toilet funneled, I snatched a sticky note off the mirror and stared at myself for who knows how long.

Raking my blondish hair over my protruding ears, I fingered the end of a series of scars that ran to the center of my head. Struck by how tired I looked, I pulled my shoulders back, opened my brown eyes wider, and ran a hand over my stubble. *Yeah, some coffee and a shave oughta help.* I checked the date on the note and popped open the pill organizer.

Gulping down two handfuls of meds, I headed for the stairs. Then I realized—I had no pants on. Tugging on a pair of jeans, I went down to the kitchen.

As the coffee brewed, I sucked down a glass of a concoction the doctor had ordered to combat the tinnitus. It tasted like shit, but it dimmed the ringing.

The sun glinted through the window, and I crept closer to look into what had become my sanctuary. With the rose bushes in full bloom, the tomato and pepper plants heavy with fruit, and the annuals spraying a rainbow of colors, a calmness descended on me. It was all me, I did it myself, and it felt good—a respite from my madness.

As the coffee finished its cycle, I wondered if I'd watered the garden yesterday—or even the day before that. I tried retracing yesterday's steps. The coffee signaled its readiness, and I poured a mug.

I began reading through the notes my brother, Vinny, left. Oh yeah, got to do those brain exercises. Did I do them yesterday? They say it helps, but I don't know about that. I put the mug to my lips. It was empty. I poured another mugful.

The faint sounds of car doors slamming came just before the doorbell rang and pounding on the door started. I rushed to suck a sip but spilled most of it on my shirt. Pissed, I scurried to the door.

Eyeing a couple of police cars through the window turned me into concrete. What should I do? Should I call Vinny? I turned to the kitchen, then back to the door as the metallic taste in my mouth swelled. A policeman tapping on the window forced me to the door.

Opening it revealed a small army of cops. A ruddy-faced officer stepped forward, "Peter Hill?"

I nodded as he checked my face against a photo.

"You're under arrest for the murder of William Wyatt."

"What? What?" I leaned into the doorframe.

The officer pulled out a pair of cuffs.

"Macquire, read him his rights."

A cop stepped forward and flipped open a fold of paper. "You have the right to remain silent…" As he droned on, I zoned out.

"Hey! Do you understand?"

I mumbled a yes, fixated on how much he sounded like the cops on TV.

Red-face grabbed my wrist and slapped a cuff on. Then he swung me around and cuffed my arms behind my back.

My mind drifted to the scene at the PX in Kabul. A fight had broken out, and the MPs rushed in, cuffing one of the drunken instigators. What was that guy's name? Chris? Kent?

I tried to remember the name as they marched me down the walk. The house across the street had its sprinklers on, and suddenly I was overwhelmed with doubt—had I watered my plants anytime this week?

Chapter 1

Bagram, Afghanistan, two years before Peter's arrest.

Opening the door, the warm air seemed sweeter. I inhaled deeply, attempting to quell my nervousness. Stepping out of the hangar, I walked around for a last look at hell.

It was weird being outside without a helmet, vest, and equipment. Even though dawn had just broke, perspiration began to sprout from my pores. I liked it hot, but man, this place was a frigging oven.

A stark stretch of dirt and sand ran for ten miles of nothingness until smacking into a wall of mountains. My eyes skimmed the brown peaks. I focused on a niche that formed a plateau, bringing back a brutal, screaming firefight. I shook the memory of the carnage from my head, cursing the loss of two buddies. My shirt was sticking to my back. I headed back in, saluting a major who was smoking.

"Heading home, soldier?"

"Yes, sir."

I wanted to say it was about fucking time, but after having my tour forcibly extended once, I wasn't taking any chances. We all knew the Marines could pull that shit. It had the power. The government bureaucrats do what they want, when they want, don't they?

Stepping back inside, I was feeling lucky to make it out in one piece, but also unsettled at the thought of leaving my platoon behind. Tony Burato was the only buddy making it out with me.

Tony's eyes flashed open as I approached. He fist bumped me as I sat, then went back to sleep. I ran my hand over my head. The blond hair was starting to grow out. *Thank God*, I thought.

Crew cuts, uniforms, routine—it was all part of the effort to force us into a unit, a "we" rather than a "me" mentality. I remember thinking it was bullshit, but midway through my first tour we really were looking out for each other. We'd become one, no two ways about it. We were closer than blood brothers.

When pint-sized Jimmy got blown to bits by an IED, I'd known him for two months, max. But losing him hurt like hell. I didn't give a crap what people thought when I cried like for days. The head doctors claimed the reaction was my fear of it being me next, and maybe that was part of it. But shit, he was just a little kid from Nebraska. Poor Jimmy: his grieving family—the void—the loss. I started to descend but forced myself out of the chair to shake the blues and take a piss.

Washing up, I stared in the mirror. I'd lost fifteen pounds but was rock-solid and in better shape than when I played high school football. Probably faster as well, I grinned. My brown, almond-shaped eyes had lost the sparkle that Mom used to say they had. I looked tired, but smiled at the thought of sleeping in a real bed, in my room, alone. Well, maybe not alone—I just couldn't wait to see Mary. I hadn't seen her in over a year. Last time home she'd been away with her girlfriends. Anyway, soon we'd be reunited.

Missing her more than I thought possible, I'd spent countless nights tucked in my sleeping bag thinking. Was I really missing her? Or was being out in a cold Afghan night the reason she was appealing? A month of mental tug-of-war led to the conclusion that the ache for her. Mary was the one for me, and about two months ago, I decided I was gonna propose to her if I got out alive.

I smiled. Yeah, things were going to change for the better. We'd get married and fix up the house a bit. I'd finally clear out my mom's things and move into the master bedroom with my bride.

Another thing I vowed to do was to make sure I'd see my brother, Vinny, as often as possible. I mean, he was the only family I had left. He was coming up to see me two weeks after I got back to Jersey. I'd wanted him to come sooner, but he—a loudspeaker barked preboarding instructions, and I hustled out of the bathroom thinking, *shit, I would even be nice to Billy when I got back.*

The fifty or so passengers were gathering their belongings as I trotted over to Tony.

"Get up, man."

"What's the hurry?"

"It won't feel real till I'm in the damn air. Nah, check that, till I'm on the ground in the States."

Tony stood. "Don't worry, bro, you're going home this time."

I slung my duffel bag over my shoulder and grabbed my knapsack. "I'm getting a move on."

Waiting at the head of a forming line, I tried to will the green C-17, to open its door for a waiting stairway. The door cracked open, and I ran out, welcomed by the deafening thunder of my ride home.

Adjusting my duffel bag, I caught a glimpse of a shining, black mass before it slammed into me, catapulting me skyward and into darkness.

***

The pressure in my head was building as I slipped in and out of consciousness. Pain blurred my vision and muffled voices.

Attempting a scream, I blacked out and came to when something was shoved down my throat. A high-pitched whine, reminding me of my father's drill, sounded.

Flipping between blackness and an enormous pressure in my skull, I felt like I was being carried. Struggling to see, shadows moving in and out of a white light were all I could make out.

What were they saying? Where the hell was I? Was I underwater? Yeah, that was it. The pressure and muffled voices made sense now. I tried to get to the surface, but was stuck to the bottom.

A voice of an angel whispered, "Peter, Peter."

Oh no, shit, I'm drowning! I'm gonna die, Mom! Mom, help me. The angel floated over. Her face was beautiful. She looked just like Mom. I reached out to her.

"It's going to be okay. Please, just go back to sleep." A drilling sound resonated, drowning out my angel. I descended to the bottom of a dark lake.

***

Dr. Mancino, the triage head at Bagram Airfield, hustled in and changed his sweat-soaked scrub suit.

On his way to the sink, he barked, "Get a diuretic line going! We've got to control the swelling. Make sure you keep an eye on his blood pressure."

Mancino wanted to prevent the swelling brain from furthering the damage. He pulled his face shield down. Hunched over Peter's shaven skull, Mancino drew a series of black circles.

"All right, let's get going." He took a drill from a nurse, kicked it into high gear, and put it to Peter's head. Skin flicked away, and blood began flowing.

"Sponge, clean the wound."

The drill sound deepened as it bore into the skull. Bone, skin, and blood sprayed as he leaned in. "Sponge it, dammit! I need to see where the hell we are."

He applied the drill, and as it broke through, a rush of cerebral fluid shot up, offering relief to the pressure on Peter's brain.

"Grab a sample of the fluid. Run labs on it."

Dr. Mancino bored openings in other spots, allowing fluids an escape route. The surgeon inserted drains before checking Peter's abdomen and right leg.

"X-ray the ab and leg. I want to be sure nothing's going on in the midsection. Then, get a splint on the leg. We'll worry about it later." The doctor shook his head. "We have to get him to Landstuhl. Stabilize him, and get him on the next flight out."

As Dr. Mancino stepped outside, he was met by Tony.

"Doc, how's my buddy doing?"

Dr. Mancino brushed by the soldier.

"Petey, um, Peter Hill. We're in the same platoon. How's he doing?"

"He's suffered a traumatic brain injury. He's out on the next flight to Ramstein. He's gonna need surgery to repair the skull fracture and a thorough going-over."

"Going-over?"

"An extensive assessment of the brain injury. We're limited here, but Landstuhl has it all. They'll decide the best course of action."

Six hours after his skull was pierced, in a drug-induced coma, Peter was rolled onto a dull-gray C-5 for the flight to Germany. His buddy Tony, who refused to board his original flight, took one of the seats lining the wall.

***

Seven hours later, the plane touched down at Ramstein Air Base. Dawn's light streamed into the cavity as a procession of gurneys were hurried down the ramp onto a special bus. Lights ablaze, the bus lurched forward for the ten-minute drive to the hospital.

Duffel bag slung over his shoulder, Tony stepped off the aircraft into a German morning. Inside the terminal, he headed to a bank of phones and called his mother. Then he tracked down Pete's brother, Vinny, locating him in Dallas.

"Vinny? Vinny Hill?"

"Yeah, you got him. Who's this?"

"Tony, Tony Burato. I'm a friend of your brother's. We served together. But he's been in an accident and is in the hospital."

"What happened?"

"He got hit by a car, hit his head. They flew him to Germany, to a hospital in Landstuhl. It's the best the Marines got."

"But nobody called."

"That's a good sign, you know. If it was bad, they'd have reached out already."

He got no response and continued.

"Anyway, I wanted to get a hold of you, since you're the only family he has."

"Thanks, but what now?"

"The Marines will probably fly you over. It's free for family, you know, and you can be with Petey."

"Who knows what's going on with Peter?"

"Call Fort Dix. They got a special system, and they'll patch you through for the latest on Petey's condition."

"Okay."

"Hey, you got his girl Mary's telephone number? I think she should know what's going on."

"Mary? Uh, I'll handle it. Don't worry about her. I've got it."

"Good. Wasn't looking forward to that call. Anyway, look, I gotta run. I'll check in on him again before I leave."

Chapter 2

Peter Hill was critical but not as bad as the six others in the latest batch of soldiers wheeled into the bustling triage area. Brightly lit, it was anchored by a circular station where a doctor, in green scrubs, scanned reports, directing teams to each of the incoming.

Peter's gurney was intercepted. He was taken for an MRI and wheeled into an operating room.

***

Revitalized after grabbing two hours of shut-eye on a cot, Tony grabbed a ride to Landstuhl hospital.

"Good afternoon, ma'am. Here to see Pete Hill."

A civilian tapped on a keyboard.

"Private Hill is in the recovery area." She cocked her head toward a nurse, "Susan will take you in, but no more than ten minutes, okay?"

They stepped into a cold, brightly lit room lined with beds hooked up to equipment emitting streams of beeps. Nurses scurried across its gleaming floor, administering dosages and checking readings, numb to an overpowering, antiseptic smell.

"How's Petey doing?"

"Good, he's been out an hour. He's still under."

"How long for the anesthesia to wear off?"

"Normally, two, three hours, but with a TBI, things get complicated."

"TBI?"

"Traumatic brain injury." She pointed. "He's the last one on the right."

Tony stopped at the foot of the bed, spreading his legs for support. Peter's face was swollen. A tube was down his throat. His head was wrapped in gauze and a forest of poles held bags with lines to both arms. Pete's right leg was elevated by a sling hanging from a winch. A urine catheter dangled from his leg.

A nurse breezed in and logging onto a laptop, mumbled, "Goddamn IEDs."

"It wasn't a roadside bomb. Believe it or not, he was hit by a car."

"I thought it was strange there were no shrapnel wounds."

"It happened at the airport right when we were going to board a flight home."

"What bad luck."

"It gets worse. He was hit by a state department car."

"What? Hit by one of our own." She frowned. "Look, I'll be back. You can get closer. He won't bite you."

Tony inched up. He stared at his buddy, and when a tear slipped out, he focused on the respirator's baffle.

When the nurse came back, he asked how he could get a prognosis on Pete. She jotted down a number. Tony took a long look at Pete, gently patted his good leg, and left.

Dr. Brown's evasiveness made Tony angry. However, when Dr. Brown mentioned Pete would be kept unconscious for two days and transferred to Walter Reed Hospital in a week for rehab, Tony brightened.

"That's better," Tony said. "Pete's brother, Vinny, will be here soon, and I'll see Peter in Reed Hospital."

***

Vinny was a year older and three inches taller than Pete. He'd left New Jersey when their mother got sick and bounced around, ending up in Texas. He rarely came back to Jersey. An upper-level manager for FedEx in Dallas, Vinny pulled strings to avoid leaning on the military's offer. Hitching a ride on a FedEx freighter to Frankfurt, he picked up a company car and drove to Landstuhl Hospital.

Pleasantly surprised at the civilian feel, Vinny was confused when he was shown into a room housing eight bedridden soldiers. A scan of the room left a lump in his throat. He zeroed in on Pete's bed. Sandwiched between a legless soldier and one with an arm missing, his unconscious brother looked intact.

The nurse hovering over Pete met Vinny's eyes.

"Must be family coming, Peter. Maybe a brother? He looks like you."

Vinny wiped away a tear. He stood at Pete's bedside, silently cursing the war. The nurse dragged a chair over. The scraping sound seemed to stir Pete, and his head lolled a bit. Vinny shot a glance at the nurse.

"It's nothing. He's out."

Vinny sat, arms crossed.

"It's okay to touch him. Contact helps them recover. He knows you're here."

Vinny shifted closer, reaching through the side rail to touch his brother's hand.

"He's cold as ice. Get him a blanket, for Chrissakes!"

"It's fine. He's just below normal, which is right where we like him to be with a TBI."

"Look, before this happened, I'd never heard of a TBI, and I still don't know what the hell it is."

"A traumatic brain injury."

"I know that, but what does it mean for my brother? What the hell's happening with him?"

"I know this is difficult, but we believe Peter can hear you. Yelling may cause stress, it won't help his condition."

Vinny stood, leaning toward the nurse. "I need to understand what's going on. Is he gonna be all right?"

"I'll ask the doctor to speak with you."

Peter was getting a sponge bath and Vinny sat in a small area by the nurse's station. Rain pelted the windows. A reed-thin doctor, in green scrubs and clogs made a beeline for Vinny.

"Mr. Hill? I'm Doctor Molanari."

The physician didn't offer his hand, sitting on the coffee table.

"The surgery yesterday went well. I repaired the fracture, removed the skull fragments, and installed a ventricular drain to relieve the cranial pressure. Even patched up the nasty tear in his meniscus."

"Is he going to be all right?"

"It's too early to tell. The head trauma he suffered is a complicated thing to gauge. We need three to five days to let the fluids drain. Then, we'll take some scans that'll give us a picture of the damage to the brain."

"Brain damage? He's going to be a vegetable?"

"I doubt he'll be in a vegetative state. We see way too many TBIs here, and frankly, Peter's is not as bad as many."

"Doc, cut the bullshit. Give it to me straight."

The doctor stood abruptly. "Like I said, it's too early to tell the extent of damage. That said, the brain is a complex organ that we don't fully understand. I believe he'll have to undergo extensive rehab but will likely recover most functionality."

The doctor turned on his heels, leaving Vinny to struggle with what functionality meant. Finding it difficult to think and breathe, he headed for a dose of fresh air.

***

Eyes riveted on the floor, Vinny trudged back into Peter's room. He stared at his brother's comatose body, lamenting that he didn't really know his brother. Vinny shifted in his chair as tears trickled down his cheek, vowing to help Peter if he made it out. The guilt of leaving Peter to deal with their sick mother weighed on him. He cursed his father, who'd been in the reserves for years, for going AWOL in Grenada. Vinny still couldn't believe he left their mother and shacked up with some girl, dying shortly afterward.

Vinny cursed the people who put his brother in uniform and closed his eyes.

"How we doing today?" A nurse, blonde hair piled high, came in.

Vinny scrambled to his feet, putting him inches away and wishing he'd shaved.

"Vinny. I'm Pete's brother."

"Thought so, you have the same eyes. I'm Angela. Nice to meet you."

She reached for an IV bag, hiking her skirt and Vinny's interest.

"You or Petey need anything, just let me know."

He looked at her with glassy eyes.

"I know it's tough, but let's give it time. He'll get better, you'll see."

"I don't know; nothing's changing."

"Well, he's breathing on his own now. He'll make more progress."

"When will these tubes come out of his head? I mean, it gives me the creeps."

"Most of 'em will come out when the draining is done." She pointed to the tubes. "You see, it's a reddish gray now. A good sign will be if it turns clear. Keep an eye on it, okay?"

"Sure, Ang, sure."

"See you later."

Vinny watched her shapely body sway away before turning his attention to the color of the fluid draining through the tubes.

***

On the third day, Vinny pushed the door to Peter's room open, got a whiff of flowers, and kept his head down.

"How you doing today, Petey? It's me, Vinny." He checked the tubes, staring at one coming from the crown of Peter's head. The color seemed a shade lighter. He compared the color to the others, but couldn't tell if it was clearer.

Angie breezed in.

"Ang, check the fluid. I could be out of my mind, but it's looking a little clearer."

She came to Vinny's side of the bed.

"Yeah!" Angela high-fived Vinny. "Good eyes. If he stays on schedule, it'll be clear in a day, day and a half."

"When's he gonna wake up?"

She paused. "It's been three days. He could start coming out of it anytime."

Vinny jumped up. "Really?"

She held up a hand. "Just don't expect much at first. No matter what, remember, it's gonna take time. I'll check back."

***

Vinny pushed through the door, relieved there were no visitors in his brother's shared room. An amputee with an eye patch caught Vinny's eye, and he smiled. Quickening his pace, he was sure he saw Peter's eyes flutter open and shut.

Vinny put his hand on Peter's cheek. He lifted his brother's hand a few inches and dropped it, repeated it a bit higher and sat down, questioning what he thought he'd seen. He sat for a minute before bolting up to check the fluid stream. It had cleared significantly. He sat, took his hand, and began praying the Hail Mary. When the second verse came up, he heard the amputee chiming in. Vinny burst into tears, burying his face in his hands.

Regaining his composure, Vinny turned toward the amputee and gave him a thumbs-up. When he turned back to the bed, Peter's eyes were open.

Vinny got in his brother's face. "Peter, Peter, it's me, Vinny. You're gonna be all right, man."

Vinny stared into Peter's unfocused eyes. Then his brother's head lolled and his eyes closed.

"Come on, man. Wake up, buddy."

After repeated pleas went unanswered, Vinny pried open his brother's left then right eye. Emptiness stared back, and Vinny slumped into his chair.

***

"Wake up and make yourself useful."

"Uh, must've dozed off."

Angela handed him a cup and lollipop-like swab. "His lips are getting dried out. Swab 'em every now and then, but don't get any in his mouth. He could aspirate."

"His eyes were open for a second."

"Good. You see how clear this fluid is?"

He leapt up. "Wow, it really cleared up!"

"That's because the bleeding's done, and it's stable. I'll inform the doctor. He'll run scans tomorrow."

As she turned to leave, Vinny said, "Wait, look, his eyes are open! Peter, how you doing, man?"

"Hello, Peter. You're gonna be fine." Angela patted his forearm.

Peter's eyes shut.

***

Peter had been up periodically before being taken for the scans. When Angela rolled him back in, he was out cold.

"How soon will we get the results?"

"Immediately, it's digital. Maggie told me the doctor and the head neuro guy were going over them now and will have an assessment for you."

Vinny frowned.

"Stay positive. I've got a good feeling about it."

"I—I just, you know; oh, forget it."

"Forget nothing. What's going on?"

"You mean besides my brother laying here like a vegetable in Germany?"

"I mean with you."

"I don't know what to do. I live down in Texas, and if he's going to need, I don't know, like a ton of care . . ." He shook his head. "We ain't got nobody. Parents dead. No brothers, sisters, nobody to help out."

"Whoa, take it one step at a time. First, let's get a handle on his condition and then take it from there. Okay?"

"Guess so, no other choice."

Angela smiled. "Oh, by the way, that girl Mary Rourke called again. Said you never called her back."

"Okay, I'll call her. And just so you know, she's a friend of Pete's, not mine."

"Here comes Dr. Molanari."

He turned and saw the doctor beckoning. Vinny flashed crossed fingers to Angela and followed the doctor out. Vinny and the doctor huddled in the busy corridor.

"Look, we were able to capture some really high-quality scans today. The resolution was outstanding. Now, we've got some good news and some not so good."

Chapter 3

The doctor leaned into the wall as nurses streamed by.

"Peter's taken a bit of a beating. It's early in the game, but it could've been worse. That said, you should be prepared for the possibility of long-term or permanent impairment in his cognitive ability and memory."

"What d'ya mean? Is he going to be slow or something?"

The doctor slipped a foot out of his clog.

"We really don't know at this stage. Let's concentrate on the positives. He's lost most of his motor skills from the shock to the cranium, but it appears temporary and recoverable."

"Okay."

"Look, in a day or so, he'll be awake, most times, and though communication will be challenging, it's best to get him into intensive rehab as fast as possible. Without a setback, we're looking at flying him to Walter Reed in five, six days, max."

"Walter Reed in America?"

"Yes, DC."

***

Peter's brown eyes moved from a spaced-out look that couldn't follow your finger, to one evidencing focus. On the third day, he was able to follow movements, and a day later, to follow instructions: blinking once for yes, twice for no. Vinny was pleased but frustrated with the glacial pace. He estimated it would take two or three years before his brother would have any independence. At that pace, how was he ever going to get back to Texas and his life?

The day Peter was going to be moved, he kept mouthing the name Mary, sending a chill down Vinny's back. Peter's face strained from the effort, and Vinny told his brother to save his strength for the flight to the States. Reacting to the news he was headed to America, Peter's head moved, and his eyes lit up. Peter continued to struggle to speak Mary's name. Vinny squeezed his hand and tried to calm him down. Pete started coughing, collapsing into a deep sleep.

Vinny unhooked his hand as Angie tended to the patient in the next bed.

"Hey Ang, Petey reacted like crazy when I told him he was going home."

"I don't know, Vin, it's doubtful he knows where he is."

Vinny got up.

"Nah, I swear he moved his head, and his eyes lit up."

"Well, you never know."

"I'll wake him, okay?"

She came to the bedside. "Leave him be. Hmm, his heart rate's elevated."

Peter coughed, and Angie asked, "He been coughing regularly?"

"Yeah, every ten to fifteen minutes or so."

"Anything come up? Like blood?"

"No."

She opened his mouth, swabbed inside, and came up with what looked like blood. "Damn."

"What's wrong?"

She hit the call button and rushed out.

Vinny watched his brother's heart rate fluctuate around 120, and he coughed twice in the five minutes it took for an X-ray machine to be rolled in.

A few minutes later, Dr. Molanari came in, trailed by Angela.

"Your brother has a pulmonary embolism."

Angela explained, "A blood clot in his right lung."

"That serious?"

"Can be deadly."

"You fucking kidding me?"

"The doctor is going to give him something to help with this."

The doctor handed a syringe to Angie. "Here's the TPA. In the left arm while I administer the coumadin."

Vinny questioned, "How the heck did he get this?"

"Combo of trauma to the leg and immobilization."

"Now what?"

"Well, he'll be on blood thinners. It's complicated by the TBI. I hate to break it to you, but he isn't going anywhere."

Vinny shook his head and headed for the elevators.

A nurse at the station called out, "Vinny! Call for you, from New Jersey."

It was Mary.

"Hi Vinny, how's Peter?"

"Well, right now, not so good."

Mary gasped. "What's going on?"

"Look, he's hooked up to a bunch of machines, and a new problem just cropped up."

"Oh my God, I feel terrible."

"Look, save your tears. You got your life to live, and Pete's—"

"How dare you!"

"How dare me? No, it's how the fuck dare you!" Vinny slammed the phone down.

***

Peter was the recipient of leg massages and was getting stuck with needles to check how thin his blood was. It was a delicate balance. The doctors were fearful that if his blood was too thin it could ignite bleeding in the brain.

Antsy, Vinny went to call his boss with the news about his delayed return.

Vinny hung up, pinching the bridge of his nose with a thumb and forefinger. The call didn't jibe with the sympathetic accommodation he'd received to date. Vinny now got the vibe his boss was losing patience with his prolonged absence.

Chapter 4

It took five days for the clot to dissipate. Peter was now ready to be moved out. The extra time allowed for improvement in Peter's alertness. He even spoke at times, though the words were muddled and disconnected. Welcomed, progress was tempered by his repeated pleas for Mary.

Vinny despised making the journey to Walter Reed Hospital on a military flight, but with Peter clearly frightened, he relented. The presence of thirty or so maimed warriors aboard made the six-hour flight seem endless.

Walter Reed Military Medical Center was the size of a small city, with a staff of ten thousand, and six thousand rooms. It had been tending to America's fighting forces for over a hundred years.

Vinny went to a meeting to go over Peter's case in a rehab room filled with equipment in use. The huge room was filled with patients and their therapists, who provided motivation, encouragement, and praise.

Vinny was directed to a stocky man with horn-rimmed glasses standing beside a set of cubicles.

"John Clalia. I'm Peter's lead physiatrist. You got to be Peter's brother Vinny, right?"

Vinny said, "Psychiatrist?"

"No, close, but its physiatrist. We're trained in physical medicine and rehabilitation."

The interior of the tiny cubicle was covered with photos of wounded soldiers. There were a lot of smiling faces on the torn-up bodies in the pictures, but they didn't raise Vinny's spirit.

"I don't know how you guys do all this, day in, day out."

"It's extremely rewarding."

"Frigging depressing is what it is."

"Your brother sustained a traumatic brain injury. What we don't know is how much function he'll recover. A significant amount of progress in these types of cases comes from the hard work that forces the brain to learn again." Clalia pushed his glasses up. "On a scale of one to ten, how would you rate Peter's drive, his focus? What happens when the going gets tough?"

"He's not easily dissuaded. He's going to do what he wants to do, no matter what. I remember as kids he was tormented by one of my friends on a football team, but he didn't give up."

"Good. You mentioned he'll do what he wants to do. What do you suggest we do to motivate him?"

"What more motivation does a guy need to get better?"

"You'd be surprised. Many of the people we treat, they get down."

"You mean depressed?"

"Yeah, it's a typical phase most go through. Expect it to happen, and if it doesn't, it's a giant plus."

Vinny shifted in his seat.

"The treatment your brother will receive here is comprehensive."

"Like physical therapy?"

"That's one component. He'll also work with a speech pathologist, a neuropsychologist, an occupational therapist, a recreational therapist, and a social worker. There'll even be someone for you to help you deal with all this."

"I'm okay. I don't need any help."

"We find most families need help with things like how to modify the house to prevent falls, or recognizing the early signs that the patient may be engaging in risky behavior."

Vinny pulled his chin in.

"Risky, like drinking alcohol or an activity that heightens the risk of a concussion."

"In other words, he needs a babysitter."

Clalia took his glasses off. "The reality is your brother suffered a serious brain injury, and the facts are that people in his condition are ten times more likely to suffer a concussion after they recover."

"Ten times?"

"Unfortunately, even if he recovers most of his physical abilities, a real danger exists. You see, a brain injury is an invisible disability. If he doesn't modify his behavior, changing his lifestyle in some ways, he's likely to suffer what could be a devastating concussion."

"I thought he was here to get better, you know, not to be—"

Clalia held a hand up. "Part of the process is to be informed of the risks going forward, a way to ensure that the progress we make here is kept in the bank, so to speak."

The physiatrist and Vinny talked for a half hour longer with the focus returning to the importance of Peter's emotional stability. Clalia stressing that the highest degrees of recovery were linked to avoiding depression.

Chapter 5

The rehab room smelled of Pine-Sol. A couple of therapists were with his brother. Vinny liked the way they took his brother's limp hand and shook it as if there were nothing wrong.

Clalia issued instructions, and the group moved Peter to a pair of parallel bars. They maneuvered Peter into a contraption between the handrails. They lowered Peter, putting his hands on the rubberized rails and his feet on the ground.

A beefy kid knelt, straightening Peter's feet, "Okay, Peter, let's go for a stroll."

Slowly, the hoist moved forward. Two therapists inched Pete's hands forward while another kept pace with his feet.

"Come on, Pete. Take a step. Help us out here. You're not going to make us do all the work, are you?"

"He's moving his hands! Way to go, man!"

Excited by the declaration, Vinny studied his brother's hands. There was no voluntary movement.

***

I was a prisoner of my body. It had to be depressing for Vinny as well, and I caught a glimpse of him cursing as they wheeled me out. I was beat and drifted to sleep.

I don't remember getting put back in bed, but they told me I'd napped for two hours. They got me up, fed me a snack, and then helped brush my teeth. When a mirror was propped up on the tray, I was glad to see that my hair had grown enough to cover the gap between my head and ears. Refreshed, I felt ready for a series of tests to determine my cognitive state—doctor speak for memory, language, executive function, and visuospatial capabilities.

They wheeled me to another wing of the hospital. A sedate suite of rooms with classical music playing in the background. I thought of a funeral parlor and began to get worked up, but a neuropsychologist named James and his smiling female assistant noted my anxiety.

"Peter, we're here to get an idea of what areas need attention. We'll administer tests, but don't worry. Your injury is still healing."

I nodded.

"Most of all, please don't get frustrated. Things that you may not be able to do today will come back quicker than you think, okay?"

I didn't like the way this sounded, but not knowing what to do, nodded anyway.

"Let's begin over here."

The doctor held up a red square. "What color do you see?"

"Uh, uh, rrr, red."

"Excellent."

The doctor went through six colors, and I nailed them. My spirits skyrocketed, but a problem arose when the doctor would show a color, hide it, and ask what color it was. When he did that, my success rate went down by half. I got irritable. The doctor moved on to another test.

The doctor showed me a picture of three animals and pointed at them. "Is this a cat? Dog?" Most of the identities I picked out. I mean, geez, they're animals. But, when the doctor asked whether a certain animal was left, right, or in the middle of the picture, I got confused and failed miserably. How the hell could I be screwing this up?

I was getting tired of all the bullshit when they moved on to a test identifying shapes.

Surprisingly, I was able to identify each one correctly and was even able to recall most of them within ten seconds of seeing it. However, when the doctor lengthened the time to twenty seconds between seeing the images, I faltered, unable to recall even one shape.

The roller coaster continued. I did well in the language area, at times jumbling the order of words, but the doctor seemed pleased.

The last testing zone was visuospatial, to gauge how I interpreted what I saw. The doctor pulled out two props: a clock where he changed times, and two glasses of water with different amounts of water. It seemed simple but was a total disaster, exposing an area where loss screamed out.

I tried to pound the table as I spit out a stream of curses. The doctor tried to talk me down. He thought he was sly, concluding the series of tests with something I'd pass, ending on a high note. I saw right through him.

***

Walter Reed had its own McDonald's, and Vinny exited it laden with dinner and the fear that his brother's mental recovery was lagging.

"Yo, Petey, how you doing?"

Peter was staring at the TV and didn't acknowledge him.

Vinny put his dinner down and tapped his brother. "Knock, knock. Anyone home?"

Peter slowly turned his head. "When you get here?"

"Just walked in."

"Is Mom coming?"

"Mom? Come on, Peter. Don't you remember she passed away?"

"Uh, yeah . . ."

Vinny handed a bag of fries to Peter. "These are yours."

"Mine?"

"Yeah, you asked me to get you french fries."

"I did? I don't like fries."

"Geez, yes you do. Just eat them. All right?"

"Did Mary call?"

"How would I know?" He took a bite of his Big Mac instead of running out of the room.

"I want a phone. Why don't I have a phone?"

Vinny shrugged.

"Where's my fucking phone!"

"Hey, take it easy. Here, use my cell for now."

Peter took the phone and stared at it.

"What's the matter?"

"Uh, I don't, remember her number."

"Whose number?"

"You know who."

"How the hell would I know her number? I'll find out, and tomorrow we'll call, okay?"

Peter barely nodded.

"Hey Petey, here's a card from Mrs. Norton."

"Who's that?"

"The next-door neighbor, the brown house; her husband is Bob."

Peter nodded.

"When you get this?" Vinny picked up a shiny cane that was next to a walker.

"Clalia brought it today. Said I'm about ready."

"Man, it's light but strong." Vinny tapped it on the ground and read the label. "Made out of some titanium alloy. Geez, everything's hi-tech today. It'll be good to see you using this."

Peter turned his attention to the TV.

The next evening, Vinny carried his dinner up from the cafeteria, hoping that Peter had either forgotten about calling Mary or would fall asleep as he ate dinner, as was often the case. Disappointment was routine for Vinny, and before he could put his tray down in his brother's room, it visited again.

"You get the number?"

"Yeah, I got it."

"Good. Come on. Dial it for me."

"Can't we eat first?"

"Now!"

"Shush." Vinny pulled his phone out, dialed, and handed it off. "Just push dial."

"What button?"

"The green one."

"It's ringing."

"Whoop-de-do."

"Mary, Mary, yeah, it's me, Petey."

Vinny strained to hear what she was saying.

"I'm doing good, real good. When you coming to see me?"

Vinny cringed at the thought of her coming.

"Oh, oh, that'd be great. I just can't wait."

A brief silence was broken when Peter spoke.

"Mary? You still there?"

"Oh, okay, okay. You know I'm missing you. I mean, I miss you so much, and, and I love you."

Vinny watched Peter's beaming face darken.

"Okay, see you soon. I love you, Mary."

Vinny took the phone back. "So, when's she coming?"

"Next week, she said she'd try. She'll call you to let you know."

"Eat."

"Ain't hungry."

"What's the matter?"

"I don't know, she sounded different. And when I told her I loved her, she said she knew."

"So?"

Peter stared at his lap and said, "She didn't say it back."

"Look, things are different now."

"What do you mean?"

"You know, time passed. Things change. That's all. Now eat. You need your strength."

***

I graduated from a walker to using that special cane and had regained good stability when walking. It was still a struggle if I tried to jog on the treadmill, but the doctors were confident it'd get better. Besides the buzzing in my ears, sensitivity to bright light, and a metal taste in my mouth, a big problem was my eyesight. It was better than before, when I couldn't see jack shit unless it was right in front of me, but far from normal. Every time I reached for something, I couldn't get it the first time, so I went to see a specialist.

Vinny and I went into a darkened room, and the doctor, an Austrian dude with an accent, had me sit in each of several machines that lined the wall. When he said my name, he hung on the first syllable, making it sound like *Peetur*. He reminded me to keep my chin in each of the machine's cups. I kept forgetting, and after a while it must have bothered Vinny, because he put his hand on the back of my head and pushed me forward.

The doctor asked me to stand. I struggled before reaching for the cane.

"Okay Peetur, sit back down and get up, but close your eyes."

Surprisingly, I got up without much effort.

"Now close your eyes again and try it without the cane." He took my cane. "Don't worry, Peetur, I'm right here to help if you need it."

I got up pretty easily, just wobbled a bit.

"Good, Peetur, good." He handed me the cane and took a pen out, centering it on my face. "Now follow this and let me know when it disappears from view."

He moved it to the left and right and up and down, "You're operating with a fair amount of peripheral vision. Your left eye is significantly weaker, though." He curled a finger. "Follow me."

We went into another low-lighted room where a large, black disk with red lights occupied an entire wall.

"This tests the peripheral vision with a reaction component. It not only measures if you see it, but when your eyes focus on it and react to it."

There were foot imprints on the floor, but the doctor dragged over a tall chair.

"Now, lights will appear randomly on the disc. As soon as you see a light, move your closest hand toward it."

At first it was pretty easy to get my hand in the right direction, but the speed increased, and it was challenging. Still, all in all, I thought I did well.

"Okay Peetur, one more test, and we're done."

We went back in the room with the machines and sat at a narrow table. The doctor gave me a small aluminum rod.

"What I want you to do is stick the rod inside each of the objects I hold up."

He took a ring the size of a hula hoop from under the table and held it up. My first thought was this was some kind of a joke, but then I panicked, thinking I might not be able to do it. Fortunately, I was able to do it easily with both hands. Then the doctor pulled out a pie-sized ring.

I poked through with my right hand but hit the rim with my left, but I still made it in. We stopped when I couldn't get either hand to pierce a circle the size of a tennis ball.

The doctor opened a drawer and took out a pair of glasses that had one lens blocked out.

"Put these on, Peetur. You have a couple of problems: peripheral and reactionary, but depth perception is affecting you the most. The lack of depth perception is limited to your left eye. It is really more than just a lack of, it's, well, I've seen this in other TBI cases. Somehow the brain mixes the data it receives from each eye. In many cases the strong eye, say in vision, will compensate, but it could be the injury caused some damage that may or may not come back."

I tried to follow him but was lost.

"I'm going to have a special pair of glasses made for you."

"Like the ones I wore? I can't go around like—"

He held up a hand. "They'll have a script that will help the focus of your right eye. The left lens will be cloudy. A film will be applied to it that will help correct depth perception." He pointed to my left eye. "The eye will see certain parts of the spectrum but allow your right eye to determine relative distances."

The glasses took some getting used to, but I had to admit they worked. I gained a new measure of normality, if you can ever be normal walking around with pirate-like glasses. Looks aside, they were a critical step in getting me released to go home.

Getting back home was made easier by Vinny, who'd left two days before to get things in order. He'd had the utilities turned on, the place cleaned, and made some modifications that Clalia said would make things easier and safer. Vinny also had my mom's old car jump-started and serviced.

Riding back to New Jersey in Mom's car brought back a bagful of mixed emotions. I still missed her and had not forgiven Vinny for taking off, leaving me to take care of her when she was sick. I didn't have the energy or stream of thoughts to put it into words, but when I tried to gather my thoughts as we rolled up the turnpike, I started crying. When

Vinny asked what was going on, I sidestepped it, saying I was happy to be heading home but scared of being on my own. He repeated his pledge to stay by my side as long as it took. I was surprised how genuine he sounded, but given his history, pools of doubt remained.

The street looked familiar, but if you'd asked me, I couldn't say it was where I grew up. Then we pulled up the driveway, and the house looked different somehow.

Stepping through the front door, I was hit with the smell of Windex and stale air. I paused, leaning on my cane as I scanned the living room before taking another step.

"Wasn't there a giant, you know, one of those Chinese carpets in here that Mom loved?"

"Yeah, it's rolled up in the garage. Clalia said to take all the area rugs out. You could trip over them."

I nodded and started to cry.

"What's with the tears, man? The rug will go back. Don't worry—"

"It's not the rug. I'm, just, glad to be home."

Vinny put his arm around my shoulder. "Yeah, man, it sure is good."

"Couldn't have done it without you."

"Me? You kidding me? I didn't do nothing. It was all you, man. You fought like a bastard. I'm proud of you, bro."

I reached for a picture of our mother and started crying again.

"Come on. Let's eat something. I stocked the fridge with real food, not that hospital crap."

We headed to the kitchen, and Vinny cleared a stack of papers five inches high from the counter.

"What's that?"

"Ah, papers, bills, the mail."

The reality of life reappeared.

"Uh, who's been taken care of things?"

"Like I told you, I got it handled. Let me worry about the bills. You just get better."

"But I could help. I can use my Marine pay, and you've hardly been working."

"Look, let's take one step at a time, okay? I'm gonna be going back to work. FedEx's got a big place in Eatontown. I'll get a temporary gig there. It'll work out."

***

Vinny had gone to work, and after thumbing through a pile of magazines that neighbors had brought over, I went into the kitchen and came upon an envelope that a green certified mail card on it. It was from the Middletown Township tax collector.

It said a lien had been put on the house for twenty thousand dollars in unpaid taxes. That seemed like a lot of money to me and was way more than my military salary. Not knowing what to do, I put the envelope between my shirt and tee shirt so I'd remember it when I went to bed.

The next morning, when Vinny came down to eat, I waved the envelope at him.

"You found the love note from our friends in town." He wagged his head. "I went down to see them. Told them everything, even though they fucking knew what happened to you. Said they couldn't do anything. It's the law, blah, blah, blah. Heartless bastards, said to file for a federal grant or some bullshit."

"What're we gonna do?"

"Don't worry."

The faint ringing in my ears began to elevate.

"But can't we lose Mom's house. Then where—"

"I said don't worry. We'll get it paid."

A mouthful of rusty metal settled in my mouth.

"How?"

"Well, remember when we filed those papers a while back when you were in Walter Reed?"

I nodded, but had no idea what he was talking about.

"Well, it's your disability, and they said you'd get it backdated and get a lump sum amount if they approve it."

"Is it that much money?"

"Not exactly, but I said I'll handle it, and I will. I don't want to use your money. You need it. But we'll have to use it until I make up the ground I lost."

"When we gonna get the money?"

"I wish I knew when. I've been calling for a month."

***

Vinny was yelling into the phone. I rushed down the stairs and scraped my knee. I hobbled into the kitchen as he slammed down the phone.

"What's the matter?"

"You believe this shit? Fucking government morons turned down your disability."

"How? How can they?"

"Some bullshit about it not being a battlefield injury. Like you had a fucking choice being there!"

"Now what?"

"I got half a mind to call Fox News and tell him how you're getting dicked around. They'll help us, I bet."

***

I pulled another drawer out and rummaged through it. *Where is it? When the hell is Vinny getting home?*

The front door opened. "Vinny! Where's my blue shirt?"

"Look in the closet, Petey."

"It's not there. What happened to it?"

I heard Vinny trudge up the stairs, then he came into my room and said, "What the hell's going on? The place is a mess."

"Nothing. Just getting ready for Mary to come over. Where's my shirt?"

"She ain't coming till this afternoon."

"So? I gotta be ready. Where's the shirt? The blue one?"

Vinny stepped over a pile of clothes, reached into the closet, pulling out a blue shirt. "Here it is. Now, can I get some sleep?"

"Not that one, the one with the white collar."

"Pete, I don't know what you're talking about. This is a perfectly good shirt, and I'm beat."

"But it doesn't have a white collar, and Mary likes colored shirts with white collars."

"Stop being so anal, okay? I'm gonna take a nap. When I get up, I'll check around, but at least you got something nice to wear."

I finished getting ready, hobbled down the stairs and turned on the TV. I sat carefully, so my clothes wouldn't get wrinkled, and flipped through channels until I hit an episode of *Gilligan's Island*.

I'd been up most of the night thinking of what to say to Mary. Man, I missed her. I wanted to get things back to the way they were before I went to Afghanistan. Vinny told me it would take time, and I guess he was right, but geez, I was tired. I started to nod out and spread out on the couch to get comfortable.

"Petey, time to get up."

"I must've fallen asleep."

"That's okay. You need the rest."

"What time is it?"

"A quarter to one."

"Oh no! Mary's coming at one. Right?"

"Yeah. Take it easy."

"Why didn't you get me up earlier?"

"I was sleeping too. You forget I work the night shift?"

"I want to be ready."

"Look, you're ready. I picked up the donuts, like you asked."

"Did you get raspberry? She loves raspberry."

"Yes, boss. I'll put a pot of coffee on."

I grabbed my cane when the doorbell rang. As Vinny headed for the door, I smoothed my shirt and said, "Let me get it."

I opened the door, and there she was. I just froze, staring at her. She looked me up and down, making me nervous.

"You gonna let me in, Peter?"

"Oh, sorry. Come in."

Why'd she call me Peter? I thought as Mary extended a thin box with a card. She pulled it back when she saw me switch hands on the cane and reach out.

"It's okay. I can handle it."

"I got it."

"I can handle it!"

"Take it easy, Peter. It's no big deal."

Vinny came to the rescue, saying, "Hey, Mary. How's it going?"

As we headed into the kitchen, I took a couple of deep breaths and forced a smile.

Vinny said, "Look, I've got some errands to run. I'll see you guys later."

As soon as Vinny left, I said, "Man, did I miss you, Mary. Where's my kiss?"

I didn't like her hesitation, but she got up and pecked my cheek.

"That's it? That's all I get."

She slid the box and card over. "Aren't you going to open it?"

I ripped open the card. I was surprised there was nothing personalized on the card and pissed she signed it Mary, not Love, Mary. I stared at the card for a moment before I tore off the wrapping paper, revealing a box of chocolates.

"Thanks."

"So how are you doing, Peter?"

Peter again? "I'm doing great. Really, you should have seen me. I was banged up." I looked at my hands. "Why didn't you come to see me in the hospital?"

"I wanted to, but I couldn't get off work."

"But you could've come on the weekend."

"I'm here now. That's all that counts." She reached out and patted my hand.

My heart jumped, and I clasped her hand in mine. I thought I felt a little pullback, but it passed. "You got me through Afghanistan. Without knowing you were waiting for me; I don't know what I'd have done."

"It must have been tough over there."

"The toughest part was being away from you." I squeezed her hand.

Mary coughed. It sounded fake to me, and she pulled her hand from mine to cover her mouth.

The coffeemaker beeped, and she leapt up, pouring two cups.

"I got you some raspberry donuts. They're right there." I pointed my cane, nearly hitting her.

It was all small talk, make that tiny talk, as we had our snack. I didn't know if it was me, but everything seemed forced. It was like she was a saleslady or something.

Mary got up and cleared the table. When she sat back down, she looked me in the eye for the first time.

"So, you're really doing okay?"

"Oh yeah, like I said, I was a mess for a while, but now I'm doing great."

"That's good, Peter. I was worried about you."

There she goes again with Peter. "I'm gonna be fine, back to my old self. Just got a few things to work on." I lifted my cane up.

"Well it's good to see you."

I reached for her hand, but she stood and said, "Look, I've got to go. Getting my hair done."

"Oh, come on! You just got here."

She mumbled some nonsense, pecked my cheek as I struggled to get up, and said. "Sit, sit. I'll let myself out."

Just like that, she was gone.

I played the visit over and over in my head until Vinny came back. He told me to keep things in perspective, that it was the first visit after a long time, and things were expected to be awkward. It made sense, and I felt better about it.

Chapter 6

We got to the Blue Robin around seven. The place was quiet and stank of stale beer. It was the first time I'd been in a bar since I went to boot camp. Vinny said I was limited to one, maybe two beers at most, since I ate fistfuls of pills every day. I insisted we sit at the bar, even though he had to help me onto a stool. I didn't want to hang my cane on the bar where everyone could see it, so I laid it across my lap. The bartender, a kid who looked familiar, came over when we settled in.

Vinny knew him from way back when and introduced me. The guy said he'd heard what happened to me and shook my hand. He thanked me for serving, though it felt like he forced it.

"So, what you having to celebrate?"

"Ah, ah—

Vinny jumped in, "Coupla draft Coors."

The bartender pulled on the tap, filled two glasses, and set them on the sticky bar. We clinked glasses, and the bartender, I forgot his name, whooped his approval as we took a draw on the brews.

I burped as my brother said, "Another milestone."

"The burp?"

"Man, after all the shit I seen come out of you, a burp or even a frigging fart is welcome."

We laughed as a group barreled through the door, catching Vinny's attention.

"Yo, Ricky, what's up?"

"Shit, Vinny, where you been hiding?"

"Hanging with my brother." He put his arm around my shoulder. "You remember Pete?"

"Sure, man. He's a fucking hero, man. Pride of Middletown."

"Come on. Stop it," I mumbled as the procession shook my hand and pounded my back, telling me how good I looked and how proud they were. I had to admit, it did feel good, even though I knew it was bullshit. Hardly anyone, had reached out to me the entire time I'd been back in the States.

My cane kept clattering to the floor, causing a cascade of arms to compete to get it. Not only was it stickier each time the winner handed it off, but I was getting the feeling they felt they had done me a huge favor.

Another guy, with a goatee, came in the door. I couldn't place his face as he traded hugs with the others and made his way to Vinny and me.

Vinny pawed his chin. "Looking like a painter, Luke. You remember my brother, Pete?"

He extended a hand. "Sure, used to go with Mary, right?"

I shook it. "I—I still do."

He cocked his head. "Yeah? I thought she was going with, uh—"

Vinny jumped in, asking him what he was drinking. I saw Vinny raise a finger up to his lips, and the conversation went into a lull before Vinny jerked it to sports.

Vinny tried to get me into the sports conversation, but I was angry about the Mary comment, and I couldn't or wouldn't talk. Vinny easily shot the shit with his friends, but my silence was the dead duck in the room. Vinny nudged my arm, but when I didn't respond and instead asked for another beer, he challenged, "Hey, what do you say to nine ball, five bucks a game? You on?" He tugged my arm.

Before he realized his mistake, I slid off my stool, and he caught my arm before I hit the ground.

"Ah, yeah, sure."

"'Born in the USA'" began to blare out of a beat-up jukebox and kicking off a ringing in my ears. It triggered a mental brawl whether it was the song, Springsteen himself, or the volume that was at fault. I ambled over to the pool table as Vinny pulled balls from the pockets, filling the rack.

He shifted the rack, tightening the balls. I leaned against the table and chalked my cue.

"Hey, we're supposed to flip for the break, but since tonight is like breaking your cherry, it's all yours."

Hooking my cane on the corner pocket, I leaned over, and slowly stroked my stick, feeling eyes boring into my back. I tried to concentrate. *Breathe in and out, focus. Steady. Breathe, man, breathe. Good, good. Okay, steady, stroke, be fluid—*

"You waiting for an invitation, or what?"

I thrust the stick forward, but the impact only sent the cue ball on a pathetic path into the pack. The balls broke apart but without the force necessary to scatter them or the hope to pocket one.

"Maybe you should've worn the new glasses, bro."

"Yeah, well, after the Captain Hook jokes at the doctor's last week."

Vinny pumped in two chip shots before missing an easy one.

"Shit."

"Look, I don't need any charity, man."

"What?"

I looked over the table for the easiest shot and was glad to see the eight-ball hanging on the side pocket lip, a chip shot. I lined up the cue ball and was ready to pocket it when Vinny broke in, "What you doing, man? You sink the eight and the game is over. You forget we're playing nine ball?"

Confused, I lined up a different shot but flubbed it. Vinny missed one as well, but as much as he tried to throw it to me, I just couldn't do it. My eyes were betraying me. I thought I was making good shots, but, well, let's just say it didn't happen.

***

The following week's therapy went pretty well for me. I was making progress physically, but wasn't happy because things weren't normal with Mary. I couldn't figure it out. I don't know, maybe she was scared, as she always kept her distance. I mean, she came over every now and then, but it was kiss on the cheek stuff, and she never, ever stayed long, always claiming she had somewhere to go. When I pressed her, she said she needed more time, said she was confused. I guess my condition scared her. But why? I mean, couldn't she see how much better I was? Anyway, I still really felt that when I got all the way back, things would be good with her again.

I looked around the garage at the tools hanging on the pegboard. Then I saw Mom's old car out the garage door window. Vinny had let me drive a couple of times, but after scraping the curb three outings in a row, I had to take it slow.

I was used to the glasses and all, but in a car, things sped up, making it tougher. A garbage truck rumbled down the street. I watched it till it was out of sight, and then I went back into the house after trying to recall what I came in the garage to get. I kicked the wall and put a hole in the wallboard. It was frustrating.

I'd really been struggling with my memory. It was better than when I first got to Walter Reed, but the last few weeks I couldn't remember jack shit. Vinny was always saying he had told me that already and said I was zoning out a lot. I don't know about that, but I never forgot a thing about Mary and thought about her all day long.

***

In an hour or so, Mary was coming over again. I was amped up.

"Hey, bro, can you do me a favor?"

Vinny looked up from the newspaper.

"You're going to work soon, anyway. Why don't you take off while I jump in the shower, so I can have some privacy when Mary gets here?"

Vinny closed the paper. "Sure thing, Romeo. I gotta pick up your refills at CVS anyway."

"Thanks, man."

Vinny grabbed his keys off the counter. "You want me to put a pot of coffee up or anything?"

"Nah, I got it."

"You sure? It's no problem. She won't be here for, like, almost an hour."

"Geez, what am I, a fucking invalid?"

"Take it easy, tiger." He headed to the door and looked over his shoulder. "Don't forget to shave, lover boy."

The phone was ringing.

"Hello?"

"Peter, are you home?"

"Yeah, why?"

"I've been ringing the doorbell for ten minutes."

"Oh, sorry, sorry." I dropped the phone, grabbed my cane, and hustled to the door.

Mary was wearing bright red lipstick and a pantsuit. She looked great.

"Come in, come in."

"You okay, Peter?" She showed genuine concern, warming my heart.

"Yeah, fine. Why?"

"Well, you look, uh, I don't know, tired or something."

"Really?" I looked in the foyer mirror and realized I had never showered, or shaved, for that matter. "Well, I—I was sleeping. Went for a walk, a real long one, you know, and guess I must've dozed off or something."

She smiled, pecked my cheek, and handed me a box of crumb cake.

"I'd love a cup of coffee. Why don't you go get changed, and I'll put a pot of coffee on?"

"Yeah, I was thinking the same thing. Be right back."

When I got ready to shave, I was horrified to realize I'd been wearing my dorky glasses.

"Peter! Peter! You all right up there?"

"Yeah, I'm fine. I'll be right down."

It was good Mary was in the kitchen. I struggled to get down the stairs, forgetting how tough it was to do without my special glasses.

I squinted at the doorway into the kitchen and shut one of the lights. I stepped in and smiled.

"Better?"

"Yes, but what on earth were you doing for so long?"

Uh oh! I didn't like the sound of that. "Was it that long?"

Mary nodded.

"I—I was looking for that shirt. You remember, the red one with the pockets. You always liked it."

"It's okay, Peter. Really, don't worry. You want a cup of coffee?"

"Sure, but how about you?"

"Had two already. You want a piece of crumb cake?"

We made small talk as I drank my coffee. Mary kept calling me Peter. It had always been Pete or Petey.

"You okay Peter?

"Yeah, why?"

"I don't know, you seem fidgety."

"Gotta take a pee. Been holding it for a long time." I got up with a hand on my crotch like a five-year-old trying to prevent a leak.

When I came out of the bathroom, she was putting the cups in the sink.

"I really gotta run."

"Already? You just got here."

She nodded and said, "It's just that Cathy needs to talk. She's got some major issues going on. You remember Cathy, don't you?"

A metallic flavor seemed to coat my throat.

"Of course, I fucking remember! Everybody thinks I'm some kinda moron."

"That's not fair, Peter."

"Yeah? Well, it's not fair that you're leaving. I, we need to talk about the future, our future."

Mary moved to the door. "It's not a good time right now. Some other time, okay?"

She went to peck my cheek, and I grabbed her arm.

"Ow, that hurts. Let me go. Now!"

"Aw, come on, Mary."

"Peter!"

Her screech pierced my ears and I released her. "Sorry, I didn't mean it. Just wanted to, you know . . ."

She headed down the walkway and I, to a date with the blues. Vinny found me staring at an infomercial when he came home.

"What're you doing up? It's frigging four in the morning."

I shrugged. "I donno. Guess I couldn't sleep."

"How'd it go with Mary?"

I picked up the remote and flipped through channels.

Vinny headed to the stairs. "I'm beat, man. I'm going up. You coming?"

I kept changing channels.

"Look, Pete, you gotta stop fixating on Mary. What's gonna be is gonna be, man."

I raised the volume and Vinny stormed over, grabbing the remote out of my hand.

"Look, you wanna stay up all night? Fine with me. Just have some damn courtesy and lower this so I can sleep."

Vinny lay in bed and decided to put his anger toward Mary aside and enlist her help with Peter.

As soon as Vinny got to work the next day, he called Mary, asking her to let Peter down easy, play it along a bit, not crush him. Mary said she would do almost anything to help, but when she told Vinny about Peter's behavior, he made an appointment with the neuropsychologist.

***

Dr. Rombauer's office was in a low-slung building in Colts Neck, near Delicious Orchards. The setting was tranquil and bucolic. The smell of cut grass put a tickle in both brothers' throats as they entered. Vinny smiled at the receptionist, hoping she wouldn't bring up the past-due coinsurance amounts they owed.

If *Psychology Today* carried pictures of what a head doctor should look like, they'd use Rombauer as a model. Tall and erect, with the beginnings of middle-age flab, his face was punctuated by a gray goatee hanging off his chin without the aid of a moustache.

When Vinny made the appointment, he alerted Rombauer about Peter's increasing forgetfulness, erratic behavior, and verbal outbursts. Vinny hoped his brother's irritability and anger could be nipped in the bud.

***

I picked up and put down just about every magazine in the ten minutes we waited until being shown into Rombauer's office. The doctor was sitting perfectly still, hands folded in his lap as if posing for a portrait. He looked like a statue to me. Rombauer studied me and stood, smoothing his white coat as he came around his desk.

"Peter, it's nice to see you again." We shook hands. "Please, please take seats, gentlemen."

Rombauer eased into his leather chair, "Tell me, how are you feeling, Peter?"

"Pretty good."

"Is there anything bothering you?"

I said, "Usual stuff, the ringing never really goes away, and bright lights—"

"Tell him about the memory stuff, Pete."

"It's not so bad. I can live with it."

"Peter, the objective is to achieve the highest degree of functionality we can. There is no reason to accept anything less, unless, of course, we cannot improve it. Does that make sense?"

I nodded.

"Good. We're hoping the tinnitus and sensitivity will fade somewhat over time, but let's see about the memory and cognitive areas. I'd like to run some of the same tests we've done in the past and a couple of new ones as well. This will give us a picture of where you are and how it compares to previous results. We can go from there."

I nodded again; everyone expected me to.

Rombauer stood. "Let's get started."

The first test seemed simple enough, I thought. Rombauer gave me a sheet of paper and pen.

"There are four objects I want you to try to remember. You ready?"

"Okay."

The doctor held a picture up and said, "These are the four objects: dog, house, duck, spoon."

I silently moved my lips.

"Now draw a picture of a clock with the time showing one o'clock."

I hunched over and scrawled away. When I finished, Rombauer asked me, "Now what were the four objects?"

I felt like a deer in headlights. "Dog, uh, spoon. Uh, uh, dog, spoon—fuck!"

"Good, that's fine. No need to get angry. We're here to find solutions, okay?" He reached for the sheet of paper and scanned the oval-shaped clock I'd drawn, which had only one hand.

"Let's move on. This is what we call the Doors and People test." The doctor smiled.

This sounded good. "Makes sense, people go through doors, right?"

Rombauer smiled. "First, I'll show you a picture of four colored doors." He held up an image. "You'll need to remember them."

He paused for five seconds and put the picture facedown and turned over a new sheet with ten different doors on it. "Now, point out the doors from the previous sheet."

Moving my index finger over the doors, I tapped. "This one here, and this one, no wait, no." I pointed again. "This one, yeah this one for sure." I moved on. "Mmm, this looks like one, but . . ." I sat back. "Geez, they all look pretty much the same."

"Good, good. Now, let's do the people part. I'll recite four names, which I'll ask you to repeat. Ready?"

I swiped my hand across my mouth, trying to get the rust taste out, and nodded.

"John, Mary, Joe, Malcolm."

"Mary, Mary, Joe, and Malcolm."

"Good. Now I'd like you to repeat them again."

Again? I blinked. "Uh, Mary, Mallory, and Joe, and uh, uh." I slammed my fist on the table.

"There's no need to get upset, Peter. I know you may feel frustrated, but remember, we're here to help you."

I rested my chin on my hand.

Rombauer handed a sheet to me that had twenty randomly numbered circles. "I want you to start at circle number one and draw a line as quickly as possible from one circle to another. Now you have to go in numerical order, one, two, three, etcetera. Locate the first circle, and we'll begin."

This I could do. I mean, it was just like counting. I put his pen on the first circle, and Rombauer clicked a stopwatch.

It took just shy of two minutes for me to slam down the pen and a smiling Rombauer to slide the test back across the desk into a drawer.

Rombauer presented another sheet to me. "We'll do one more and then take a five-minute break. I want you to read the three sentences aloud, but the point is to remember the last word of each sentence."

"The swan is on the lake. Is the soup ready? Throw me the ball."

Rombauer took the paper. "Okay, what were the last words?"

"Throw the ball."

"The last word of each sentence."

"I—I." I sighed heavily. "Let me read it again."

"It's okay—"

"Give me the fucking paper!"

Rombauer calmly stood and smiled. "Let's take that break now."

***

The following day Rombauer called Vinny.

"I'm pleased that you had the foresight to bring Peter in before his regular appointment. I've had a chance to review his latest test results against the last couple of series." The doctor took a breath. "Your brother has slipped in a number of areas, primarily in the memory area."

Vinny sighed. "I knew it. Here we go again."

"Well, let's not jump to conclusions here."

"It's the only thing I'm good at."

"I see. Well, as I was attempting to express, Peter's memory facility, more specifically, his episodic and semantic capacities—"

"What?"

"His ability to retain facts and autobiographical information: what he did, when he did it, with whom, all the details and recollection."

"Now what?"

"I'm going to change some of his medications. It may be that he has built up a resistance to some of the nootropics, the memory-enhancing drugs. There are a number of studies that support such a thesis. In any event, I've made several changes. Now, keep in mind this may be trial and error, and we'll need to retest frequently to see what's working and what's not."

Vinny rolled his eyes at the thought of more tests, as the doctor continued.

"Vincent, your eyes are going to be critical to the process. We'll need to know as early as possible of any changes in his behavior, memory, anything. It'll take some time to identify the right combination of drugs and then more time for the medications to build up to an effective level."

"What's a realistic time line?"

"Well, that's difficult to predict. The brain is continually building new links, and a drug's efficacy is impacted . . ."

Rombauer droned on. Vinny had heard it all before.

***

Vinny watched closely, hoping the change in medications would get his brother back on a path of recovery. Within days, however, Peter seemed to be falling asleep more often, and his memory certainly didn't improve. Vinny called Rombauer.

"Doc, I gotta tell you, I don't think the new pills are working. He seems to be getting worse."

"What signs do you believe indicate the new regimen is not effective?"

"Well, he's falling asleep easily during the middle of the day."

"Yes, that can be a side effect, and while we should keep an eye on it, I am reluctant to make changes at this point."

"Yeah, well how about this, two times this week he asked me when we were going to eat."

"An increase in appetite is—"

"Hold on, Doc. He asked within an hour of having eaten. When I tell him we just ate, he seems to have forgotten completely. I'm telling you; it's gotten worse. I'm real concerned, as I've got to take a trip soon, and I just can't postpone it."

The doctor agreed to change course and prescribed different medications.

Chapter 7

I couldn't put my finger on it, but I knew I'd slipped, causing a dilemma for Vinny. You see, not only was his lease up in Texas, but the hold on his regular job was slipping away. He didn't know what to do. I simply hadn't recovered enough to allow him to move back to Texas like he wanted, so he decided to go down and move his stuff into storage to buy some time. I felt bad. I knew he wanted to go back to his old life, or at least take me down there, but the doctors said I had to stay in a familiar area. When Vinny suggested getting a sleepover nurse, basically a babysitter to stay with me while he was gone, I fought with him, and we ended up with a compromise of sorts.

Vinny took off for Texas on a drizzly morning, leaving a list of instructions and sticky notes everywhere. It was depressing. It drove home how dependent I'd become. The meds I was taking helped sometimes, but the problem was that I needed damn reminders all the time. I turned on the TV and plopped on the couch with a notepad he had tagged with a giant, lime green identifier. After checking the date, I started to read the day's instructions but got caught up in *The Price is Right*. I loved that show.

The doorbell rang a few times, and I trudged over, opening it for Melika, a Russian lady Vinny hired to check on me. She eyed me up and down, frowning.

Then she drummed in her hand the newspaper I'd left outside. "It's three thirty, and you're not dressed yet?"

I looked down my robe to my bare feet and pulled the belt around me. "I, uh, was—"

"You gonna let me in?"

I stepped aside. She rushed in, flipped on the lights, and shut the TV. Then she told me—no, commanded was more like it—to get dressed.

When I came down, she was tidying up. She frowned with her hands on her hips.

"No shower? What did you have for lunch?"

"I, ah, um, I didn't have anything, yet."

"What about breakfast?"

I couldn't remember if I ate or not and stood there thinking as she stormed into the kitchen. I plopped back on the sofa and started to read the pad of notes Vinny left. Halfway down the first page I read something that made me smile. Thank God Tony was coming tomorrow. It would give me a break from the gestapo bitch for a day.

Man, it was gonna be great to see Tony again. He visited twice or maybe three times when I was in Walter Reed, but it'd been a while. I couldn't remember how long since I last saw him.

***

My buddy came right before lunch, carrying subs and salads from Dearborn Farms.

"Yo, bro!"

We embraced for a long while, and a couple of tears plopped out.

"Man, you're looking good, Petey!"

"I don't know . . ."

"How you feeling?"

"Uh, sometimes good, but the frigging memory—I don't know. It seems to be getting worse by the day."

He pointed to his eyes. "What's with the specs?"

I shrugged. "Lifesaver, man, they help me with, you know, the, the, uh, what's it called? You know, how far things are . . ."

"Depth perception?"

"Yeah, see, I told you. Can't remember a frigging thing. This short-term memory crap—"

"Don't sweat it, bro."

"It's funny, I can remember things from a long time ago. Like when we were in the fucking hellhole, Afghanistan, clear as a picture, but remember to brush my teeth?"

"What do the docs say?"

"Bunch of mumbo jumbo. Anyway, they gave me another couple of pills to help. Let's see if it works."

"How about the ear thing?"

I shrugged. "Kinda the same. I can live with it most of the times, but sometimes—"

"Come on. Let's have some chow. I'm starving."

You know, they're right, service buddies are friends for life. After being filled in on what some of our buddies were doing, we caught up on the romance end of things—Tony telling me he'd met someone he felt he'd marry, and me telling him I thought things were getting a little bit better with Mary.

The afternoon flew by, fueled by more stories of our time in Afghanistan. We were somber at times, but the joy of being home together drove the day into evening. Tony reminded me he was staying overnight to celebrate his brother's birthday before heading back to Cherry Hill.

"I gotta get going, Petey."

"Sure."

"Hey, why don't you come to the party tonight? You know Joey."

I'd met his brother a few times. "I don't know. I'd feel funny, and Vinny wants me to stay in."

"Come on, man. You got to get back in the swing of things. What you gonna do, watch frigging TV?"

"Who's gonna be there?"

"Just some family. No big deal—you gotta eat anyway."

"I—I don't know, Tony. How am I gonna get back and forth? Vinny'll kill me if he knows I drove alone."

"I'll pick your ass up at seven."

***

I was glad I went. There weren't a lot of people there, and their mother was nice and a great cook. After we ate, they had a birthday cake, and it quickly quieted down. Joey was meeting up with his friends at the Lincoln Lounge on Route 35 to continue, or should I say, start the celebration. Tony pushed me to go with them, saying it was on the way to my house anyway. He promised to take me back after a game or two of pool, and knowing Mary went there sometimes, I quickly agreed.

The Lincoln Lounge was an old neighborhood bar with pool tables. The place reinvigorated itself by bringing in a DJ to play dance music after the old-timers went home. Joey's friends were shooting pool and hoisting beers when we came in.

"Yo, birthday boy!"

"What's up, old man? What are you, like, forty?"

"Fuck you."

I scanned the place for Mary as bear hugs and fist bumps erupted.

"This is my bro, Pete. We served together."

"Yeah, sure. You're Vinny's brother. Good to see you on your feet, man."

I nodded and shook a few hands as a familiar face cut in.

"Hey, Pete, how you doing, man? Heard you got injured."

It was an old classmate with red hair whose name I couldn't recall. "Okay, I guess."

Tony said, "Okay? Man, you should've seen him! I hate to say it, Petey, but I really didn't think you'd make it. He was hooked up to so many fucking machines."

I peered over Tony's shoulder for signs of Mary. I moved outside the circle for a better view as a barmaid took our party's drink orders.

As she began to move to the bar, Tony said, "Don't forget my man, Pete. You remember him, no?"

"Yeah sure. You used to go with Mary before she hooked up with Billy."

Used to? "I—I, we still, uh, I mean, we're—"

"I hear she and Billy are getting hitched soon."

I froze. Leaning on my cane.

"So, what can I get you? A beer?"

My mouth was slammed with the taste of rusting iron and my mind with confusion.

"Is Heineken okay with you?"

I nodded. "Billy who?"

"Wyatt."

I collapsed into a chair as images of my nemesis taunting me in the first-grade schoolyard flooded my head. It was the start of the end of my relationship with my brother. A year older, Vinny didn't intervene when Billy Wyatt, my age but six inches and twenty pounds heavier, punched me in the belly and I lost my breath. I was hunched over, hands on my knees, trying to gulp air as tears streamed down my face. A circle of first and second graders watched as Billy pushed me to the ground.

Mrs. Murphy rushed through the throng of kids and pulled me to safety as my brother said, "Get up. Don't be a sissy."

I refused to go back to class, and they called my mom to get me, serving to embarrass me further. The tear flow exploded when I saw her. I told her what happened and that Vinny didn't help me. She comforted me and confronted Vinny when he came home. I listened from the hallway as he lied, saying he didn't see what was going on and only came when he saw Mrs. Murphy running. But my mother knew, as moms do, when their kid is lying. She punished him, but it didn't help. In fact, it made things worse as he blamed me for having to stay inside the entire weekend.

Vinny and Billy Wyatt became inseparable through middle school, and I didn't trust either one of them. When it came time for high school, Vinny and I went to Middletown South, and Billy to North. However, the fierce rivalry between the schools' sport teams did nothing to damage their relationship. Vinny hung out with Billy and the kids from North, while I hung with my South classmates. I kept my distance from Billy, who'd built a huge reputation as a bully. I longed for the day someone would put him in his place.

Becoming the quarterback for the North's varsity team fed right into Billy Wyatt's aggressor karma and led to another humiliating experience for me in front of almost everyone I knew. The two Middletown football teams had a scrimmage against each other at our home field. Since we had a heated rivalry going, the practice game was well attended. After the scrimmage, we were headed to the locker rooms when I was hit above my ear with a football. I turned around, and the throng of kids parted, leaving a smirking Billy as the obvious prankster. I searched for the coaches, but they were inside already, so I marched up to him, but before I could say a word, he swung his helmet into my gut. I doubled over, and like ten years before, had the breath knocked out of me. The humiliation I suffered led me to search for a way to restore my pride, but the opportunity always evaded me.

The barmaid tapped my shoulder. She took a bottle of Heineken off her tray and held it out.

I banged my cane on the ground and pulled myself out of the chair and into the tray. As the bottle crashed to the floor, I stormed over to Tony.

"I wanna go."

"What's the matter?"

"Nothing. Take me home."

"But we just got—"

"Now, goddamn it!"

Tony threw up his palm, put his beer down, and we left.

Tony tried to figure out what was wrong, but I wouldn't open up. Simmering as he drove, I fingered the cell phone in my pocket with a trembling hand. I closed the car door as Tony made plans to visit again.

I pulled out the phone on the way to the front door.

She answered on the second ring.

Chapter 8

Monmouth County Prosecutor William Stanley had called a meeting with John Cline, an assistant who headed the county's Major Crimes Bureau, and County Sheriff, Bob Meril. A troubling rise in murders to four a month versus one in years past, combined with an alarming rise in burglaries, were testing their ability to keep the peace. The media was running multiple stories a day, scaring residents, while providing Stanley's opponents with plenty to campaign against in his reelection bid.

Stanley, a wiry man with steel-blue eyes and a creased forehead, was known as a man of action but also as incredibly stubborn. The prosecutor wanted to tackle the increase in burglaries, which often tracked an uptick in drug use. He flopped open a file.

"The rise in drug use is almost all attributed to the increased use of crystal meth." He tapped the table with his forefinger. "This meth is wreaking havoc on our communities." He offered a sheet to his associates. "Addictive Services reports there are no available beds, with a nine-month wait for inpatient treatment and a minimum of four months for outpatients."

The sheriff slid the report back, grumbling. "I donno how they smoke that crap."

Assistant Prosecutor Cline offered, "The traditional law enforcement response would be to increase surveillance, bust street-level dealers—"

Stanley furrowed his brow. "Sure, choking availability would reduce the meth supply, but it would drive up prices."

"And a junkie's desperation," Sheriff Meril added.

"Exactly where I was heading, Bob. Everything we know tells us that meth abusers become psychotic and extremely aggressive. I'm concerned these addicts will get even more violent, desperate in their pursuit to satiate their cravings."

Cline nodded. "It's something I witnessed when I was with the DA's office in New York. We had a crack cocaine epidemic, and it was nasty. Crackheads were popping dealers left and right to get their hands on that junk." He held up three fingers. "We had three bodies a day to deal with."

Stanley said, "I've been thinking, maybe we ratchet enforcement up a bit. Hit the projects, parks, wherever the dealers are." Stanley looked at the sheriff for a second. "Not too much, Bob, just raise it a notch. At the same time, I'm going to lean on the governor's office for a substantial funding increase in treatment dollars. Any way we can get these addicts off the street . . ." Stanley left it hanging and searched his associates' faces.

"It's worth a shot."

The sheriff grinned. "And the upside is it won't suck up my overtime budget."

"Good, then I'll leave it to you, Bob. Just not too heavy a hand. If we can tamp this down a notch or two, it'll fall out of the papers."

The group finished the meeting by discussing how most of the new wave of homicides involved robberies, and a fair share exhibited patterns pointing to the possibility that one person or group was responsible for up to a third of the crimes. They agreed to keep an eye out for patterns, and left Stanley's office.

Stanley was hopeful, calling in a favor with the state police to get twenty troopers and their vehicles to patrol in Monmouth. But he had to go to the freeholders to get the funding for the show of force and increased treatment dollars. He scanned his email before putting on his jacket and heading to see two freeholders at town hall.

The structure that housed Freehold Town Hall was a stone-faced edifice off bustling Main Street. As he traversed the building's small plaza, his phone rang. He checked the number before answering.

"Hey Paul, let me get back to you. I'm heading into a meeting with—"

"What?"

"Where?"

"Damn! Who's on it?"

"Okay, I'll get back as fast as possible."

Stanley hung up and hustled to his meeting.

The news about the latest murder had already beaten him to the freeholders, and though the heat on him increased, Stanley was able to use it to support his cause for more funding. The freeholders agreed to bust the budget but made it crystal clear that results were needed, and quickly, or their political support for his reelection bid would be difficult to maintain.

Chapter 9

The patrol car that responded to the 911 call encountered a sobbing woman surrounded by neighbors standing outside despite a steady rain. The responding officers checked with the throng, drew their weapons, and entered the house.

Sneakered feet were visible at the end of a small foyer. Eyes sweeping for possible threats, they inched toward the body belonging to the gym shoes. One officer kept guard while the other knelt on the brown carpet, trying to find a pulse on the body. He shook his head, wiping dried blood from his finger.

The officers cleared the rest of the house, called for the homicide detectives, and secured the crime scene. A neighbor offered her Cape Cod house to the woman and onlookers as a refuge from the rain as they waited for the investigators.

Lights flashing and wipers clearing windblown rain, Detective Frank Luca pulled onto Keansburg's Seventh Street, joining four black and whites at number nine. He pulled up his collar and followed his partner, JJ Cremora, to the officer guarding the front door.

"Hey, Luca, JJ, we got ourselves another nasty one. Poor guy had his head just about turned to pulp."

Luca grabbed the clipboard and signed in. "Who's the responder?"

The officer called inside. "O'Reilly, homicide's here."

Luca's blue eyes sparkled as he smiled. "O'Reilly again?"

Middletown's skinniest officer waved them in. "Come on in."

Luca put on bootees and stepped inside. "We gotta stop meeting like this, O'Reilly."

"And how."

"What do we got here?"

"Male, late twenties, name's William Wyatt. Looks like it was severe head trauma that punched his ticket."

"Who found him?"

"Girlfriend." He looked at his pad. "Name's Mary Rourke. Says she found him lying right there."

The detectives exchanged glances and Detective Cremora asked, "Any signs of forced entry?"

"Not that I saw, but we didn't comb it over closely. We secured it and called in the cavalry. Oh, we shut the TV off."

Luca asked, "Coroner here?"

"Nah, had something in Trenton this morning."

"Check on his ETA for me."

Police photographer, Stevie Gianelli, was busy snapping pictures of the body and the crime scene with his trusty old Nikon. He looked up at the detectives, winked a hello, and repositioned for another shot.

"Gianelli, make sure you take a complete video as well, inside and out."

The photographer nodded. "Sure thing, handsome."

The detectives bent over and examined the victim. Lying on his stomach with his head turned to the left, Billy Wyatt, a man in his prime, had begun to stiffen. A fifteen-year veteran, Frank Luca had checked his emotions at the door.

"No signs of a gunshot wound."

"Or knifing," JJ added.

Luca felt the victim's leg and belly. "He's pretty stiff and ice cold."

"What d'ya think, Luc?"

"I don't know, maybe twelve to fifteen hours."

"Looks like he was hit from behind, no?"

"Yeah, maybe. When the doc gets here, he'll see if there're any bruises on the right side."

"His legs are tangled up."

"Could've gotten that way trying to get away."

"Other than the head, seems to be no other wounds. You see anything else?"

Luca pulled out a magnifying glass and went over the body again.

"Nothing under the fingernails that I can see either, but the doc will scrap 'em."

Cremora called out, "Yo, Gianelli, you get close-ups and all?"

"It's not my first day, bro."

The veteran detective pored over the corpse and inserted his gloved fingers in the victim's back pockets.

"No wallet. JJ, lift the body a bit. I want to check the front pockets."

Luca grunted as he fished out a set of car keys from the right pocket. Cremora lifted the left side of the body enough for Luca to probe the other pocket. He came up with a fistful of cash.

Cremora said, "Guess that rules out robbery."

"Maybe."

Luca put the cash in an evidence bag, and they stood over the victim for a couple of minutes before Luca took a final survey of the room and corpse.

"No signs of a struggle in here. Let's check the rest of the place out."

They circled the living room, where the body was lying. Yesterday's *Asbury Park Press* lay open on a velour sofa showing wear. A marred coffee table hosted a half bottle of Bud, three remotes, and a crumb-filled plate. Luca looked for a crumpled napkin but couldn't locate one. They headed to the next room.

No surprise, he thought, when they entered the galley kitchen where the sink was crowded with crusty dishes. A loaf of Wonder Bread and a can of tuna sat on the Formica countertop beside a butt-filled ashtray.

"JJ, make a note. It was tuna the victim was dining on. It may help Fitch with nailing down a time of death."

Cremora nodded.

An alcove off the kitchen held a washer and dryer and a door to a small yard.

"O'Reilly!"

The wiry responder slid into the kitchen. "What's up, Luc?"

"This door—was it open when you got here?"

"Yeah. I told you, we didn't touch anything but the TV."

Luca cocked his head at Cremora.

"Get it dusted for prints."

Then he pulled out a pencil, pushed the door fully open with its eraser, and stepped onto a concrete pad.

Luca eyed the unkempt yard. It wasn't fenced but was shielded from the other houses by a mixture of overgrown holly and rhododendrons. Noting the trash cans and an old bicycle to his left and a rotting shed in the center, his eyes settled on two cans of beer and a pack of Marlboros on a redwood table to the right. Examining the ground for footprints, Luca changed his shoe covers and approached the patio furniture, carefully sidestepping several cigarette butts littering the area. The rain had slowed to a faint drizzle, but the pack of cigarettes was soaked.

Luca's partner stepped into the yard.

"Anything interesting?"

"Put on a new pair of bootees, J. The bench is pulled out, someone was sitting here. Just don't know when or who." Luca pointed to the butt that lay an inch or so away from the table's edge. "Looks like it burned out on its own."

JJ looked closely at the burn mark and butt, nodding. "It's a Marlboro."

They considered the two cans of beer, one used as an ashtray. Luca poked the other can with his pencil, testing its weight. He looked around the yard slowly, declaring, "Let's bag up the butts and cans, and check with the girlfriend on what brand her lover boy smoked."

***

Luca munched on a turkey hero as Cremora slapped his office door with a file.

"Autopsy report." He eyed the sandwich. "Maybe we'll wait till you're finished?"

Luca took a bite, wrapped the rest of the sub into a ball and tossed it in the garbage can.

JJ came around Luca's desk and plopped open the file. "No surprises. Death caused by trauma to the head with a blunt instrument. No other wounds."

Luca paged through the headshots. "Doc say what he was hit with?"

"Could be a bat, pipe, something circular in nature. And no doubt he was hit from behind."

"The vic high on anything?"

"Blood alcohol of .04, a little buzzed. He's, or was, one hundred and seventy."

Luca read on. "Shit, nothing under the fingernails. What's this about the knuckles?"

"Doc wasn't sure. Said it could've happened on the way down."

"Maybe throwing a punch?"

"He said no, but you were right on the TOD."

"You mean, again?"

JJ elbowed his partner. "Time of death was about fourteen hours before O'Reilly found him."

"Not much to go on, but we know he bought the farm about eight last night."

"I'll check with the captain, see if the foot soldiers brought anything back from talking with the neighbors."

"Don't let the door hit you in the ass." Luca said, picking up the phone.

Luca felt the customary pressure to make significant progress within days of the murder or risk the trail going cold. Looking for something to work with, he was going to push forensics hard for any clues they could reveal before he headed to an emergency meeting.

***

Luca slid onto a barstool next to his date. "Sorry, Deb."

She sipped her vodka. "I knew it was too good to be true."

"Aw, come on, Deb. It's been crazy. The pressure is really on."

Debra frowned. "Same old story."

"No, it's true. The brass is on our backs."

"Come on, Frank. I'm sitting here like some bimbo for almost two hours." She shook her head. "You always put the job ahead of everything."

"That's not fair. I've changed. It's just that right now with the Wyatt kid murder and a shitload of assaults, the suits in Freehold want results."

"Guess after a couple of," she fingered quotation marks, "dates, I got my hopes up too high."

Luca kissed her cheek. "No, this time it's gonna be different. I'm telling you." He bored his blue eyes into her. "You'll see."

"It better be. Let's get something to eat. I'm starved."

They ordered off the bar menu. All through dinner Luca worked at making this latest transgression fade away. He assured Debra that his proposal of moving back in with her was right for them. Fact was, he missed her terribly and wanted them to be a couple again. Knowing it was his fault, Luca had secretly vowed not to let the job define his life, and maybe even more importantly, wouldn't violate his marriage vows again, no matter what sexy tail came along.

They had met when Luca was commuting as a junior at John Jay College, and the good-looking couple was inseparable. A whirlwind courtship ended with an engagement, and they married a month after he graduated from the academy.

Anxious to prove himself as a rookie, Luca relished the "low man on the totem pole" assignments and never complained, despite Debra's protests. As a new bride, she wanted her husband home, but the overnight and weekend shifts left little time for a honeymoon period.

Luca felt that trying to build a career benefitted both of them and began resenting her complaints. A proverbial wall had gone up by their second anniversary, and things fell apart when Luca, a George Clooney lookalike, started receiving calls at home from a woman officer he found impossible to resist.

The damage from his wandering took three years to fully mend. After a tentative restart, the couple enjoyed a two-year period whose bliss was shattered by a miscarriage. The couple regrouped, but Luca quickly became impatient with his wife's anxiety over the loss. Restless, he began studying to become a detective.

He passed on the first go-round and had been working in plainclothes for over a decade. Luca's new career path got off to a rocky start on his first case when he and the lead investigative detective succumbed to pressure to solve the murder of a county official's family member. The young man jailed for the crime, Dominick Barrow, hung himself, and the uproar exploded exponentially when another suspect confessed. Luca, the junior officer, didn't want to make waves in the efforts to frame the kid, and carried a heavy load of guilt over the case.

Attempting to dislodge the guilt from the Barrow case, Luca began working way too much. Debra was understanding at first, believing the guilt he felt drove him to work excessively. But as the years and cases passed, she tired and the couple separated.

Chapter 10

Sergeant Richard Gesso led the hastily arranged gathering. Given it was midmorning on a Saturday, he had only a handful of officers to work with. The fit, sixty-something Gesso stepped in front of the blackboard.

"We got another homicide to deal with." He touched the end of his wide, black moustache. "We need to wrap these up and wrap 'em up quickly. The community is scared, and no surprise, the press is making us look bad again." He lowered his voice a notch. "Frankly, I'm tired of getting heat from the county, not to mention the calls from every old lady within forty miles."

Gesso paused to pick up a sheet from the lectern and dug out his reading glasses.

"Keansburg section again, second time this month." He wagged his head. "Twenty-six-year-old male, William Wyatt. Head bashed in last night. Forensics is collecting at the scene, and there's a push from Freehold to get the autopsy done tonight." Gesso pushed up his glasses and continued. "There are no suspects and no sign of a break-in, so he may have known his assailant." Gesso peered over his glasses before continuing. "Wyatt lived alone. Girlfriend, a Mary Rourke, found him. She's not ruled out. Detective Luca's gonna handle her." He stopped reading. "Wyatt's a local kid. Geez, I remember him as the quarterback for South. Led them to two state championships. Then the kid went to Rutgers but couldn't make first team and dropped out." He went back to his paper. "Wyatt went to DeVry and then got a job as a technician over at Philly's in Hazlet a couple years ago. His parents moved down to

South Carolina, so I'll get the locals to interview them, see if anything comes up."

Gesso surveyed the room. "We gotta put the leather to the pavement. Johnson, you and O'Brien take four officers and cover Wyatt's neighborhood. Door-to-door it; see if you can uncover anything: a car, someone on foot, something suspicious. You know the drill."

Two youthful detectives jumped up. "We got it, Sarge."

Gesso pointed to a map on an easel. "And be sure to check the houses on the street behind Wyatt's. There's a cul-de-sac backing up to Thompson Park where the stream is."

The detectives nodded and left. Gesso continued.

"Mulligan, you and Griffin dig into his background: coworkers, any family you can find, his girlfriend. Check that. Luca's got her, unless you hear he was two-timing her. Talk with the people he went to school with. I want you talking to everyone, even his bowling buddies." Gesso took his glasses off and gestured with them. "This was a brutal beating. Nothing seems to have been stolen. He was missing his wallet but had a wad of cash in his pocket. Who knows, maybe it was a revenge thing or something. So, the rest of you keep your eyes and ears open on your patrols and lean on your contacts. Look, Stanley's got the sheriff crawling up my ass already, so I'd appreciate some results here and pronto."

***

Arriving at the crime scene, uniformed officers fanned out, hitting the houses on the surrounding blocks, while Johnson and O'Brien covered the houses on Wyatt's street. When neither next-door neighbor said they'd seen nor heard anything unusual, they split up, with Johnson heading across the street to a brick-faced colonial. A woman in her forties in a blue housecoat answered the door.

Johnson flashed his badge. "Ma'am, we're canvassing the neighborhood for any information about last night's incident. Were you home last night?"

"It's terrible. He was a good kid. Served in, uh, Iraq. No, it was Afghanistan. What a damn shame. His poor family." She closed her eyes. "We're frightened as can be. We have a seventeen-year-old daughter."

"Calm down, ma'am. There's no reason to panic. Now, did you or anyone in your household see or hear anything unusual, anything at all, no matter how small a detail?"

"Well, we—me and my husband, Mike—were watching TV, and really, we didn't hear anything. That's the scary part, you know. It just seems like a normal night, but meanwhile, right across the street, a young man is killed. Why?"

"So you and your husband"—he looked at his notes—"Mike, didn't hear or see anything unusual. No cars out front, nobody walking, no sounds, anything?"

"Nothing."

"Anyone else live here?"

"Yes, our daughter Kathy. Her name's Kathy."

"Was she home?"

"No, she went with some friends to stay over at a girl's who used to live in town." She wagged her head. "Poor thing doesn't even know what happened." She looked at her watch. "It's only eleven thirty. They said they'd be back around four."

"When she leave?"

"Right after dinner. I made a tuna casserole. Her friend, Patty, picked her up."

"What time would that be?"

"Around six thirty, seven."

"Okay, ma'am. Here's my card. If you remember anything, let us know. Look, when you talk to your daughter, ask her if she saw anything, and call me."

At six o'clock the two cops headed back after interviewing nearly thirty neighbors. Two saw a tall man running through backyards. One woman estimated him to be in his mid-thirties, but another neighbor said he looked much older, maybe as old as fifty. They also collected three reports of a dark sedan driving slowly and a compact car parked in the dark on the road behind Wyatt's home.

There were four neighbors who weren't home, but other than the tall-man sightings and the sedan, the foot soldiers were not hopeful that what they had would lead to a breakthrough.

With the heat rising on the police force, O'Brien and Johnson were working Sunday and went back to hit the neighbors they missed. They pulled up to a brown ranch whose rear yard backed up to Wyatt's. A potbellied man, sporting a stained tee shirt, opened the door.

O'Brien held his badge out. "Good morning, mind if we ask you a couple of questions about what happened behind you?"

"Figured you boys would come 'round. Damn terrible thing." He stepped outside. "Wyatt was a nice kid an' all, but they fought like cats and dogs."

"Who?"

He popped a cigarette in his mouth. "The girlfriend and Billy."

"How do you know that?"

He lit his smoke. "Well, I hear 'em going at it from the back porch. The wife, she doesn't let me smoke inside, so I gotta come out back."

"Did you hear anything, any fighting, on Friday, May fifteenth?"

The neighbor took a deep drag. "It was raining, and the wind was blowing that night." He lowered his voice and pointed to a hanging chime. "I remember, 'cause my old lady's damn chimes were clanging away. One of these days I'm going to rip 'em down."

"But on other nights you stated you heard them fighting?"

"Sometimes, depends on what else is going on. You know, sometimes these kids on these motorcycles; they're so damn loud I can't hear my own thinking."

"Was there anything else about that night you remember?"

He blew smoke through his nose. "Well, now that you say it, that kid Jimmy Johns, heck, he ain't no kid now, but he used to go to school with my boy Tommy."

When he took another deep drag on his cigarette, O'Brien prodded, "Go on. What about him?"

"Well, I seen him cutting through my yard."

"What direction was he moving?"

The neighbor pointed. "Kinda on an angle, moving this way."

"So, coming from Wyatt's street?"

"Seemed like it was that way."

"So how do you know it was this guy Johns?"

"Shit, I know it was him. I had him doing some yard work. My wife had run into him, and he was down on his luck, so we had him come, you know, take out some of the brush and all, about six months ago." He shook his head. "You know, the bastard had the balls to steal some of my old lady's Hummels when he came in to use the john."

"I see. Did you file a report at the time?"

"Nah, poor kid's just desperate. Besides, she got too many of them things anyways."

"Do you know where this Jimmy John kid lives?"

"It's Johns, Jimmy Johns. Don't know exactly, but the kid is from Keansburg. I think around Second Street or so. They used to be over on Bay Avenue when his momma was alive."

O'Brien took a description of Johns from the neighbor and continued pounding doors.

The neighbor whose daughter had gone out around the time in question called O'Brien, and the cop stopped off to interview the kid on his way home.

O'Brien was shown into their small living room and took a seat in what must have been the father's recliner, as both mother and daughter perched themselves on a plaid sofa. There were so many tchotchkes in the room that the place looked like a flea market stand.

"So, Kathy, I'd like you to take your time and try to recall anything you may have seen, heard, or even smelled the night in question."

"Well, it's not really much, probably nothing, but my mother keeps hounding me." She rolled her eyes.

"Well, sometimes even the smallest things can be helpful." O'Brien flipped open his notepad. "Shall we?"

The kid popped a piece of gum in her mouth. "Well, my girlfriend, Patty, Patty Shields, she lives over in Fox Run. Well, she was coming to pick me up. She has her license already, and her parents got her a car already." She glanced at her mother, and when she tilted her head, her ponytail lay on her shoulder.

"Okay, go on."

"So, like, she came, I think like six thirty or so, and when I was getting in the car, another car came up like real fast and kinda like screeched, no, not screeched, but like came to a stop, like real fast and all. But that's it. We didn't see anything 'cause we left then."

"Okay, so where did this car stop?"

"Across the street by that poor guy's house." She stopped smacking her gum and looked into her lap.

"In front? Directly in front of the Wyatt house?"

"I guess so." She pulled on her ponytail.

"Take a second and think about it. Where were you when it pulled up?"

"In front of my house, by Patty's car."

"Did, uh, your friend stop right in front of your house?"

"Basically."

"When you were getting in her car, you could see this car directly to your left."

The teenager blew a bubble, and nodded.

"Okay, tell me about the car you saw. What color was it?"

She closed her eyes. "Uh, kinda red, like a dark red, maybe burgundy?"

O'Brien jotted a note. "How old would you say? Was it new?"

"No, not new. I don't know much about cars. Just that I want one." She giggled.

"Anything else you remember about the car? How many doors? Or special wheels or anything?"

"No, I'm sorry. It's just that we didn't pay attention. We didn't know anything was going to happen."

"Of course. Now, you told your mother that you didn't see who was driving. I want you to take your time and think about it. Could it have been a man? A woman?"

"I—I don't know, but maybe it was a man."

"What makes you say that it was a man?"

"I don't know. It just seemed like a car a man would drive. It was kinda fuddy-duddy, if you know what I mean." She giggled.

"So, it was an older car?"

"Kinda, not a junk box, but not new, for sure. It had that big front thing, uh, uh, what you call it?"

"The grill?"

"Yup, that's it."

"The car had a large grill?"

"Yeah, I think so, like, you know, those cars that kinda looked like a, those real expensive cars over in England?"

"Rolls Royce? Bentley?"

"Yeah, I'm pretty sure it was something like that."

"Sounds like it may have been a Chrysler. I hate to impose, but do you folks have a computer we can look at pictures of cars on? It'd be really helpful."

Chapter 11

Luca and Cremora were greeted at the door by Mrs. Rourke, Mary's mother, and were shown into the apartment's small kitchen. Even without makeup, the twenty-something Mary was a stunner. Her shoulder-length auburn hair had a glossy sheen to it, but it was the perfectly apportioned body that Luca nearly gaped at. Braless, Mary's nipples were pushed against her white tee shirt. Luca had to make a conscious effort not to stare, but he thought he could make out the dark circles surrounding her nipples.

"Mary, these are Detectives Luca and Cremora."

They extended hands, offering their condolences.

"Sorry it's so cramped in here."

There were only three chairs around the half-moon table.

The mother said, "Sit, sit please."

"It's okay. I've been sitting all day." Cremora leaned on the fridge as Luca and the mother settled into chairs.

"Again, we're truly sorry for your loss, Mary, and we're sorry to bother you at a time like this, but it's important for us to interview people while the information is fresh in everyone's mind."

"I understand," Mary said as her mother squeezed her hand.

"How long did you know Billy?"

"Almost my entire life, like from grade school."

"And when did you start dating?"

"Well, we always seemed to have a thing for each other, but we got serious a year ago, and we were gonna"—she sniffled, and her mother offered a tissue—"get engaged for my birthday."

"Can you think of anyone who would want to hurt Billy?"

"Nobody. Everybody liked Billy. He was a prince." Mary dabbed her eyes.

Luca held up his palm. "Just give it a second and think about it. Anyone he had a beef with, someone from the past, maybe at work?"

Luca watched her tits bounce as she wagged her head. She looked him in the eye, and by her barely perceptible smile, he knew she'd caught him. "Like I said, everybody loved him, right Mom?"

Luca shifted in his seat as the mother chimed agreement.

"Did Billy like to get his way, be the center of attention?"

"Kinda, I guess."

"Who wouldn't?" the mother added.

"It's just that we hear Billy was quite the bully."

"Mom!"

"How dare you, the poor boy is not even in the ground yet."

Cremora stepped forward. "Sorry, ma'am, we're just trying to see if anyone harbored a grudge or something."

The women pursed their lips and remained quiet.

"Did Billy carry a wallet?"

"Uh, yeah, except he was always losing it, like leaving it behind when he paid the check," Mary said.

"Do you know if he lost his wallet recently?"

"I don't know. He didn't say anything to me. Why?"

"We couldn't locate his wallet on his person or in the house."

"Did you check his car? He'd put it in the console all the time. Said it bothered him when he sat."

Luca glanced at Cremora, who said, "Pretty sure we did, but thanks. I'll check it out, just to be sure."

Luca ran his hand over his silk tie. "Okay, Mary, I'm going to ask some questions about the morning you called 911. Take your time, and if you need to take a break or anything, just let us know. So, tell me about the morning you found him."

"Well, it was Saturday, and we always went to the gym together on Saturdays."

Ostensibly to knock the picture of her in gym shorts out of his head, Luca nodded.

"And what gym is that?"

"WOW on Route 35."

"The one by Shoprite?"

Mary nodded.

"Kinda out of the way for you to go all the way to his place, wasn't it?"

"Um, yeah, I guess so. I was out already and figured, you know, to just get him."

"Where did you go?"

"When?"

"When you were out."

"Oh, I don't know, the store or something."

Luca made a mental note. "You have a dark red car, right?"

"How'd you know?"

"It's parked in front of your unit. Lucky guess. So, you were shopping, right?"

"Um, yeah, and when I got to the house, Billy's house, I found him. He was lying there and all the blood and . . ." She broke down, and her mother consoled her.

"Was the door open?"

"No, I have my own key."

"Okay, what did you do when you found him?"

"I went straight to him. I tried to rustle him, but I knew; I just knew he was . . ." She cried again.

"Take your time, Mary. Did you notice anything unusual? Anything out of place?"

She shook her head. "I didn't know what to do. I started to scream, and then I just ran out."

"Did you touch anything?"

"No, I don't know. Billy, I touched him, and I don't know what I did . . ."

"Isn't that enough, officers? My poor baby's upset."

"We're almost through, ma'am."

Mary wiped her eyes and nodded to her mother.

"Did you and Billy fight often?"

The mother bolted upright. "That's it! Get out! Get out!"

***

Luca dropped the receiver into its cradle.

"If I have to talk to another crackpot with visions of who did it—"

"School me. This kinda shit never gets covered in the TV shows."

Luca checked his watch. "Wow, it's almost six. Time flies when you're having fun."

"I'm outta here by six, six thirty latest."

"Me too. Meeting Deb for pizza and a movie."

"What're you going to see?"

"She loves DiCaprio, so that remake he's in—"

"Heard it sucked."

"Hope so, I could use the nap."

After a square Sicilian pie at Luigi's, they settled into their seats at the Hazlet Cineplex, where Luca nodded out a quarter of the way through the flick. Debra enjoyed the movie and filled Luca in on what he'd missed.

As they prepared to hit the sack, Luca said, "Boy, you must really like that Leonardo dude."

"What does that mean?"

"Just that you seem so happy. I'm ready to get a poster of him for the bedroom."

Debra shook her head as she capped the toothpaste. "See, all it takes is the simple things, Frank. I don't need diamonds. They'd be nice, though. Just keeping a promise for a little thing like going to the movies is really all I need."

Luca came up behind her and nuzzled her neck. He slipped his hand under her robe and caressed her breast. Pressing his hips into her, he steered her onto the bed.

"You know what? I think there might be a diamond under your pillow."

***

Luca bolted upright, awakening Debra.

"What's the matter?"

Luca was breathing heavily.

"Nothing. It's okay."

Debra reached out and touched his back. "Geez, you're soaked," she said.

Luca sighed heavily.

"You're still having those nightmares?"

"Not like I used to, really; just every now and then."

"It wasn't your fault, you know."

"I know, it's just that I can see Barrow's father's face like it was yesterday."

Chapter 12

Joanne was a pretty nineteen-year-old who lived with her parents in the same neighborhood as Billy Wyatt. She developed earlier than most girls in her school and owned a rack that had interested older guys since junior high. Attracted to older men, Joanne found herself in a relationship with a married man while she was still in high school. When her parents discovered it, they went ballistic and confronted the man. It was an ugly ending for all and quickly became the talk of the neighborhood.

The devastation and embarrassment made her ripe for a rebound lover, and she secretly began seeing a Hazlet policeman. Thirty-five-year-old Steve was married and had a three-year-old son but was hot and heavy with the teenager nonetheless.

Joanne would feign going out with friends when she left the house to meet with him. Steve would pick her up two blocks away from her home, and they would drive west of Morristown, where no one would see them.

Steve pulled up to the curb. "Hey, good-looking! How's it going?"

Joanne looked both ways and hopped in the car as Steve leaned over to peck her cheek.

"No one saw you, right?" she said and sank her frame as low as the seat would allow.

"Of course, what're you worried about?"

"Well, everyone's spooked, and like, there are cops everywhere."

"Take it easy. They're just canvassing to get information about the murder."

"What's going on with it? Did they get anyone?"

"Nothing yet; it's a tough one."

"Nothing?"

"Couple of pieces, clues. Looks like maybe a robbery gone bad or something."

Joanne sat quietly as they headed for the parkway.

"Don't worry, we'll get him."

"I think, maybe, oh, it's probably nothing."

"What? Tell me, Jo."

"Well, Friday night, I left to meet you and walked right by his house."

"Whose house?"

"The kid that got killed."

"Okay, go on."

"I was across the street, the side without lights, and I was just past the house when a car came flying up and kinda screeched to a stop in front of his house."

"Whoa, hold on there."

Steve pulled into the Cheesequake rest area, and Joanne told him she saw this reddish, or maybe it was a brownish car pull up in front of Wyatt's house. Then a man—she was certain it was a man, who was about thirty—got out carrying a pole or something. She said she saw him walk up to the door. Joanne said she didn't think much of it until she heard what had happened and checked to be sure it was the same house. When it was, she was scared and didn't know what to do.

"You gotta tell the detectives handling the case! We're going now." He started the car.

"No, no, I can't." She started crying.

"You have to."

"No, I won't."

"Jo, a man's been killed, brutally beaten to death, and the killer is still out there!"

Her chin fell into her chest. "I know, but . . ."

"No buts, you have information that may help us find who did it."

"My parents—they'll find out about us."

"We'll handle that."

"We'll? You mean you and your wife?"

He slammed on the brakes. "That's not fair, and you know it!"

"Yeah, well, what about me?" The tears flowed as Steve pulled off the entrance ramp and parked.

"Come on, Jo. Well, maybe we can say you were meeting your friends or—"

Her lips quivered. "Can't we just forget it?"

"I can't. I'm sorry, but our guys are busting their asses to track down this guy. He's a killer, Jo. No one's safe with him out there."

She blew her nose. "I know, but can't we do it, like, anonymously, like on a hotline or something?"

Steve drummed his fingers on the steering wheel. "Look, I know the guy running the investigation. He's a good guy. I'll reach out to him."

"You gotta promise me, Steve; don't use my name. I'm begging you. My parents—they'll throw me out. I couldn't face them."

***

At the end of his shift, Steve knocked on Luca's office door. The detective was reading a report and peered over his reading glasses.

"Hey, Stevie, how's it going?"

"Good, got a minute?"

Luca looked at his wristwatch and frowned.

"Shit, Debra's—"

"It's important, Luc—the Wyatt case."

Luca snapped off his glasses, motioning to a chair that Steve took after closing the door.

"What do you have?"

"Well, I don't want to beat around the bush, so I'll give it to you straight. A girl I've been seeing, and we obviously got to keep that buttoned up, she thinks she saw something that might help with a suspect."

"No worries, bring her in and—"

"Well here's the thing . . ."

Luca settled back into his chair as Steve laid out the situation.

"Look, I'm not gonna lecture you, but geez, the kid's only nineteen." He shook his head as Steve hung his. "All right, let's get moving. I don't have to tell you the pressure we're under."

***

Vinny called me as soon as he heard the news.

"Pete, I can't believe what happened to Billy."

"Yeah. How's it going?"

"How's it going? I mean, holy shit, Pete, Billy was murdered, for God's sake!"

I didn't know what to say other than, "So what?"

"What the fuck is that supposed to mean?"

The words just tumbled out of my mouth. "The prick deserved it."

"Geez, we were friends our whole life. What's wrong with you?"

I didn't really feel bad about it. "Well, maybe he shouldn't be going around with other guy's girls."

"What're you talking about?"

Why couldn't my brother see how bad Billy was? I mean, he was always making people miserable the entire time I knew him. What was Vinny, blind? "Fuck it. Look, he was a piece of shit, a fucking bully, and he got what he had coming, is what I'm saying."

"You know what, man? You're fucking crazy." Vinny slammed the phone down on me. He spent the rest of the two days he had in Texas doing his thing without checking on me. I kinda enjoyed not being babied.

***

After meeting with Steve and his young lover, the detectives huddled in Luca's office as the station emptied out. Luca told his partner about the new source, and Cremora shook his head.

"Stevie's taking some big-ass risks here. This shit leaks, and it's not only his wife he's gotta worry about; Gesso will be forced to suspend him."

"Yeah, I promised him I'd keep it under wraps, so let's try and keep it there."

Cremora threw up a hand and nodded.

Luca flipped open a file. "This kid, she corroborated the car color to be in the red family. So, let's rule out brown for the moment. Best of all, she said it had a big grill. I showed her some pictures. She thinks it's a

Chrysler. Why don't you put in a request for a DMV report? It may give us something to run with."

"Let's hope so."

"Kid also said it was a male, just like the neighbor said. I don't know about you, but Wyatt's girlfriend didn't leave me warm and fuzzy."

"Yeah, that whole story about being out and going to pick him up for the gym."

"If she was, she didn't call him before coming over. There's no record of a call going to the house that morning."

"You run their cell phones?"

"Not back yet."

"So, we know Wyatt was or seemed to be alone when someone driving a red Chrysler and, in a hurry, pulled up to his house. This someone had a bar, stick, or bat, according to Stevie's squeeze. Wyatt either knew this person or for some reason let him in. Maybe an argument broke out, and bam, he gets whacked in the skull."

Cremora rubbed his forehead. "Could've been a revenge type thing. He was a bully. That'd give us motive."

"Neighbor did say he and the girl were always fighting."

"We need to dig deep, Luc, see if he ever got physical with her. Maybe he hit her or did something to enrage her. She's got no history of any violence, so she'd have to have been pushed over the edge."

"Yeah, but nine times out of ten it happens right then and there. I don't know, to me this seems like it could've been premeditated."

"Wyatt was out back, smoking and having a beer sometime that night."

"If someone was there, they weren't drinking with him. The one can was his, but the other was old, according to the yeast sample test."

"How about the smokes?"

"The cigarettes were his brand. We got his DNA off most of the butts except one, a menthol, Newport. No DNA, but there were trace latent prints on the butt. I've got the lab doing their best, but there just doesn't seem to be enough of a print."

Cremora crept to the edge of his chair. "Newport's a chic brand, no? Think the girlfriend smokes?"

"Mary? Don't think so. We were with her for a while the other day, and interviewing is when they all seem to want to puff their brains out."

"I'll check it out."

"You know, maybe there were two of them?"

"Huh?"

"Could be two people involved. The guy driving the car, and a neighbor saw someone cutting through the yards."

"I don't know. Both girls who saw the car pull up said only one person was in the car."

"Maybe he dropped him off on the street behind and was waiting out front."

Cremora shook his head. "Usually, the getaway car is hidden on the block behind."

"I know, I know, just brainstorming."

"You mean brain drizzling."

"I gotta get moving, or Deb's gonna throw me out before I move back in."

***

When Vinny walked in the door, Peter was doing exercises with his therapist in the living room. As he said his hellos, the phone rang, and Vinny took the call in the kitchen.

"Hey, Vinny, it's Tony."

"Hi Tony, how are you doing?"

"Good, man, how's Petey?"

"Okay. He's doing PT right now, but making progress."

"Good, good. I tried calling him like five times but never got through. Left a bunch of messages, but—"

"Yeah, I got them and told him, but he's pretty forgetful these days."

"He still pissed about Mary?"

"What?"

"You know, when we went out for my brother's birthday, out of nowhere he got all pissed off and made me take him home. I didn't know what was going on, and he wouldn't tell me. But when I got back to the bar, I found out he heard about Mary getting married and all, and that was what set him off."

"Oh, uh, well, he's, he's doing okay, pretty good. Look, I gotta run. Can I have him call you back?"

***

Just after the therapist left, Vinny came into the living room where I had already palmed the remote. As I flicked through channels, Vinny approached.

"That was Tony, again, said you never called him back."

"Oh, guess I forgot."

"Said that night he was here you guys went out."

"Yeah."

"Anything happen?"

"What do you mean?"

"He said you heard about Mary and Billy and freaked out."

"So? What did you expect me to do? Dance? Get 'em a fucking engagement gift?"

Vinny snatched the remote out of my hand and shut the television just when *The Price is Right* was coming on.

"We gotta talk."

"But my show's—"

"What happened that night?"

"Uh, what night? I don't know what you're talking about."

"Not good enough. When you heard about Mary." Vinny lowered his voice a notch. "It's okay, you should be mad, but what happened?"

I turned my attention to the ceiling. "We were at the bar, and I was having a good time, then this bitchy bar girl blabbed her mouth off about Mary and that fuckhead Billy."

"Okay, so you were pissed. Then what?"

Pissed? That's the understatement of the year. "I donno. I wanted to get out of there, so we left."

"Tony brought you home? Straight home?"

I kinda remembered the ride home, and I nodded.

"Then what?"

"Nothing."

"Nothing? You came home and that was it?"

"Yeah, I think so."

"You think so? What did you do when you got home?"

I couldn't really remember even walking in the house. "I don't remember."

Vinny crouched in front of me and softened his voice. "Did you go anywhere? Do anything?"

"I don't think so."

"Petey, you gotta be straight with me, man. I'm here to help you."

"I told you, I don't remember. What's the big deal?"

"The big deal is, that's the night poor Billy got murdered."

I was really getting sick of hearing about Wyatt. "Poor Billy, my ass! Now leave me alone."

***

That night, still at work and preoccupied with the day's developments, Vinny picked up the phone.

"Mary? It's Vinny. I know it's late, but do you have a minute?"

"Yeah, sure."

"How you doing and all?"

"I miss him terribly."

"I know, me too. Look, I know you have a lot on your plate, but I'm really worried about Pete."

"What's going on?" Mary asked.

"I don't know. He seems down, depressed and stuff. I know he found out about you and Billy getting married and—"

"Yeah, but you know what? He seemed cool with it. He called me when he found out that night, but he was, like, not mad or anything. I was kind of surprised, but happy that he seemed to be finally moving on."

"What do you mean? He called you the night Billy got killed? What did he say?"

"Yeah, that night. It seems like yesterday." Mary paused. "Anyway, he just asked if it was true what he'd heard. I told him yes, and he was quiet. I expected an outburst, but he kept it together. He just asked me if that was it. I told him I was sorry if I hurt his feelings, but he cut me off and said, like, well I hope you're happy."

"Has he been calling you?"

"He left a message the day after Billy was, you know, uh—"

"You call him back?"

"No, too upset, anyway, I figured he just wanted to offer condolences."

***

When Vinny pulled into the driveway after work, he remembered that when he returned from Texas, the car was closer to the garage than where he normally parked. At the time, he didn't give it much thought, but now it added to the whispering in his head. Vinny sat in the car for a few minutes before gingerly stepping through the front door.

Peter was snoring on the couch as cartoons played on the television. Vinny tiptoed over to the sofa and grabbed his brother's cane. Then he took the cane into the laundry room, looked it over closely, and then washed it down with bleach. He examined it again, washed it with soap and water and leaned it back against the couch.

Chapter 13

Luca punched the keypad, and the door buzzed open. The detective sipped his morning java as the door clicked shut behind him. Running late, he breezed past dispatch as a new girl, who Luca thought was hot, called out, "Detective, someone from DMV dropped off a report for you. I put it on your desk."

Luca flashed his best smile. "Thanks."

Cremora was at his desk chomping on a bagel when Luca asked, "You go through the DMV report?"

"Toilet paper, Luc. Seems red Chryslers are pretty popular in Jersey."

Luca thumbed the five-inch stack centered on his desk.

"Shit. Why don't we have 'em run it against the database of assault convictions?"

"Made the call while you were still getting your beauty sleep."

"Look at that, a good cop, and funny too."

"They promised it quick. Told Carey the info was needed for a grand jury."

Luca rolled his eyes.

"You never know. Hey, I forgot to tell you that Mary Rourke doesn't smoke, never has."

"It was a long shot."

"Yeah, and to boot, the cell phone logs confirmed her version of the morning she found Wyatt."

Luca couldn't help but think the news about Mary lined up with one of three things every case he'd been on had—information that seemed like it would be a key to solving the case slams right into a stone wall.

The detectives were about to call it a day when the fax machine hummed, spitting out a cover page from the DMV and a page that Cremora scooped out of the tray. Luca's partner put the still-warm page of detail on Luca's desk.

"That's it? Thirty, thirty-five names?"

"Guess so. Cover page said only one page attached. I'll call to verify."

"Okay, I gotta run. I'm getting together with Deb."

Luca grabbed his jacket and nearly ran into a uniformed officer in the hallway.

"Uh, sorry, Detective. Sarge said to let you know we got a hit on a Wyatt credit card."

"Where?"

The young cop pointed to a piece of paper. "This morning, Keyport 7-Eleven by Route 36, near the intersection with 35."

Luca grabbed the sheet from the officer and thanked him. The detective pulled his cell phone out and stared at it. He quickly dismissed the thought Debra would understand that something had come up. Luca then pondered going to the 7-Eleven in the morning before punching in her number.

The parking lot was busy with a stream of hopefuls buying tickets to a heavily promoted Powerball jackpot, interspersed with commuters picking up essentials, and night carousers grabbing their six-packs of beer.

Luca slid up to the counter, caught the eye of the fellow pumping out lottery tickets and flashed his badge. The kid nodded, jabbered something in Pakistani to a woman ringing up cigarettes, and told Luca they'd get the manager.

A balding, heavyset man with a stained shirt appeared and waved Luca over to a glass cubicle. The detective stepped into the small area and was hit with the pungent smells of the food laid out on the man's desk. The guy, Tarif Sahib, who turned out to be the owner, pushed his dinner to the side.

"What's wrong, Officer?"

Luca scanned the six screens displaying feeds from security cameras and said, "A credit card used this morning is connected to an ongoing investigation. We'd like to see any video footage you have during that time period."

"Of course. No problem. No problem at all."

Luca showed the Visa printout to Sahib. Sahib swept his hand toward the monitors. "We've got many cameras. The whole place is covered. I even have one the workers don't know about."

"How long do you keep the tapes?"

Sahib smiled, revealing a mouthful of gold fillings.

"No, no tapes. We use DVDs, and we keep them one month." He stepped to the side and opened a drawer lined with DVDs.

"Don't write over any of those until we have a chance to see if we'll need anything further."

"Okay." Frowning, he shut the drawer. "You want to see the counter feeds?"

"Let's start there. The printout gives us a transaction time of 10:07 this morning."

Sahib loaded the DVD and hit the fast-forward button. Images blurred by as the time stamp morphed from six in the morning into the ninth hour of the day.

Luca spoke as it passed the half hour. "Okay, slow it down to real time."

The detective leaned in, staring at the herky-jerky images of the morning's patrons. As the time stamp crossed ten, Luca asked him to slow it down, and he inched closer to the screen.

A lull in the flow of customers from 10:02 to 10:05 was broken by a young man buying what looked to be Red Bull. As he left the counter, a man in a baseball cap and tee shirt, whose head was down, sidled up to the counter with what looked like two six-packs of beer. Luca noted a large blotch on the man's forearm, pegging it as a tattoo. The clerk turned around, grabbed two cartons of Newport cigarettes and set them next to the man's beer. The customer then handed off what must have been the credit card in question. Luca checked the time stamp, and sure enough, it had moved to 10:07 as the clerk swiped it. The customer pocketed the credit card, stacked the six-packs and piled the cigarette cartons on top. He slid the goods off the counter onto his hip and walked away, head down, through the exit.

Luca watched it three more times but couldn't make any determinations other than it was a male about six feet tall. He moved on to the parking-lot footage, but nothing seemed to tie the credit card user to a specific car.

Luca ran the counter footage again before deciding to confiscate all the footage inside and outside the store from nine to eleven. He hoped the guys down at the lab could manipulate the images and give him something to work with.

Chapter 14

There were thirty-four people convicted of assault who had red Chryslers in Monmouth County. Luca cautioned his partner to pursue the angle with restraint as it was limited to Monmouth County and precluded someone borrowing a car.

The detectives discussed the list and eliminated any of the targets who had just one assault and those records that were over seven years old. They also excluded the six women in the report, narrowing the focus to the seven men with multiple arrest records. Then Luca asked Gesso to dispatch officers to visit the reduced list of suspects.

Gesso's men quickly boiled the list down to three, as one suspect had been in the hospital and another in a locked-down drug rehab at the time of the crime. A third man, suffering from late-stage cancer, was also discounted.

Gesso dropped in to see Luca about the remaining suspects and handed over three files.

"Luc, we hit 'em all and—"

"Who'd you send?"

"Donofrio and Messina."

"Both top notch. What's their gut telling 'em?"

"Didn't like this Griswald character."

Luca shuffled the files. "Okay, give me Griswald first." He beckoned with his hand, opened Don Griswald's file and looked at a mug shot stapled to the left-hand side.

Gesso settled into a chair. "Big dude, said he put on fifty pounds since his last arrest."

"He'd be slower, and Wyatt was an athlete back in the day."

"Biker and Skull member. In and out of prison his entire adult life."

Luca paged through his rap sheet. "Yeah, a real upstanding citizen."

"Donofrio said he was a cagey bastard. Claimed to be in a gin mill. Originally said he couldn't remember what bar it was. Pressured, he said it was Heels, that titty joint in Keansburg. But they swung by it, and nobody seems to recall seeing him. You ask me, and it'd be pretty hard to miss such a big bag of shit."

Luca chuckled. "Where'd they leave it?"

"Donofrio wanted to lay on Griswald, but I told 'em we gotta run it by you."

"Thanks. Leave it with me at this point. What else they got?" He opened the next file. "How about Waters?"

"Seems this Waters guy knew Wyatt pretty well, but he said he was working at Pacer on the night shift loading trucks, and it checked out."

"You sure he was there all night? Couldn't he have broken away?"

"It seems that way. They looked at the video feed on the loading dock, and from six to eight he was there."

He shuffled the Waters file to the bottom. "Let's move on to Brown."

Gesso stroked his moustache. "Brown claims to have gotten religion. Says he became a devout Muslim in the can. Said he was at a brotherhood meeting. Those bigots backed him up, but you know those bastards; they'd lie to the cops to protect one of their own."

"You're telling me? Have 'em nose around some. Talk to the brothers we have leverage with. See if any cracks appear in his alibi."

Luca had a patrol car pay a visit on Griswald to ask him to come in and talk. The threat of arrest for obstruction if he didn't, worked.

Luca waited over an hour, letting him stew, before he opened the door. A hulk of a man in a black, sleeveless tee shirt scowled at him. Luca thought he was thirty pounds too heavy to get away with the tough-guy, tee-shirt look and smiled in return. Griswald, who turned away, had a matching set of skull tattoos on either side of his neck and a huge dragon tattoo that snaked its way up one arm and down the other, grabbing Luca's attention.

Luca eyed the biker chain that hung on his grungy jeans, wondering how the hell he was allowed to keep it on.

"I'm Detective Luca."

Griswald jumped out of his seat. "What the fuck am I doing' here?"

Luca hit a button under the desk. "Easy, big boy, we need to talk. Now sit back down!"

As the detainee pawed the chair, the door opened, and a uniformed officer poked his head in.

"Everything okay, Detective?"

"My friend's a little upset." He looked at Griswald and cocked his head toward the two-way mirror. "Why don't you keep an eye on things in case our friend gets claustrophobic?"

The officer left the room and Luca began.

"We asked you to come in for a chat."

"Asked me? What bullshit! You threatened to arrest me, man."

"You shouldn't have lied to our guys about your whereabouts."

"Look, I donno what you want, but I didn't do nothing."

"Good, then this should be easy. Where were you on the night of May fifteenth?"

Griswald squirmed in his chair. "May fifteenth?"

"Yes. Friday, May fifteenth, the day William Wyatt was beaten to death."

"Hey, man, I had nothing to do with that. Don't go trying to pin that shit on me, man."

"Well, where were you?"

"I donno. I think I was out drinking. You know, we roamed to a few places."

"You claimed to be at Heels, right?"

"Yeah, yeah, that's it, I think."

"Didn't check out, Donny boy."

"Look, man, I swear I didn't do anything. On my mother's grave, man." Griswald put his hand over his heart.

"That's means a lot, you swearing and all, Donny. It's not that I don't believe you, but you see, here we deal with facts, evidence, things like that." Luca poked a forefinger across the table. "And the fact is there's no evidence you were at Heels that night." Luca leaned in and clasped his hands. "We talked to a couple of your biker pals. Nobody saw you there, or for that matter, anywhere that night. So, where were you?"

Griswald shrugged.

"Look, Donny, if you don't start talking, I'll lock you up right now."

"Hey, wait. You can't do that for not talking. I got rights, you know."

"Sorry, my friend. Remember you lying to us? That's obstruction, and in a homicide case, it's serious business, buddy. Judges don't look too kindly at that."

Griswald gnawed on a fingernail.

"What's it going be? You gonna tell me, or should I get my officer friend"—he gestured to the window—"to escort you to booking?"

"You don't understand, man." He rapped his knuckles against his temple.

"Then help me understand."

Griswald began cracking his knuckles. Luca looked at his watch and stood up. "We're about out of time. Start talking, or you're going to spend some time as a guest of the county."

***

Luca and Cremora paged through the file on Jimmy Johns, who was seen by the back neighbor the night of the murder.

"Man, what a mutt. He's got some history."

"Yeah, mostly drugs to go along with five assaults. Another fucking meth head."

"The last two assaults were recent, and the prick clubbed his victims."

"Yeah, and they ran him in on yet another one: some junkie dealer whose head was bashed in. Said it wasn't him, and Johns pinned it on another zombie."

Luca smiled. "So, a rat to boot."

"Last known address is his sister's basement."

"Where does the sister live?"

"Keyport. The address should be in there."

"That's only six, seven blocks from Wyatt!"

"Let's get him in here."

***

"Well I'll be damned," Cremora said and smacked his thigh.

Luca had told him that Griswald wasn't involved in the Wyatt murder. He said Griswald was banging the girlfriend of the biker gang's leader, a violent guy serving time for a brutal assault, on the night of the murder. Griswald and his secret squeeze were holed up in a hotel just over the Jersey border in Easton. His alibi was confirmed by the hotel's surveillance cameras and Griswald's credit card.

"You know, I'd have almost bet he had something to do it with it."

"It was kinda weird, big, tough biker dude, pleading to keep it quiet. I swear, he might've cried if I pushed things."

Cremora snickered. "Well, that Blemmer is one sick puppy, remember the time he—"

Gesso barged into the room.

"Got a couple of things on the Wyatt case. Kennedy checked out Brown—he's got a lot of contacts in the black community. Said Brown seems to have been at one of those Muslim things the night Wyatt got hit."

The detectives looked at each and Luca spoke. "He sure?"

"Yeah, got it from two sources, and besides, seems the kid's really been keeping his nose clean."

"So that leaves us with the meth head."

Gesso put up his palm. "Well, the other thing is, a lead just came in."

Chapter 15

Gesso began telling the detectives about the call from Mary Rourke's mother. He thrust his chin at Luca and said, "She said she didn't want to talk to the detective who was too rough on her daughter."

Luca spoke. "Just trying to poke holes in what was a—"

Gesso waved him off. "With the pressure I'm getting from Stanley"—Gesso looked around and lowered his voice—"man, what a pompous asshole. Anyway, she said that Mary thought you should check out her ex-boyfriend. Said this guy's just back from Afghanistan, and the story is complicated, but when isn't it?"

"Kid wants to be a detective, Luc," Cremora said and laughed.

"Okay, what do you got, Sarge?" Luca asked.

"Well, Mary was dating this guy, Peter Hill, for a couple of years, but when he went overseas, she started going with Wyatt. She said this guy, Hill, was gone a long time. Served two tours while things got serious with Wyatt. Seems Mary never got around to telling Peter it was over." Gesso shook his head. "Then the poor kid got injured. Seems it was a real serious head injury, and she didn't have the heart to tell him."

Cremora said, "She wanted to be nice after two-timing the guy?"

"Sad and all, but that's it." Luca threw his hands up.

"No. Here's where it gets interesting. Mary said that Hill found out she was two-timing him, as you say, the night Wyatt turned up dead."

The detectives shot glances at each other.

"And Mary said she didn't know too much, but that there was a little history between them."

Luca leaned forward. "Between Hill and Wyatt?"

"Seems so. She said Wyatt was close friends with Hill's brother, and when they were kids, there was some friction."

"Does Hill have a record or anything?"

"Nothing came up." Gesso put his hands on his hips. "Look, nose around, but do me a favor and stay away from the girl unless you really get something. Okay, guys?"

The detectives nodded, and as Gesso left, Luca swiveled his chair to face Cremora. "I know it's a long shot, but can you get your guy at DMV to run this Hill guy and see what car he drives?" Luca stood. "I'll grab us some coffee in the meantime."

When Luca came back holding two cups, Cremora told him there was no record of auto ownership for Peter Hill. They ran routine background checks as they drank their java and then headed out to see the new lead.

As Cremora swung the car into a space across from Peter's house, Luca said, "You see what I see?"

"But Santiago said there wasn't anything on record."

They popped out of the car and headed for the driveway where a burgundy Chrysler was parked. They peered inside the car and checked the car's grill. The detectives nodded at each other and went to the front door.

Peter was laid out on the couch, glued to some soap opera, and never moved when the bell rang. When the knocking began, Vinny put his coffee mug down and trudged barefoot to the door.

"You know, Pete, you could get off your ass, man, and help me once in a frigging while. I just got up."

"Shush." Peter inched his head toward the television as Vinny opened the door to two men in suits.

"Can I help you?" *Too old for evangelists*, Vinny thought, scanning their faces as the coffee he'd drank began backing up.

"Peter Hill?" Cremora flashed his ID.

"No, I'm his brother, Vinny. Vinny Hill."

Luca peered over Vinny shoulder. "Is Peter home?"

"Uh, yeah, but"—Vinny pulled the door and lowered his voice— "he's not well, you know. He got badly injured in Afghanistan."

Cremora nodded. "Yes, we understand, but we have a few questions we'd like to ask, informally, of course."

"About what?"

"The Wyatt murder."

Vinny squeezed the edge of the door. "Billy was a good friend of mine, uh, of ours. What do you want to know? I can probably answer for you."

"So, you knew William Wyatt well?"

"Sure. We were buddies, best friends, man, through school and all." Vinny shook his head. "I just can't believe what happened. I'm sick to my stomach about it."

"Can we speak with both of you?"

"Ah, well, you see, it's not a good idea. He's on a ton of meds and needs a lot of help. I take care of him."

"It'll only be few minutes. I promise."

"I—I don't think I can allow that. I mean, the doctors, you know, like I, we'd like to help the police and all, but his condition . . ."

Luca said, "Sure, we understand. Say, would you mind answering a few questions, and we'll see if that clears things up, so we don't have to bother your brother."

"Yeah, sure, sure." Vinny looked down at his bare feet and smiled. "Just got off the night shift at FedEx. Let me throw some things on, and I'll meet you out front."

Before the cops could respond, the door closed and the lock sounded.

The garage door rose on a space full of furniture and boxes that Vinny snaked his way through.

Cremora hiked his thumb at the Chrysler. "Got to say this car reminds me of one my uncle had. Is it yours?"

"Uh, no. It's my mom's. Well, used to be. She passed away about two years ago."

"Sorry to hear."

"Yeah, frigging sucks." Vinny frowned. "So, what's up?"

"We just have a couple of questions for you about your brother."

"Shoot."

"So, how's your brother's recovery going? Must be tough."

"It's been a nightmare, but he's come a long way."

"Good to hear he's making progress," Cremora said.

Luca hiked a thumb to the car. "He back to driving?"

"Ah, not really. I mean, sometimes I let him drive with me."

"But he's able to drive."

"As I said, a little. What, are you guys from the DMV, or what?"

"Just routine. Trying to get a sense of his everyday life."

A blue sedan pulled up to the curb and Vinny said, "Look guys, I gotta run. That's Peter's physical therapist."

"We have a few more questions. Say, you work at the FedEx place off Hope Road. Why don't you swing by on your way in next week? Does Monday work?"

Spine shivering, Vinny quickly agreed and pulled down the garage door. Spooked as he entered the house, he wondered how they knew where he worked.

***

Franco Greco had graduated from John Jay College with a degree in forensics. The forty-year-old now ran the county's crime lab and was the closest thing Monmouth County had to a fingerprint specialist. When Luca arrived at the Freehold lab, he found the balding technician hunched over a microscope.

"Frankomino, you looking at porn again?"

Startled, Greco picked his head up and reached for his glasses.

"Hey, what d'ya know. It's George Clooney himself."

Greco started to take off his gloves, but Luca stopped him.

"I know you're busy, but did you get a chance to check out what I sent down?"

"Yeah, in spite of how crazy it's been, I did."

"And, what did you find?"

"It'd be easier to show you what you got me dealing with."

Franco led Luca to a windowless chamber cluttered with laboratory equipment that had a row of monitors along one wall.

"Yikes, place looks like my high school chem class."

"Tell me about it. We're so stretched for space, I had to put the new digital system in here."

Franco took a seat and tapped away at a keyboard, bringing the bank of monitors to life.

"Here's what we got off the evidence."

Two screens displayed blue colored prints that were partial and smudged.

"Two? That's it?"

"Sorry pal, but even using ninhydrin, these were the only prints that met the guidelines."

"How do they match up with Johns?"

"Hang on, Luc."

Franco posted the prints of Johns' thumbs, fore, and middle fingers, and Luca stepped closer, looking from image to image, trying to see the similarities.

"What's nice about the new system is we can overlay the prints."

When the combined images appeared, Luca said, "Wow, it's like an exact match!"

Franco shook his head, "Sorry, bro, but not even close."

"What?"

"What we have is inconclusive at best."

"Look at this, man. These here line up perfectly." Luca traced two lines that started on one side of the print and ran out the other side. "And look at these loops here." The detective pointed to three lines that started at one end of the print and circled back to their starting point before being smudged.

"Look, there are some ridges and loops that match." Franco then pointed to the center of the second image where a pair of circular ridges overlaid each other. "There's even a pretty good match on this whorl."

"So, what's the problem?"

"For starters, there are about a hundred and fifty ridge characteristics in the average fingerprint."

"Ridge?"

"Points of identity. So, while we have a couple of lines that match, the smaller, more definitive points, which we call minutiae, truly define the individuality or uniqueness of the print, and they're just not there."

"But—"

"And they're off, shall we say, poor quality prints, to boot."

Luca leaned against the wall and rubbed his chin. "Okay, okay. Hear me out a second. I know we might need more matching, but doesn't this mean anything? It can't just be a coincidence."

"Luc, I wish I could help you here, but to make any kind of judgment, we need ten or more points of identity to match. Otherwise, it'd get thrown out of court in a heartbeat."

Luca shifted his weight. "I see, but in a general sense, in an investigation, not a courtroom, would you say this data, no matter how incomplete, puts the focus on this guy?"

"I really can't say, Luc. It's just not science, man."

"Fuck the science. Think like a cop, man."

Franco put his palm up. "Look, let's just say it doesn't give us enough to say it's him, but it certainly doesn't clear this guy, okay?"

Chapter 16

Luca barely kept his promise to be home for their first dinner together, arriving an hour late. Debra ignored him when he walked in, but a supermarket bouquet of flowers he picked up pacified her somewhat. The detective recognized he'd have to be sensitive if it was going to work this time, and since he wanted it to, he was going to try working at it.

Tenuously reunited, the couple's awkwardness receded with the draining of the first bottle of wine.

It was Friday night, and knowing he'd spend the weekend running through the list of things he promised Debra he'd do, Luca focused on the night's dinner and the pleasure of getting back into the bed he'd missed so much.

After a leisurely meal, they rolled around on the couch while watching TV until Luca persuaded Debra to move the action upstairs.

Luca showered quickly, and feeling more content than he had in a long while, dozed off. When Debra hopped in beside him, he came to life, pressing his growing hardness against her. Luca pulled himself back to concentrate on pleasing Debra, and the couple enjoyed each other before falling fast asleep.

Sunlight streamed into the kitchen as Debra poured a second cup of coffee for Luca. She reminded him, "Don't forget to fix the drip in the shower. I could hear it all night. Didn't you?"

He grabbed her by the waist. "Drip? What drip? I slept like a baby." He snuck his hand under her shirt. "Your body's a sleeping pill for the Lucmeister."

She smiled and pulled away. "Easy, tiger, you got some work to do, and who knows? If you're a good boy—"

"Hey, that's not playing fair."

Debra teasingly pulled her nightshirt up a bit as Luca's cell phone rang.

"Luca here." The detective pursed his lips. "Okay," he said, and added "shit" as he hung up.

"What's the matter?"

"Uh, emergency meeting. Sorry, hon, I gotta go in."

"What? But—"

"I know, but it's all hands on deck. Last night we had another murder and two vicious assaults."

"You promised it'd be different."

Luca approached her. "It will be. I know the timing sucks, but I can't control it."

"Exactly. Bad people are always going to be doing terrible things."

"I promise I'll get back as soon as possible."

"Yeah, right."

"Don't worry. I'll get everything done, even if I have to stay up till three."

Debra turned away and headed into the bathroom, saying, "You still don't get it, do you?"

With Debra locked in the bathroom, Luca quickly pulled a suit and shirt out of his garment bag and changed. After buttoned his shirt, he strapped on his holster, draped a jacket over his arm and tiptoed out of the room.

The squad room was loud with banter and a mix of uniformed officers and detectives. Luca waded through, greeting and ribbing his colleagues as he made his way to the front, where the detectives and senior officers sat.

He chatted with a couple of captains for at least twenty minutes before JJ strolled in, and the partners paired off.

Luca was telling JJ about the mess this meeting caused with Debra when the door swung open, and Sergeant Gesso held the door for his boss, Captain Fusco, who was followed by Sheriff Meril and the county's top law enforcement officer, Prosecutor Bill Stanley.

Luca muttered as he took a seat, "Oh boy, Stanley's making an appearance. This ought to be fun."

Fusco, who'd been more of a political animal for the department than a captain who ran the precinct, took the lectern.

"Morning, ladies and gents. Thanks to those of you who came in on your day off for this meeting, but we believe it's a necessary sacrifice. Prosecutor Stanley would like to say a few words before we get into specifics vis-à-vis tactics."

Fusco moved aside as William Stanley, running for his second term as prosecutor and rumored to have an eye on the governorship, stepped up and grabbed the lectern's side rails with both hands.

"Thank you, Captain. As we all unfortunately know, the county's been beset by an alarming rise in crime. Now, it's true that we've been through spikes in the past, and things may eventually quiet down, but our mandate is to use the resources we have to secure things." Stanley tapped his bony forefinger on the lectern. "We *must* provide our residents with the ability to conduct their lives without fear for their safety." Stanley paused and surveyed the room. "We've all been around a few years." He smiled and looked over at the sheriff and captain. "Who knows, maybe too long." He got a few chuckles before continuing, "But what's not funny are the scores of calls we're getting, both in my office and the sheriff's, from residents fearing for the safety of their children and businesses."

Luca's mind drifted as Stanley drowned the attendees in a flood of statistics. Luca checked his watch and searched for an idea on something to bring home or do to get back on track with Debra. Then Stanley got his attention by slamming his hand on the podium as he said, "And I mean aggressive!"

Luca shifted in his seat as Stanley continually emphasized the immediate need to quell the rising fear in the county's neighborhoods. The detective was troubled by Stanley's call to bring anyone under suspicion into custody, which ignored the investigative end that produced evidence to support an arrest. However, it was quickly overshadowed by the panic he felt when the prosecutor laid down deadlines to solve violent crimes.

Stanley then made it clear that the focus would be on what he called headline crimes, mentioning the Wyatt case by name, along with two others. The prosecutor finished up by asking them to temporarily put aside work on less violent investigations before ceding attention back to Captain Fusco, who held a file.

"Let's take a break. We'll reconvene in an hour." A cascade of groans sounded, and Fusco put up his hand before flipping open a file. He read off names and rooms where people were to gather after the break. Fusco asked them to review the cases they headed before reporting to their assigned rooms, then he dismissed them.

Luca and Cremora moved along in the lunchroom line for a cup of java.

"The timing sucks. All of this sucks." Luca complained.

"You want the bad guys to make appointments?"

"Not them, you, bozo. This meeting, it's screwing the whole thing up with Debra. I need some damn space. Otherwise this shit's gonna come apart again before it gets a chance to get going."

"Hang in there. You'll be back by two, three o'clock the latest."

"I'll have to wear my flak jacket if she hasn't changed the locks by then," Luca said, pushing back a handle that released a stream of steaming coffee.

They put their focus back to the matters at hand and chatted about their cases as they retreated to Luca's office.

"Guess there goes the Giuliani Doctrine," Cremora said, referring to the New York mayor's intolerance of any crime, no matter how small. The policy was believed to be the linchpin in restoring the nation's largest city to a safer and higher quality of life.

"Fucking politics, you ask me."

"Out of the six zillion actives we got, guess the hierarchy is only interested in the Wyatt case."

Luca nodded. "No doubt. Dollars to donuts, Stanley's gonna push for an arrest."

"Donuts? You say donuts?"

Luca balled up his napkin and tossed it at his partner, then said, "Let's go through the Wyatt file in case we find ourselves in the lion's den."

Afterward, Cremora and Luca took seats in the empty room used for writing reports.

"Well, this is a good sign."

"Where'd they say Stanley and the captain would be?"

"I don't think Fusco said."

They heard the door in the adjoining chief officer's office close, and seconds later Sergeant Gesso filled the doorway.

"Sorry to keep you waiting, boys."

Luca said, "No problem, Sarge."

Gesso took a seat and yawned. "I'm beat. Been here all night."

"So, what's really up here, Sarge?"

Gesso smoothed his moustache and said, "They're on me about the Wyatt case. It's all over the papers."

"They?"

"Stanley, and to a lesser degree, Fusco."

The detectives glanced at each other and nodded. Luca took the lead and said, "I don't know what anyone expects here, boss. We can't pull a damn rabbit out of a hat, you know."

"Come on, Luc. Everybody just wants to get a handle on things. That's all."

"Well, that's not the impression I got from hearing Stanley pontificate."

Gesso glared at Luca. "Watch it, Luca."

"Sorry, Sarge, it's just nobody wants to get the bastard more than us, and it sticks me when he's out there creating the impression that we're not doing enough."

"Nobody is saying anything like that. Now, can we take a step back and go over what we have?"

The detectives went over what they had on the discovery of the body and the murder scene. Cremora paged through an evidence list.

"The scene didn't give us much. We got a couple of partial prints, but they weren't conclusive."

Luca jumped in. "Maybe not in a positive way, but a couple of the prints on the cigarettes didn't exclude Johns."

Luca explained the print matched on some larger, general points, but there just weren't enough on the prints to get any of the minutiae matching points that would hold up in court.

Gesso rubbed his chin. "Not enough for a judge, but if we can't exclude a suspect, then we put the focus on 'em. Basic police work, in my opinion."

Luca wiped the smile off his face and nodded as Gesso continued. "So what else you have on Johns?"

Cremora looked at Luca, who responded, "Guy's got a pattern, a history of violent assaults. His alibi doesn't hold up."

Gesso beckoned with his hand.

"Look, Sarge, we're developing it. We need time. Something just ain't right—my gut's telling me."

"One thing we don't have is time, between Stanley and the press. Look, nose around, but move on if you can't get hard evidence of a connection. Now where are we at with the Hill kid? He's got no alibi either."

Cremora nodded. "Yeah, said he was home alone. His brother's been taking care of him, and on one of the only nights since he was injured that the brother ain't home, Wyatt ends up dead."

Luca said, "Wyatt was dating Hill's ex-girlfriend. Sure, Hill was pissed off, but it's a leap to suspect him of murder, if you ask me. Shit, if everybody did that, we'd need a thousand homicide detectives."

"But the kid's got some mental issues, no?"

"Mostly memory. We made some discreet inquiries, but with all the patient confidential privacy bullshit . . ." Luca shook his head. "I've got a call into Foster, the county shrink, to see what perspective he can give us."

Gesso thumbed through the file. "Look, Hill's got a lot of history with Wyatt, and none of it good."

Luca leaned forward. "Ancient history, Sarge. It goes back to when they were kids. His brother was tight with Wyatt. It just seems like normal kid's stuff."

"I don't know. We got nothing else. I'd say it's high time you bring him in."

"Sarge, let's hold off. We have the brother coming in Monday."

"Monday?" He slammed a hand on the table and stood up. "You guys didn't get the urgency message? Get him in today, tomorrow the latest."

The detective held his tongue as Gesso stormed out.

Cremora called Vinny Hill, and they settled on him coming in around two o'clock. Luca checked his watch. It was past noon already. He trudged to the parking lot to call Debra. When it went to voice mail, he left a rambling message.

Chapter 17

Vinny approached the precinct like he was going to a house after learning it was broken into. He sidestepped an animated group exiting and advanced to the busy front desk.

After ten minutes, an officer led him to a drab interview room where Cremora and Luca were. Seeing the video camera setup, Vinny stopped in his tracks.

"Oh, come on, man. This is bullshit."

"Easy, Mr. Hill, we just need to document it—state law, you know. It protects you as well," Cremora said.

"Yeah, right, just trying to help me." He plopped into a plastic chair, resisting the urge to flash the finger at the one-way mirror.

Luca tried to put him at ease. "Look Vinny, we appreciate you coming in to talk with us. You have nothing to be afraid of. You're not a suspect in the Wyatt case."

"Yeah? But ain't you trying to nail my brother for it?"

"We just want to get the facts. You knew the victim very well, and you may provide information that may help clear your brother."

Vinny smirked as he shook his head.

Cremora hit the record button, and Luca covered the formalities for the record before asking, "You and William Wyatt were good friends, right?"

"Yeah, me and Billy met way back in grammar school and were tight as hell all the way through high school."

"When's the last time you saw him?"

"About a year ago. I came up from Texas, and we hung out. It was when Pete was on leave."

"Oh, so the three of you got together?"

"Nah, Pete didn't really like him, well not like, but, you know, he didn't, shall we say, enjoy his company."

"And why was that?"

"Hey, you can't get along with everybody, right?"

"We understand you were down in Texas the night of the Wyatt murder, correct?"

"Yeah, my lease was up. I had to clean out my place."

"So, your brother was home?"

"Yes."

"Alone?"

"I, uh, had a lady come for a couple of hours every day to clean and cook. You know, keep an eye on him after all he's been through."

Luca nodded. "But the night Billy was attacked, Peter was alone, right?"

Vinny leaned forward a couple of inches. "Not really. His buddy from the service came up."

"But he dropped him back at his house at about six thirty."

"If you talked with Tony, then why are you asking me all this?"

Luca took a sip of coffee and leaned in. "Would you characterize Billy Wyatt as a bully?"

"I donno. People were kinda jealous, if you ask me. Billy was a popular kid, great QB and all. He liked to bust balls, but we all did."

"Did Wyatt bully your brother?"

"What? Shit, they haven't seen each other in years."

"Tell me about Wyatt terrorizing Peter in grammar school: first grade, I believe."

"You guys kidding? That was like twenty years ago." He shook his head and smiled right into the camera. "If this is all you got on Petey, it's time for me to go."

"What about the couple of times Billy beat your brother up, embarrassed him in front of everybody?"

"Let me get this straight. You think things that happened years and years ago, nothing more than schoolyard bullshit, if you ask me, drove Peter to kill Billy?"

Luca noticed the glistening on Vinny's upper lip. "How do you explain that Peter tried several times to seek revenge for his humiliation?"

"Revenge?"

"We understand you were present at the Hazlet Train Station when Peter tried to push William Wyatt onto the tracks as a train came through."

Vinny pounded the table. "That's bullshit! Pete tripped and fell into Billy, that's all. Nothing happened. It was an accident."

"Not according to several witnesses."

"Who? Tell me who's making accusations now, after all these years?"

Luca noticed the dark circles forming below Vinny's armpits. "We also know that at Arrowhead Camp, Peter put shards of glass into Billy's bed the night after Billy pushed him off the dock into the lake."

"Kid stuff, man."

"Really? Peter couldn't swim, could he?"

Vinny shot out of his chair. "Where you digging all this ancient shit up from? You guys have anything that happened, in like, the last ten years? It's no wonder you cops got such a bad reputation."

"Take it easy. Sit down."

Vinny put his hands on his hips. "Nah, forget it, the show's over. I'm going home."

Chapter 18

An unmarked car picked up Jimmy Johns after he scored on the corner of Third Street. Leaving a girl sitting in his car and without getting his fix, the narcotics officers cuffed him and ran Johns in to the station.

Luca paused at the one-way mirror and studied the six-foot suspect. Jimmy Johns wore John Lennon glasses and was thin, almost hollowed out. The addict fidgeted and smoked a cigarette that was down to the filter. Johns' hair was slightly matted, and he'd been nowhere near a razor in three to four days. Luca wondered what brand of cigarettes was buried in the pocket of the suspect's green tee shirt.

Johns snuffed out the butt and dug out the pack for another. As soon as Luca saw a green box of Newports emerge, he barged in.

This guy looks worse close up, Luca thought, noting a light scratch on his face and neck as he pulled out the chair opposite Johns.

"I'm Detective Luca."

Johns squirmed in his seat as he rubbed a forearm tattooed with a giant scorpion.

"I'm starved, man. You got anything in here to eat?"

"How about something sweet, say a bar of chocolate?"

Johns' eyes lit up a shade before he coughed. "Yeah, sure, why not."

Luca got a glimpse of Johns' corroded teeth as he phoned in the request.

"Jimmy, your file says you never gave up a source to cut a deal for yourself."

"I ain't no rat."

"We need some help. Maybe you can—"

Johns had a coughing fit before he said, "I don't spill on no one, you hear?"

The door opened, and a uniformed officer handed off a Snickers bar. Johns ripped the wrapper off and chomped a piece off with the side of his mouth.

"Hungry? Or you getting a case of the heebie-jeebies?"

"Look man, don't play with me. I'm not feeling too good."

Johns stuck a finger in his mouth to dislodge of piece of caramel and quickly took another bite.

"That meth eats away at you; makes you do some crazy things. But hey, what I am telling you about it for?"

Johns licked his filthy finger, grossing Luca out as he held up Johns' rap sheet.

"You know what it does. Look at the trouble you been in getting the money to support your habit—stealing, putting the hurt on people."

Johns scratched his stomach and wagged his head. "It can make you crazy."

"Where'd you get those scratches, Jimmy?"

"What scratches?" Johns dug out his pack and popped another cigarette in his mouth.

"Newport? They're the menthol kind, right?"

Johns nodded as he lit it.

"Beat anybody with a bat lately?"

Johns took a deep drag and slowly blew the smoke at Luca. "Don't be trying to pin anything on me, man."

"Where were you last Friday night, May fifteenth?"

"HHome."

"Really? Seems you were seen near the backyard of the Wyatt house."

"Bullshit, I was home."

"Couple of neighbors said it was you that night."

Johns coughed again. "No way."

"You sure you weren't lurking around Seventh Street?"

"I told you, man, I was home."

"Okay then, when did you get home?"

"I don't know, like six o'clock, something like that. I kinda remember as it was just getting dark."

That struck Luca as bullshit as it was still light out in May till about seven.

"What were you doing?"

"I don't know. Watching TV, I guess."

"You were high?"

"Uh, I—I—"

"Come on now, Jimmy boy. You need your meth every day, no?"

Johns nodded slightly.

"Can get pretty expensive. How much is a gram these days?"

"About eighty bucks."

"A gram's nothing to someone whose been hooked as long as you. What you doing now, eight balls?

Johns nodded.

"How long that eight ball last you? A day?"

Johns' glistening eyes darted around before he hung his head and stared into his lap. "I remember when I first started using, it'd last up to two weeks, man. Now, shit, with me and Val, just a day."

"I feel for you, having to score every day."

The drug talk heightened Johns' squirming and hacking.

Luca leaned his arms on the desk. "Where do you get the money to buy?"

"Odd jobs."

"Yeah? What type of work?"

"This and that."

Luca slammed his hand onto the table. "Cut the bullshit, Jimmy! Who'd hire someone looking like you?" He narrowed his eyes. "Where do you get the two hundred plus a day to support your habit?"

Johns hung his head again, whispering, "Well, you know, my sis; she helps me out. She understands the situation."

"Bullshit. We interviewed her. She swore she would never enable you. In fact, she said she kept the door locked to prevent you from stealing from her, like you did in the past." Luca shook his head. "Low as you can get, stealing from your sister, who provides you shelter."

"Look, I did a lot of things I regret, and I don't need reminding about it from a copper."

Luca knew Johns had lost his respect, but he pushed on despite the smidge of sympathy he began to feel for him. "You and your lady friend turning tricks for money?"

"Fuck off. I ain't no fucking queer."

"So, a pimp or a thieving bastard, then?"

"You leave her out of this. I'd never push her to walk the streets, man. What the fuck you think I am?"

Luca sat back down. "Okay, okay. Look, Jimmy, you wanna get out of here, you gotta be honest with me. So, tell me, then. You steal to get your fix, right?"

The suspect shrugged, mumbling, "Only if there's no work to be had."

Luca threw his file on the desk. "You've got quite a record of breaking and entering."

Johns shrugged and picked at his thumbnail.

"Did you break into Billy Wyatt's house on the fifteenth of May?"

"No man. I told you all I was home."

"You thought the house was empty, but Billy surprised you by coming in from the yard, and you whacked him in the head."

"I didn't do it, man!"

"Yeah, what about Ron Briest and Lew Garp? You assaulted them with a bat, didn't you?"

"No, man, you got it all wrong. They attacked me, and it was like self-defense and—"

"Yeah, right, self-defense, after you broke into their homes."

A coughing Johns cupped his forehead with a hand and leaned on the table. "Look, man, nothing's got to do with nothing."

***

Luca was in the office rifling through files when Cremora entered. Luca asked, "How's your Pop?"

"Good, thank God. Doctors said just a flare-up of his herniated disk, not a heart attack."

"Good. I was worried—the way it sounded."

"Tell me about it. My mother was frigging hysterical. So how did it go with that creep, Johns?"

"You didn't miss much. He denied everything, but I keep getting a bad vibe from him." Luca shook his head and briefed Cremora on the interview.

"What a creep. So how you want to play it?"

"Well, I had our guys revisit the backyard neighbor, and he stuck to it being Johns there that night."

"He's tall, so it meshes with another neighbor's sighting."

"I know. I'm thinking he definitely was there that night. The question is, doing what?"

Cremora asked, "So what's next?"

"Look, let's nose around and lay on his sister a bit. She was forthright, but I'm sure she's holding back something. He's her brother, after all."

"Blood's thicker than water."

"Look, at the end of the day, this piece of shit needs to find several hundred a day for his fix. And stealing and robbing are what he knows. Who knows? Could've been a robbery gone bad, really bad."

Cremora volunteered, "I'll take a run at his dealer on Third. You never know."

"Before you go, take a ride with me. I wanna check something out."

Chapter 19

Vinny trudged up the stairs just when Billy Wyatt got slammed on the head. Was I dreaming or in another trance? This time the episode was really vivid. Details of Wyatt's house were exactly as they were. It felt so real that I began to panic. It couldn't be a dream, could it? Holy shit, was it really me who hit him? I struggled to pull off my sweat-soaked shirt, and I hit the ground with a thud.

"You all right, Peter?"

The light came on as I pulled myself onto the bed.

"Yeah, I fell outta bed."

"Geez, how'd you do that?"

The scene of Billy getting hit was replaying in my head, and I blinked.

Vinny studied me. "You sure you're okay?"

I wanted to tell him about what was happening in my head, but I couldn't. "Yeah, just having these, these scary thoughts and things."

"Just nightmares, that's all."

"You're probably right."

"With all the shit you're going through, who wouldn't have nightmares?"

I hoped he was right. "Guess so."

"Go to sleep. I'll see you in the morning."

***

Luca cut the yellow crime scene tape and opened the door. He took a step in and stopped, causing Cremora to bump into him.

"What's the matter?"

"Nothing. Just taking a fresh look. You never know."

They circled around the marker outline of Wyatt's body, trying to unlock clues, when Luca said, "Look, you go out front, and when I tell you, hit the doorbell nonstop."

Luca made his way slowly through the kitchen and out the rear door. He closed the door and stood by the picnic table.

"Okay! Go ahead, JJ!"

Luca strained his ears but couldn't hear the bell. He discarded his idea and trudged to the back door. Swinging it open, he could easily hear the bell chiming. Luca paused as a smile creased his face.

"JJ! Come on out back!"

Luca waved his partner over to the picnic table.

"We know Wyatt was here out back smoking and having a brew that night. Let's say the killer rings the bell, and Wyatt goes to see who it is."

"Could be why the back door was open."

Luca nodded, "Or he may have left it open."

"Yeah, could've been left open a lot. Remember, the neighbor out back said he could hear them fighting."

"True, so it would seem Wyatt must have known who rang the bell or was fooled into letting in whoever did it."

"Maybe, but we can't rule out that it could be someone who was here already and was premeditated or provoked somehow."

"True."

"Or even someone who had a key, like his girlfriend."

"Yeah, guess I'd fallen into a trap by focusing on Johns."

"I donno about any trap, but there just doesn't seem to be a connection between Wyatt and Johns."

Luca nodded. "Yeah, guess you're right. A streetwise guy like Wyatt wouldn't let a character like Johns in his house. It's just—"

"Why don't we take a closer look at Mary and some of Wyatt's friends?"

"Sure, anything we can do to confirm or eliminate someone gets us closer. Let's check with any friends of Wyatt's who visited. Mary can help there if she's cleared."

"You want me to lay off Johns' dealer?"

Luca drummed his fingers on his chest. "Yeah, for now, anyway. Let's get a move on. I wanna to go to Freehold. I know the prints we collected aren't worth a shit, but I'd like to see if Franco can give me anything to work with."

"Drop me at the station. I'll check into Wyatt's girl and any possible visitors."

Luca dropped his partner off and was about to head to the Freehold lab when he made a sudden detour and took Route 35 into Route 36, turning east into Keansburg. He parked a block away from the asphalt boardwalk and eyed a corner where two guys were camped out in front of a dilapidated house. As he walked toward the corner, a rundown car pulled up, and one of the dirtbags in front of the house approached the car's window.

The hood took cash from the passenger and handed it off to his partner. Luca crouched out of view as the man with the cash surveyed the area. Satisfied it was clear, he signaled his buddy, who lifted a plank from the porch, grabbed a packet, and stuck it in the car window. As the car pulled away, Luca popped out and flashed his badge, bringing the car to a halt. The corner dealers started to flee, but Luca knew them well and called for them to stop.

Luca took the bag of crystal meth from the car. "Now scram. I don't want to see your ragged ass here again. I can guarantee you the next time you won't get a pass."

Luca ripped open the glassine envelope and shook out the contents as he approached the dealers. He pointed to the senior guy, who was casually lighting a Marlboro.

"Franklin, tell your boy to take a walk."

The dealer hiked his head, and the hood walked off.

"Getting brazen, Franklin? It's the middle of the day, for Chrissakes."

"What you talkin' 'bout, man?"

Luca smiled and shook his head. "Look, if I was here to bust you, your ass would be in a wagon already. I'm gonna give you a pass today, but you gotta give me something."

The dealer took a step back and smiled. "What you want? Some candy?"

"Information on one of your buyers."

He took a drag on his cigarette. "I can't be talking to no coppers, man. It'd ruin my—"

"Your call, Franklin. I understand." Luca beckoned with a wave. "Come on, then. Let's take a ride to the station."

"Whoa, now. Who you be wanting to know about?"

"Jimmy Johns."

"I ain't know no Johns cat."

"Look, we got photos of him buying."

The dealer crushed his cigarette with his sneaker but kept quiet as Luca stepped closer.

"Look, Franklin, I ain't got time to play games. Put your hands behind your back."

"Take it easy, man. This Johns, he a tall guy, granny-assed glasses, tattooed arms?"

"Yeah, that's him. What can you tell me about him?"

"What's to know? He's a regular customer, that's all."

"I'm interested in a Friday, May fifteenth, to be specific."

"Shit, man. You think we keep fucking ledgers and shit?"

Luca smiled. "Well, then, maybe you remember being arrested that night for dealing at Hiccups?"

Franklin spat on the sidewalk.

"You got that case coming up, and with another arrest today, I'm sure the judge would revoke your bail."

"Man, what you want from me?"

"Any information about Jimmy Johns that night, May fifteenth."

"I donno, but the motherfucker came asking for credit—like I'm running a fucking bank."

"So, did you give it?"

"What, you think I'm crazy, man?" He shook his head. "He's a junkie, man."

"So, you said no. Then what?"

"He told my boy he'd be back."

"Did he?"

Franklin nodded.

"How long?"

"I donno—an hour?"

"What time was that?"

"I donno, man."

"Come on, Franklin. Think. I need a time."

"Maybe eight, nine?"

"You know where he got the money?"

He smiled thinly. "Probably like everybody else—stealing and shit."

Chapter 20

"How'd it go with Deb?"

Luca rolled his eyes. "I'm trying to crawl out of the doghouse, but the warden's making sure I serve the full sentence."

Cremora burst out laughing and put his hand over his heart. "I feel your pain, bro."

"Yeah, right. You get ahold of Foster?"

Cremora settled into a chair. "A ton of moving parts, Luc. Basically, they don't know a lot about traumatic brain injuries, like the one Peter Hill suffered. There are a whole slew of reactions and symptoms. Each case can be different, but memory loss and erratic behavior are hallmarks of the damage."

"Erratic behavior. What about violence?"

"Doc said it really varied, but that outbursts could definitely be attributed to the trauma. He said the damage caused the, um, the nerves to misfire."

"Getting into the weeds here."

"Trust me. You should have heard Foster blab away."

"The doc say anything about old memories resurfacing?"

"You mean, like what went on years ago between him and Wyatt?"

"Bingo."

"It didn't come up, but it's a good point." Cremora frowned. "Sorry, I didn't think to ask."

"That's why I get the big bucks, J. Call him back, pronto."

"They said the doc would have to call me back. They said he was"—Cremora fingered quotation marks—"indisposed at the moment. Who knows, maybe he's got a loony on the couch?"

"All right, let's talk this over. I don't want to be barking up the wrong tree, and if you ask me, Hill's not even a sapling."

"Yeah, but Hill does have some history with Wyatt."

"Make that ancient history, when they were just kids."

"I know, but some people are funny. They hold a grudge like it's a bag of fifties. Remember that Asian kid who waited ten years before he blew away that guy and dumped him in Island State Park?"

"Yeah, but the guy killed his mother drinking and driving."

Cremora said, "Just saying it is possible."

"Unlikely, but you're right. We certainly can't rule it out. Now, Hill did know Wyatt, and we know most victims are acquainted with their killers."

"Hill's got a car that meets the description of one at the scene that night, though his brother says he's not able to drive alone."

"Question is, in his condition, could he have driven under pressure?"

"Maybe he's faking it. He was alone that night, kind of a large coincidence that he always had someone with him. Maybe he waited for an opportunity."

"No way, J. That makes no sense. The reason he's a suspect is he found out about his girlfriend and Wyatt that night."

"You're right, but he still has no alibi."

Luca nodded. "I know. Says he can't recall. That's the one thing that bothers the shit out of me."

"I know. Way too easy, if you ask me."

"Yeah, it's convenient, to say the least, but then again, the kid suffered a bad injury and—"

Cremora reached for the phone ringing on his desk. It was the county shrink returning his call. Cremora posed the question about whether old memories could resurface after a brain injury and had a conversation with the doctor before hanging up.

"Things are getting interesting."

Luca leaned forward. "What did Foster have to say?"

"He said it was highly unlikely that Hill would have forgotten about the humiliation he suffered as a child. In fact, he believes that painful memories as a child influence you throughout your life."

"Makes sense to me."

"But here's where it gets interesting. Foster said that though it is disputed by most psychiatrists, there are some that believe memories can be displaced."

"Like they didn't happen?"

"No, no. Get this. He said an old memory could be perceived to have just occurred, and a new memory can be pushed back in time."

"That's a crock of shit. It makes no sense. In this case, he was a damn kid. Don't tell me that something that happened when he was ten, he thinks happened like yesterday."

"I'm only passing it on, Luc. It ain't my theory."

"Look, man, we ain't got much on Hill, if you don't count"—Luca reached for his ringing phone—"the voodoo bullshit."

Luca slammed the phone down. "Motherfucker!"

"What's up?"

"Fusco wants Hill brought in for questioning. He said they have a witness that could put Hill at the Wyatt house."

Chapter 21

Vinny pulled into the parking lot and found a space on the second level. As he turned off the car, he said, "It's gonna be all right, Petey. Don't worry."

"I don't know. I wish you could come in the room with me."

"Yeah, me too, but Edwards said to let him handle it. Come on. Let's get this over with." Vinny swung open the driver's door as I grabbed my cane and got out. We took the elevator up to the prosecutor's office, where my lawyer, Eddie Edwards, sat reading a file in the reception area.

Edwards flipped the file closed and rammed it into his briefcase. "Hello, boys." Standing, he shook our hands. "Sit down, fellas."

Edwards moved to a seat next to me. "You ready, Peter?"

I shrugged. "Guess so."

"I don't know about this, Mr. Edwards," Vinny said.

"Don't you worry; your brother's in good hands." Then Edwards turned to me. "There's no need to be scared. There's a couple of ground rules. You listen to me. If I say not to answer, don't answer. *And never* offer any additional information. The shorter the answer, the better. You understand?"

I rubbed my ringing ear with a fingertip and nodded.

"Good. Now listen, if you're unsure of a question, ask for it to be repeated. If you're confused and want to talk something over with me before answering, just ask for a break. You got that?"

I nodded.

"Good, now they'll try to pressure you, try to force you to make some mistakes." Edwards put his hands on his knees. "But just stay calm.

If you need a break, it's no problem. We can take as many and as often as we want. Remember, I'm here to protect your rights."

"Okay," I said.

"Good." Edwards rose. "Let's go, then."

We followed him a few steps, and Edwards turned around, noticing I'd left my cane behind. The lawyer lowered his voice. "Peter, get your cane and use it. It'll look better." Edwards winked, then turned to Vinny. "This is likely to take some time. Why don't you go for a walk or something and come back, in say, ninety minutes or so?"

Edwards and I were ushered into a windowless room furnished with a square table and six folding chairs. The table we sat around had a microphone attached to a recording console and a multibuttoned intercom. I didn't like being there without Vinny.

"When we need to talk, don't say anything till I shut the mic off." As Edwards pointed at the two ceiling-mounted cameras, the door swung open, and Luca, Cremora, and assistant DA Boyle stepped into the room.

Luca said, "Counselor. Mr. Hill."

"Gentlemen."

Luca and Boyle put down their coffees and files and settled into their chairs. The assistant DA and Edwards exchanged nods, and Boyle hit the intercom.

"Freddy, we're set to begin."

A beep startled Peter, and Luca offered, "Sorry, Mr. Hill. It's just a warning that the room's live."

⁎⁎

Cremora rapped a document on the doorframe. "Let's get moving. Bristol's signature is still warm."

Luca flashed a thumbs-up and grabbed his jacket off the back of his chair. As the detectives headed to their sedan, Cremora said, "We didn't get everything we wanted. Judge said there wasn't probable cause to warrant a full search and limited it to his car."

"What? That's bullshit!"

"Luc, we didn't have much to go on. Bristol could've denied it entirely."

"When are these damn judges gonna help us instead of hinder us?"

Cremora screeched to a halt behind Johns' car. Luca grabbed the warrant off the seat and jumped out.

"You stay with his car."

Luca went to the side of the house, skipping down the stairs. He pumped the bell and pounded the door with the heel of his hand.

"Police, we have a warrant to search, open up!"

Luca stood on his toes, straining to see anything through the door's small window as a window above opened.

"What's going on?"

Luca saw Johns' sister peering out the window.

"We have a search warrant."

"Hold on. Please don't break the door down. I'll be right down." The sister disappeared before Luca could respond. Luca could hear the sister's pleas.

"Jimmy! Open the door. Please, the police are here. They smash the door down, and you're out of here. I swear, this is it!"

A gravelly voice rang out, "All right already, I'm getting it!"

The door creaked open, and Luca thrust the warrant at Johns, whose bare chest revealed yet another scorpion tattoo.

"Get the car keys."

"Car keys?"

"The search is limited, for the time being, to your car."

Johns smiled.

"Get moving, before we pry it open!"

"Uh, hold on." Johns disappeared into the basement apartment.

Luca quickly pushed the door fully open and peered in. He was surprised the place wasn't a pigsty. The detective thought this guy's not a total junkie. He's still got a good measure of control. He put one foot in the apartment and craned his neck. He spied the kitchen—no plates piled in the sink, and the countertops were spotless. He pulled back when he heard Johns' keys jangling as he headed up the stairs.

Barefoot, Johns met the detectives at his car and silently turned over the keys as his sister approached.

Johns followed them, trailed by his sister. "Don't worry, Jessie. They ain't gonna find anything. It's just a bullshit fishing expedition."

Cremora said, "Keep back! You move from that sidewalk, and we'll haul both your asses in for obstruction."

The detectives pulled on latex gloves and opened the trunk, revealing a spare tire that was flat, a jack, a hazard light that worked, and a raggedy but neatly folded pair of jeans.

Expecting a load of items to sort through, the detectives emptied what was there and checked all the nooks and crannies, to no avail. They searched the pants pockets, but also came up empty. Cremora said, "Should we bag the pants?"

"Yeah, send 'em to the lab. You never know."

As they tossed the remaining items back in the trunk, Luca said, "No lug wrench or lever for the jack?"

"Didn't see one."

"Interesting."

Luca took his notepad out as they moved to the car's interior, which was clean and orderly as well. Luca checked under the front seats and came up with a crumpled tee shirt. He backed out of the car and unraveled the shirt, inspecting it closely.

"Hey J, check this out. See this?"

"Looks like blood to me."

"Oh yeah! Man, do I wanna nail this guy."

Luca opened an evidence bag and gently inserted the shirt.

"Let's keep looking."

Cremora pulled the back seat out but came up empty. As his partner wrestled to get the seat back in place, Luca checked the glove box. Sitting on top of the owner's manual was a receipt.

"JJ, check this out." He handed the bill to Cremora.

Chapter 22

Luca swung out of the busy intersection and into a gas station. He took the receipt from Johns' glove box and popped his head into the station owner's tiny office.

"Philly, got a sec?"

The affable owner raised a finger and quickly finished his call.

"Luc, how you doing?" Phil said as he got out of his seat.

"Good, good. Look—"

"Hey, I heard you're back with Deb."

Luca nodded.

"Behave yourself this time."

"You should talk."

Phil raised his eyebrows. "So, what's going on with Billy's case?"

"That's why I'm here." He showed him the receipt. "Someone I got my eye on was here the week Wyatt was murdered."

"Shit! You kidding me? Who was it?"

Luca raised a hand. "So, this guy, he had his flat fixed. I need to talk to who did it."

"Gerry usually does the flats. What day was that?"

"Wednesday."

"Yeah, he's on Wednesdays." Phil pulled open the door from his office to the garages. He whistled over the rock music and waved Gerry over.

Gerry was wiping his hands on a dirty towel when he came in the office. "What's up, boss?"

"Detective Luca needs to talk with you about some creep whose tire you plugged."

"Philly, can we get some privacy?" Luca said.

Phil nodded and sidestepped his way out the door.

Luca showed the mechanic the receipt. "We think a guy named Jimmy Johns brought his car in with a flat on Wednesday, May thirteenth."

Gerry sat on a corner of Phil's messy desk. "Yeah, I remember. He was here. What did he do?"

Luca shook his head. "It's an active investigation. What can you tell me about his visit that day?"

"He came in riding the frigging rim. Tire was shredded to shit. He wanted his spare fixed." He shook his head. "Just like him, riding around without a spare."

"You know him?"

"No more than anybody else. He's been in here every now and then."

"How'd he seem?"

"I don't know, he's kinda a weird dude, druggie type."

"He say anything?"

"Nah, not much. He wanted to borrow money, but I told him I was flat broke and didn't get paid till Friday."

"Friday's payday?"

"Yep. Philly dishes the cash out on Friday."

"Cash? You get paid in cash?"

Gerry nodded.

"Would Johns know you get paid in cash?"

"Yeah, I think so, 'cause last time he came in, I lent him, like, twenty bucks. It was a Friday, and he seen me get paid, so I couldn't say no."

***

Luca identified everyone in the room for the record, then began his interrogation.

"Mr. Hill, what can you tell us about your relationship with William Wyatt?"

I moved my hands from my lap to the table and back again and replied, "I—I, we knew him a long time. He was my brother's friend."

"Did you get along with Mr. Wyatt?"

I looked at Mr. Edwards, who nodded.

"Not so much—he was my brother's friend."

"Can you tell me why?"

The ringing seemed to get louder or maybe higher pitched. I could never tell, so I jiggled my ear. "He did some things, I don't know, that weren't nice."

"You mean like bullying?"

Bringing it up still stung. "Yeah."

Eddie Edwards interjected, "I'd like the record to reflect that the time frame for the events you're questioning are more than fifteen years ago."

"Noted, Counselor. Let me move on to, shall we say, more recent events. Peter, where were you the night of Friday, May fifteenth?"

It bothered me that I couldn't pin who this detective looked like, so I leaned over to Mr. Edwards and pointed at Luca. "Who does he remind you of? Some actor, right?"

"Well, some people say I bear a resemblance to George Clooney."

"Yeah, yeah, that's it. He was in that movie; what's it called, remember . . ."

Edwards said, "Let's get back to business, Peter. Detective, can you repeat your question please."

"Sure." Luca looked into my eyes. "I wanted to know where you were on May fifteenth, a Friday night."

Averting my eyes, I picked at a cuticle. "Home, I guess."

"You guess?" Cremora said, chuckling.

Edwards raised a hand. "My client has suffered a traumatic brain injury while serving our nation. Please show him the respect he deserves."

"I'm sorry if I offended you, Mr. Hill. We're trained in a certain manner, and well, let's leave it at that. But I really am sorry if I offended you."

Luca looked over at Edwards, who nodded slightly.

That's better now, I thought, nearly smiling.

"It's okay, just that sometimes my memory is not so good and all."

Luca took over. "Well, we'll take it slow. If you need a break, just ask. No problem at all. Would you like something to drink?"

Unsure if I should ask for a break or not, I wagged my head. I didn't want to seem too anxious to stop the questioning, but I was getting nervous.

"Okay, let me clarify the date in question. On May fifteenth, a Friday, we know your brother, Vinny, was away in Texas, and that your friend Tony Burato visited with you."

I rubbed my hands as I tried to stop squirming in the chair. I sighed heavily, and Edwards asked, "Would you like a break?"

For some reason, I shook my head no.

"Detective, can you repeat the question, and keep in mind that compound questions are more difficult to process for my client."

Luca pulled his chin in and raised an eyebrow.

"I have the psychiatric, er, neurological evaluations, if you'd like."

Luca raised his palms. "Understood. No problem. I'll keep that in mind." He looked at me and spoke slowly. "Your brother, Vincent, was away on May fifteenth, correct?"

What's he think, I'm a retard? I answered, "Yes, he went to Texas. I think he wants me to move there, but my doctors, they don't—"

Edwards tapped my arm and gave an okay sign.

Luca continued. "That same day, did your friend from the service, Tony Burato, visit you?"

"Uh." I tugged my ear as a rusty taste hit my mouth. "Yeah, pretty sure."

"And what did you do?"

"Uh, he's getting married, and there was a party."

Cremora exchanged glances with Luca and questioned, "Married? We thought it was his brother's birthday."

I thought about it and mouthed the word birthday. "Oh yeah, right. Tony's brother's birthday." Then I stroked my chin. "You sure he ain't getting married?"

Luca pressed on. "Back to that night, his brother's birthday. The party moved to a bar. What did you do at the bar?"

I puckered my lips and swallowed. "I don't know."

"Come on, Peter. Think harder."

I mean, geez, I can't frigging remember. I slammed a fist on the table. "Whatever you do in a fucking bar, like drink!"

Edwards grabbed my forearm. "Let's take that break," he said.

Luca checked his messages and called back Franco. "What d'ya got for me?"

"Hello, Frank. I'm fine, and you?"

"Look, bro, I'm in the middle of an interrogation, so I got no time for sweet talk, got it?"

"All right, all right, look, the blood on the tee shirt didn't match Wyatt's, and—"

"What? How can that be?"

"Look, Frank, the lab results weren't a match."

"This is fucking nonsense."

"I'm sorry to disappoint you, but that's what came back."

After calling his office, Edwards joined Vinny in the hallway outside the bathroom Peter was using. Edwards filled Vinny in on the proceedings and asked, "He always like this?"

Vinny said, "It's a day-to-day thing. Sometimes the meds work, and sometimes they don't."

"It's critical we keep him calm. Being belligerent is throwing red meat to the cops."

"I don't think he can control it. It's the injury, you know."

"Then we've got to assemble a full medical accounting of what Peter's been through and the residual effects."

Vinny kept his eyes on the bathroom door. "You'll need a small truck."

"The more the better. They may think this is all an act."

"Act?"

"Peter not remembering. Law enforcement is naturally skeptical. They'll think it's convenient he can't recall events. I'm not making parallels here, but think along the lines of temporary insanity."

Vinny pushed open the door. Peter was hunched over the sink scooping running water into his mouth.

"What are you doing?"

Peter pulled his fingers out of his mouth. "Can't take the metal taste anymore. It's driving me crazy."

Vinny dug into his pocket for the chalky candy a doctor had suggested. "We gotta go back in. Have one of these."

Before restarting the interview, Luca composed himself by stating for the record the time and the participants. Then he pasted a smile on his face and looked at me.

"If you need another break, just let us know. We have plenty of time. Okay?"

I stared at my clasped hands.

Luca flipped open a file. "All right, so you are out celebrating with your service buddy, Tony, on the night of May fifteenth, right?"

Talking about that night made me real nervous and brought back the images, or whatever they were, of Billy getting hit on the head. I took a couple of quick breaths as my hand began to tremble.

Edwards said, "Mr. Hill is not disputing that he was at the Lincoln Lounge with his friends on the night in question."

Edwards turned the mic off and whispered into my ear.

"Okay, Counselor. Peter, do you know a Mary Rourke?"

"You know I do. What're you playing fucking games with me for?"

Edwards brought a finger to his lips as Cremora said, "Trust me, Mr. Hill, this is no game."

Luca fired, "And what is the nature of your relationship with Ms. Rourke?"

My breath quickened. "We were going out, you know, for a long time. She was my girl"—I still couldn't believe she cheated on me and shook my head—"until that bastard stole her."

Edwards leaned over, put his hand on my forearm, and whispered for me to calm down.

"You hated Wyatt and went to his house to confront him over Mary?" Cremora said.

I put my left hand on my right arm to try to quell the tremor. "I don't know."

Cremora slapped a hand on the table. "You don't know? Well, let me remind you, we have a witness that put you at his house the night of May fifteenth."

Witness? Holy shit, they know I did it? Tugging my collar, I said, "Uh, maybe I was there." Then turning to Edwards. "I don't remember, Mr. Edwards. I really don't."

"That's okay. Just tell the truth. We'll see how credible their witness is."

Cremora leaned forward, but Luca shooed him back with a hand, asking, "Now Peter, that night in the bar. Is that when you learned that William Wyatt was going to marry Mary Rourke?"

I rested my cheek on my hand, looked at the table, and responded, "I knew somethin' was going on. I'm not a jerk, you know. She was acting strange and all, if you know what I mean."

"Not really. Why don't you tell us?"

"She hardly ever came over." I pawed at my ear with a shaking hand. "And when she did, she ran out real fast. Always had an excuse." I felt my eyes narrowing. "I didn't believe her."

"So, you knew she was seeing someone else?"

"Guess so. Maybe it was me, getting banged up and all. But everyone said I was doing well."

Luca said, "I understand you've come a long way, Peter."

Ripping off my glasses with a trembling hand, I raised my cane with the other. "Yeah, just doing fucking great!"

Edwards asked, "Peter, please take it easy. Would you like to take a break?"

"No, let's get this shit over with."

"Can you tell us what you did when you drove up to the Wyatt house?"

I closed my eyes. I didn't think I knew, so I wouldn't say anything. That's what Mr. Edwards would say.

Cremora pressed, "Did you get out of the car?"

I looked at Mr. Edwards as the metal taste roared back. "I—I donno. I can't remember."

"Didn't you get into a fight over Mary with Billy Wyatt that night?" Cremora asked.

All eyes shifted their focus to the amplified shudder in my right arm. I grabbed my wrist, trying to control the shaking, but both arms shook instead.

"We're going to have to call an end to the interview. Mr. Hill's physicians had provided strict parameters to adhere to in order to protect his health."

***

"Hill's lying."

"I don't know, JJ."

"Come on, Frank. What're you, fucking blind?"

"We're dealing with a touchy thing here," Luca replied.

"He's hiding, giving us that bullshit he don't remember. Geez, what a crock of shit. I'm surprised, no make it shocked, that you're buying it."

"Hold on, I'm not buying anything. Fact is, with these brain injuries the memory doesn't work normal. Seems crazy, I know, but I did a lot of research last night."

"Yeah, well kinda convenient he remembers things about Mary, but when the night Wyatt ended up dead comes up, he starts shaking like a leaf."

"Tell me about it. It sounds strange, but there's actually a lot of data out there."

"Yeah? And a ton of cases where defendants block out what they did."

"I know. I keep reminding myself."

"If we didn't have a witness, Hill would be saying he didn't go to Wyatt's that night."

Luca nodded. "If we had something to prove he was in the house, it'd go a long way for me."

Chapter 23

Peter was separated from his brother and lawyer and ushered into a stark white room with six other men his age. Outfitted with eyeglasses, the assemblage shared similar height, build, and coloring. A uniformed officer handed out number tags to put around their necks and told the group to line up in order. Peter was given the number five and stood, back to the wall, near the end of the line. He stared at the one-way mirror spanning the opposite wall.

The officer left the room and turned on yet another fluorescent light. A minute later, a speaker cackled, and the latest process of the legal wrangling began.

On the other side of the window, a young girl was escorted into the viewing corridor by Marc Weinburg, one of Prosecutor Stanley's assistants. Peter's attorney, Eddie Edwards, observed the proceedings as Kathy, who lived across the street from the victim, received instructions.

"Take your time. We'll ask the men to step forward so you can get a closer look, if you would like. Then we'll have them turn for a look at their profiles. Ready?"

Kathy, standing at the rear of the corridor, nodded, and the assistant DA steered her closer to the window before backing away from her.

Kathy studied the men, moving slowly along the line, pausing in front of number three. She studied him for a moment as the prosecutor spoke into the microphone.

"Number three. Step forward."

The third man, who happened to be a cop, took two steps forward. Edwards leaned forward, hoping the neighbor would identify him.

Instead, Kathy crinkled her nose, shrugged her shoulders and moved on. She didn't waste any time on the next man in line, but when she moved in front of Peter, she pressed her nose against the glass.

"Number five, step forward, please."

Peter shifted his weight before stepping forward.

"Take another step forward, please."

Peter glanced at the speaker and stepped closer. Kathy shrank back from the window.

"It's okay, no one can see you."

She stared at Peter and nodded. "I think it's him, number five."

"You sure?"

"Pretty sure. Can I see the sides of their faces?"

The speaker sounded out instructions. "Back in line. Now, everyone turn to the left."

Kathy quickly moved down the line of profiles and paused briefly at number three again. She shook her head and moved on, stopping at Peter. She studied him and declared, "Yeah, that's him. He was the one driving the car."

Kathy was asked to verify her decision again before being escorted out to sign a statement, leaving the viewing corridor to the attorneys.

"Doesn't look good for your client, Counselor," Weinburg said.

Edwards reminded the prosecutor, "Last time I looked, driving a car isn't a crime."

"It puts him at the Wyatt scene."

"In front of the house. Do you have anyone who saw him enter the house? He may have just simply driven away."

***

Cremora burst into Luca's office as his phone began ringing. "Stanley got a search warrant for Hill's house,"

"What?"

"Gesso told me as I was coming in."

Luca picked up the phone and made an inquiry.

"Participate? Of course. Who's running this fucking investigation, anyway?"

Luca frowned at his partner as he listened to the caller before saying, "It's bullshit, Chief."

Luca held the phone away from his ear as the assistant DA shouted. He put the phone back to his ear and said, "I'm not letting Stanley run away with this. When are they heading down there?" Luca shook his head. "Okay, we'll be there."

He slammed the phone down and jumped up. "You believe this shit?"

"Take it easy, Luc. Prosecutors do this shit all the time."

"Yeah, but how about letting the lead detective in on it? I'm not a fucking rookie, you know." He swept his jacket off the back of the chair. "Let's get rolling."

Vinny was screaming at the officers as he assisted a cane-less Peter out of the house and down the walkway when Luca and Cremora pulled up. As they got out of their car, two more black and whites, lights flashing and sirens on, screeched to halt behind them. They were headed to the front door when Luca veered off, approaching the brothers who were seated against the garage door.

Peter had his hands over his ears and was rocking back and forth as Vinny continued his tirade. Luca said, "You gotta calm down. You're just gonna make it harder on both of you."

Vinny glowered at Luca.

"He going to be okay?" Luca asked.

"Does he look okay to you? Getting kicked out of our house like a fucking criminal."

"Sorry, I—"

"Sorry, my ass. You had a hand in this."

Luca walked away muttering, "You should only know."

When Luca stepped inside, he was surprised to see John Cline, who was the head of the major crimes bureau, supervising two teams of investigators on the first floor. Gut churning, Luca surveyed the living room. He paused at a wall of pictures and saw Peter's cane in an evidence bag leaning against the sofa. He checked in with Cline and headed upstairs with Cremora.

The partners poked around the master bedroom, which clearly was not being used, before moving to the bedroom next door. When they swung the door open, they were greeted by a yellow Semper Fi poster.

"This is his room. Check the closet, JJ, and keep it neat."

Luca stepped over a balled-up sweatshirt and headed to a chest of drawers topped with framed photos. Luca looked at a picture of Peter, his brother, and their mother in front of a birthday cake, thinking the brothers didn't look alike. Next Luca examined a stock shot of the Marine dressed in his formals. He studied the picture, wondering if the combat or the injury had sapped the vitality out of the veteran. The nicest frame contained a younger, beaming Peter, arm around Mary, on a boardwalk that looked like Belmar. Luca focused on her exposed midsection before catching himself. He moved on to the last photo, a high school prom shot of Peter and Mary outside their limo. Then he checked the drawers.

As Luca worked his way up the set of stuffed drawers, Cremora said, "Don't look like there's anything here, but I can't reach the top shelf."

Luca swung a folding chair over for Cremora to stand on and went through the first drawer. Sorting through the socks and tee shirts, he came upon a partial photograph. Luca pondered its meaning and what the missing rest of the picture looked like. Then his partner clicked off his flashlight.

"Nothing up here but a shoebox of baseball cards and old shoulder pads."

Luca held up the photo. "Take a look at this."

Luca placed the picture in a cellophane bag, slipped it in his breast pocket, and led the way to the bathroom, where the mirror was plastered with sticky notes. Luca shook his head as he read through the reminders: *Brush your teeth. Flush the toilet. Take your PILLS. Today is Wednesday . . .*

Cremora knocked over a pillbox crammed with the week's dosages as he was swinging open the shower curtain. There he saw a portable seat, a grab bar, and a dirty nonslip surface. He turned toward Luca and frowned. Luca scooped up the pillbox, and they left the bathroom without speaking.

The detectives moved down the hall to the last door. The smallest bedroom was almost bare. A single bed and nightstand shared the space with a pair of open suitcases full of clothes.

They rummaged through Vinny's sleeping quarters and headed down the stairs, where two bags of clothing had joined the cane as possible evidence. The detectives shadowed the investigators for the next two hours, a time that produced nothing they considered hard.

On the way out, Luca stopped to speak with the brothers.

"Sorry again. They're all done."

"So, what'd you find? Any smoking guns?"

Luca said, "Look, they're taking his cane to run some tests."

"Fucking scumbags, taking a veteran's cane. Goddamn, I got a mind to call the news and see how it plays."

"You have another one?"

Peter shook his head.

"I'll pick one up at Hazlet Pharmacy and drop it off later."

"Now you're Mr. Nice Guy, after you rifle through our house?"

"Look, Vinny, I know this is difficult, but a man's been murdered, and we've got to look at everything." Luca turned to his partner. "Let's get moving."

On their way to see Mary, Cremora's cell phone rang.

"What? Okay. I'll be right home. No, no, let's meet at the hospital."

"What happened?"

"My dad—chest pains—they rushed him to Riverview."

Luca spun the car around and dropped Cremora at Riverview Medical Center, on the Shrewsbury River, then he headed to Lincroft to see Mary.

Chapter 24

Luca assured Mrs. Rourke that her daughter wasn't a suspect and that all he needed was to ask Mary a quick question. She agreed, asking him to wait on the tiny porch. She closed the front door. A minute later, Mary, accompanied by a strawberry scent, stepped out, wearing super-tight jeans and a white shirt.

"Thanks for coming to talk to me. I promise it'll be quick."

She tossed her hair back teasingly and smiled. "I'm sure you heard it before, but you really look like George Clooney."

Luca sucked in her scent. "Yeah, a ton of times. Hope that's a good thing."

Mary smiled and seemed to move a hair closer. "For sure."

Luca dug into his breast pocket. "You remember this picture?"

Mary took the picture, and her smile dissipated into a frown. "What happened to it?"

"We don't know yet. We found it this way."

"It was Billy's favorite. I had it framed for him."

"You gave Billy Wyatt this picture in a frame?"

She nodded.

"What did the frame look like?"

"The frame? It was one of those black wooden ones, kinda simple but sleek, if you know what I mean."

Luca jotted a note, "Do you know what he did with it?"

"The picture? He had it in his living room, on the buffet."

"Who was in the picture?"

"Who else? Billy."

"Can you tell me anything about it? Where you were? Things like that?"

"It was a couple of months ago. We were going out for my birthday, double dating with my girlfriend Ann. We were all dressed up, so we took pictures, and when he saw it, he liked it. He said he liked the way my eyes looked . . ." Her voice trailed off.

Luca wanted to agree, but asked, "Anything else?"

Mary studied the picture, fingering the locket around her neck as she did.

Luca noticed it was the same one she wore in the photo, and said, "He give it to you?"

"Billy? No, Peter did."

"Peter Hill gave you the, uh, locket?"

She nodded.

Luca shifted his weight. "When did you last see the picture?"

"I don't know. I guess the last time I was there. It's not like I looked at all the pictures every time."

"I understand, but try to remember if you can recall when you saw the picture last. It could be important."

"Why? What's going on?"

"At this point it's just a hunch."

"Like I said, I think it was there the last time, uh, not the last time, you know, that was when . . ."

"Were there any copies of this picture?"

"I'm pretty sure we probably made two. We always get copies. It's almost the same price."

"Do you know where the other copy is?"

"I don't know. I may even have it. I'd have to check."

"Okay, check around and let me know." He handed her his card and said, "And thanks for your help."

✳✳✳

Luca was in a bar finishing up a meeting with another contact of his in the Russian community. The informant solidified Luca's hunch on another homicide case he was working. The inside information confirmed that Igor Butnick met his fate at the hands of the gang he worked for as payback for overstepping.

As he was leaving, a knockout of a barmaid tried to lure him over. He stopped, gave her a smile, but resisted the bait and walked out the door, resolving not to waste any more time on the case. After he slid behind the wheel of his sedan, he quickly dialed a number.

"Hey, JJ, what's going on with your dad?"

"He had a heart attack. They're putting in a couple of stents."

"Geez."

"They say he's gonna be fine—just gotta stop with all the fatty foods and get his tail into some regular exercise."

"Good, we should all take that medicine."

"You get anything from Mary?"

"Think so. I'm heading over to the Wyatt place to check on something."

"Keep me in the loop."

"Don't worry, I will. By the way, looks like Butnick was offed by the Kalomoff gang."

"Just like we thought."

"Yeah, look, you take care of your pop, and I'll let you know what's going on."

Luca met the patrol car at Wyatt's house, and after the patrolman cut the crime scene tape away from the door, Luca went straight to the buffet table. He checked the four pictures on it twice and pulled on a pair of latex gloves. Luca opened the top drawer and called out to the patrolman, "O'Brien, come over here. I want this witnessed."

The patrolman observed Luca bag the item and search through all the other drawers. The detective narrowed his eyes and slowly scanned the room before saying, "I'm gonna run this into Freehold. Secure the scene."

Luca presented the bag of evidence to Franco.

"You got me a frame for my birthday?"

Luca raised a fist. "No, I got you this."

"Where's the evidence tag?"

"I was in a hurry to get it to you. It may be nothing, but—"

Franco beckoned with his hand. "What's the story with this?"

"The Wyatt case—got it from the scene."

"They missed this?"

"Not really. It was in a drawer. It's a long story, Franco. Can you just dust it and run it for a match?"

The lab technician swung an arm around the room. "Sure, sure, I got nothing to do. I was just sitting around waiting for Detective Luca."

Luca smiled and patted him on the shoulder. "Good thing I came in, then."

Franco took the bag over to a dusting table and tugged on latex gloves. He removed the frame, hung it, and gently brushed it with a white powder. Franco put on glasses and closed in on the frame with a magnifier.

"Nice contrast at least, but there's quite a few prints on it."

"This may sound silly, but don't waste time on any that look to be a girl's."

"Not as silly as it sounds, though sometimes it's not as easy to tell just on the size." Franco focused on the lower left-hand corner of the frame. "Fat thumb print here, and it's a good one."

Luca let out a breath of air. "Now we got to see who it belongs to."

"There's a forefinger and middle finger print on the rear that are clear as well."

"Can we run a check on them?"

"I'll do whatever I have to do to get you outta my hair."

Franco took digital images of the three prints and turned on a monitor to display them.

Luca said, "Franco, I want to make this easy for you."

"Always looking out for me, ain't you?"

"Just run it against Peter Hill's prints."

Luca filled out an evidence tag, stuck it on the bag, and stared at it. The detective contemplated the second of his principles: that no matter how good a cop you were, there was always a surprise you couldn't see coming. The detective rubbed his forehead with a thumb and forefinger as Cremora breezed in.

"Headache?"

"Hey, JJ, how's your dad?"

"He's one tough cookie, man—got nine lives. They put a couple of stents in, and the say he'll be fine."

"Too bad his son ain't got any of his toughness."

Cremora picked up the bag containing the frame. "Holy shit! Hill *was* in the Wyatt house?"

"And that partial picture we took from Hill's bedroom was once in the frame."

"There goes the theory that he just drove off."

"Yeah, but it doesn't make him a murderer."

"Maybe, but it's a damning piece of evidence, Luc."

"I know, I know, but it just doesn't fit."

"What don't fit? A witness saw him in front of the house. We now know he was inside the house. He had a long history of, let's call it, friction with the victim, including taking his girl."

"It's just that, what about Johns? Shit, there's enough, if not more, circumstantial shit against him."

"Don't forget, Hill has no alibi."

"Yeah, but neither does Johns."

Cremora held the bag up. "You going to Stanley with this?"

"Not yet, we need a little time to see what else we dig up on Johns."

Cremora studied his partner a second. "You sure about this?"

"Damn sure."

"I don't know, Luc."

"Come on J. I just need a bit more time. I don't want to live with another fuckup."

"Okay, but we've got to look at Hill as well."

Luca nodded as Sergeant Gesso walked in. Luca discreetly slid the bag into a desk drawer as Gesso threw a thick file onto Luca's desk.

"Seems the Hill kid has a history of losing it." Gesso turned on his heel and headed back out, saying, "I don't know how long we can hold off. Stanley's office is pushing for an arrest."

The detectives pawed through the file that contained interviews with the men Peter Hill served with in the US Marines. Then Luca's cell phone went off.

"Shit! It's Debra. Uh, hello."

Cremora smiled when he heard Debra's barking voice.

Luca said into the phone, "Yeah, of course. I'm on my way."

Luca stood and tucked the file under his arm.

"I'll run through this tonight. You go spend some time with your dad."

Chapter 25

Luca lifted Debra's arm off his chest and slowly slid out of bed. He picked up his briefs and tee shirt and snuck out of the bedroom. He dressed in the hallway and raised his shoulders as he tiptoed down the stairs. The detective grabbed the fat file off the coffee table and opened it at the kitchen table.

Luca read through an interview with a Private Soto and slumped in his chair. Soto claimed that he thought Hill was a weirdo and mercurial, if not unstable. The private said he witnessed Hill losing his temper a couple of times and getting into at least two fights. Luca took a deep breath and moved to another conversation an investigator had with a Marine named Ippolito, who painted Hill as a calm, measured man who was always looking to help people.

Luca felt hope rising as he read through the dialogue of a third Marine, a captain named Chavez. The captain praised Hill's demeanor and had even used him to defuse tensions between the Marines under his command.

The detective excitedly flipped the Chavez interview over and read yet another glowing report on Hill from Private Faegan before skimming through the remaining reports. Relieved that nothing negative jumped off the pages, he began to take a closer look when the stairway light came on.

"Frank? You okay?"

"Yeah, yeah, I'm fine. Go back to sleep."

Debra came down the stairs. "What in God's name are you doing?"

Luca flipped the file closed. "Uh, couldn't sleep, so figured I'd read through some interviews."

Debra shook her head and smiled. "Not much has changed, has it, Detective?"

"It has. It's just that this kid, I don't know, it feels like he's getting railroaded."

Debra filled a glass with water. "Who is it this time?"

"Marine named Peter Hill. He's a suspect in the Wyatt case."

"And you don't think he did it?"

"It's not that. It's like there's a rush to pin it on him."

Debra put a hand on his shoulder and said, "And you're doing double time to avoid another Barrow."

Luca nodded, picked her hand off his shoulder, and kissed it. "Come on. Let's get back to bed."

                              ***

Luca came down the stairs.

"Coffee smells good."

He kissed Debra good morning, poured a mug, and sat at the table.

"You want something to eat?"

"Sure." He opened the *Asbury Park Press* and flicked through the sections looking for the sports segment. When he saw the Monmouth County section, he said, "Just lost my appetite."

"What's wrong?"

He pointed to the headline of the lead story: "*Murdered Football Star's Parents to Meet with Prosecutor.*"

> The parents of William Wyatt, who quarterbacked the Middletown Eagles to two state championships, are scheduled to meet with Monmouth County Prosecutor Stanley. The family is frustrated with the investigation into who killed their only son, William "Billy" Wyatt, who was brutally murdered in his home. The May 15th slaying is one of several unsolved murders that have vexed law enforcement and frightened coun-

ty residents. Prosecutor Stanley's office confirmed the visit and said they were making progress on the case. However, Stanley refused to comment further on what he termed as an ongoing investigation.

A picture of a celebrating Wyatt hoisted on the shoulders of his teammates was tucked into the text.

"What's the matter with the parents coming up?"

"Nothing to do with them. These poor people have a right. I feel terrible for them, but I just know Stanley's gonna ratchet up the pressure."

"It'll be fine, Frank. Take it easy."

"You don't know these guys, Deb. They'll hijack the case and pin it on Hill."

"Come on, Frank. You're getting paranoid again."

"You think so? Then why don't you tell me why they got the search warrant on Hill without telling me?"

Back at his office, Luca discussed with Cremora the interviews of Hill's fellow servicemen. "Besides this guy Soto, nobody had a bad thing to say about Hill."

"So, what the heck was Gesso talking about?"

Luca shook his head. "I'm getting a bad feeling."

Luca's phone rang. "Today? Okay, I'll see you later."

Luca pulled up to the house and thought things through again before getting out. He rang the bell, and Vinny swung open the door. When Vinny saw who it was, he quickly stepped outside and closed the door behind him.

"What do you want now?"

"I have a question concerning Peter."

"Look, this is getting ridiculous."

"Hold on. You may not believe it, but I'm not convinced your brother had anything to do with Wyatt's death."

"So, you're saying you're on our side now?"

"I don't take sides. My job is to investigate and develop rock-solid evidence to solve cases. Frankly, the evidence, and I'm talking a bit out of school here, is weak, but that's not going to prevent Peter from getting tagged here."

"You mean railroaded."

"Look, I have my own ideas on who may be responsible, but now I'm confused. You see, we know Peter was in front of the house that night. But there was no proof he was inside."

"That's 'cause he wasn't!"

Luca raised his palm. "That is, until we found a picture frame with his prints on it."

Vinny leaned on the door. "What are you talking about?"

Luca handed him photos of the frame and the partial picture it had contained, explaining that the torn photo they took from Peter's room had been in a frame in Wyatt's house. Vinny stared at the copies and said, "This is crazy. I'm sure there's an explanation."

Luca lowered his voice. "I'm really hoping there is. I held off logging it as evidence, but if there's no believable explanation—"

"They're going to arrest him?"

"Look, I don't think things quite fit as far as your brother goes, and you didn't hear it from me, but the county prosecutors feel he does, and they are, shall we say, anxious to close the case."

"What can we do?"

Luca pointed to the photos in Vinny's hand and said, "Why don't you take these to your brother and see what explanation he has? I'll be waiting in my car."

Vinny looked at the photos, nodded, and opened the door.

When the door closed, Luca turned around and stepped back on the porch, ears on high alert. He struggled to overhear the conversation taking place inside, picking up an occasional fragment when voices were raised. Suddenly, Vinny started yelling that if Peter didn't explain what was going on, he was going to jail for murder. Luca leaned his cheek on the door and closed his eyes. He was unable to fully decipher the exchange, but he was now convinced that Vinny was not colluding with his brother. He went to his car.

Luca pulled out his cell to call Debra but saw Vinny coming down the walkway and pocketed it as he rolled down the window.

Vinny handed Luca the photos.

"What'd he say?"

Vinny twisted his mouth. "Said the picture was his. Mary was wearing the locket he gave her. He said he thought he gave her the picture, frame and all, and it was his."

"Not how Mary remembers it. Said it was a picture of her and Billy Wyatt. Have to say that what she remembers sounds right. Otherwise, why was it torn?"

Vinny shrugged. "I don't know. You know my brother has all kinds of memory problems, and he mixes all kinds of shit together. I know it don't look good, but he didn't do it. He just couldn't have."

"I'm inclined to feel the same way, but the prosecutor's going to say Peter went to see Billy in a jealous rage over Mary on the night Wyatt was killed." He waved the pictures and said, "And now this puts him inside at the murder scene."

"What can we do?"

"We need to understand what happened when he went to see Wyatt, whatever it was that happened, good or bad. If he did it, I'd be wrong, but at least we'd both know the truth."

Vinny nodded.

"Look, your brother is the only one who can tell us. See what you can get from him. Meanwhile, I'll be following any and all credible leads."

"Thanks, Detective Luca." Vinny stuck his hand in the car. "Really, I really appreciate it."

Luca shook his hand, said goodbye, and drove off troubled.

Chapter 26

Stanley slipped into his office via a rear entrance as a clap of thunder sounded. In the two days since the Wyatt family met with the Monmouth County prosecutor, Stanley had been fielding questions about the effectiveness of the department. Though the Wyatts followed his recommendation, refusing to talk to the press, the sympathy their appearance garnered raised the heat of the spotlight significantly.

Stanley quickly scanned the overnight crime reports. Thankful nothing major had occurred, he grabbed a summary of the open felonies and sank into his chair. There were more unsolved acts of violence then at any time since he assumed office. Frustrated with the number of open cases, he asked the sheriff to organize a series of meetings for that afternoon.

Just before he entered the building, Luca repressed another urge to call Debra. It was about the tenth impulse since he was informed about the emergency meeting. He knew gloating wouldn't help, so when he could, he'd try to make things different this time around.

Luca smiled at a new secretary and took a second look at her before turning into the conference room. Huddled at the far end of the wooden table, the sheriff and Sergeant Gesso briefly raised their heads in acknowledgment. Before Luca finished his wave, a folder slapped his shoulder.

"Hey, Clooney, where's your sidekick?"

"Hey, Matt. JJ's dad had another heart attack."

The only other senior detective in Luca's precinct, Matt Duro was a good cop but rough around the edges. "Oh well. Hey, heard you're shacking up with Debra again."

Luca dropped his active case files on the table and took a seat. "It's not shacking up when you're married, Bozo."

Duro sat beside him, whispering, "What's this? Another dog and pony show?"

"I'm hoping against hope they don't push—"

"You tellin' me? These fucking lawyers should ride around with us, get a dose of reality."

The door at the opposite end of the room opened, and a scowling Stanley, followed by two of his associates, entered the room. The prosecutor quickly swapped his frown for a smile and shook his visitors' hands before taking a chair at the head of the table.

Stanley signaled Gesso, who opened the meeting.

"Prosecutor Stanley is meeting with investigators, on a precinct-by-precinct basis, to review open cases and see what resources his office can provide. He wants to help close as many cases as possible."

Duro nudged Luca with his elbow.

Stanley said, "As I said in previous meetings, we're not looking to interfere. We just simply want to see where we are in all open cases and how to move them forward. We're all here to help. Sheriff Meril also has county resources at his disposal that may help to alleviate the fear the community is in."

Gesso said, "We appreciate the offer. Any help with patrols or increasing our presence would go a long way in assuring the citizens."

"Nothing alleviates fear more than arrests," Stanley said, smiling broadly.

Duro interjected, "As long as it's not a game called catch and release."

Weinburg, who had organized the Hill lineup, said, "Fair enough, Detective, but the public notices when we take a suspect off the streets."

Luca chipped in, "Yeah, but they really notice when due process gets trampled on."

Stanley raised a hand. "Shall we get back to the matters at hand?" The prosecutor looked around the table. "We need to work together to bring those who commit crimes to justice. My office acknowledges the difficult work you do in the field and called for these reviews to see where we can assist in quickly closing cases."

"Focus on the low-hanging fruit, so to speak," Weinburg said.

Stanley cocked his head toward Gesso, and the sergeant spoke as he flipped a file open. "We've got four open homicides and ten assaults with deadly weapons in the precinct."

Cline clarified, "And that would be within the last five weeks."

Gesso pursed his lips and nodded.

Stanley said, "For the moment, let's focus on the homicides."

Gesso began the review. "Block, Henry. Fifty-seven years old, white male. Shot point blank with a shotgun behind the Middletown Arts Center. No witnesses; no suspects at this point. Appears to be a robbery."

"Shotgun blast should've left a lot of evidence."

Duro jumped in. "Not a pretty scene, blood all over, but until we can find the sucker drenched in it, it's nothing but a scene out of a horror movie."

Cline said, "Record states that the victim was a family man, lived in Middletown by the train station, and commuted to the city."

Duro leaned back in his chair. "Like the summary says, the vic stayed late for some office function and took a late train back. Wife noticed he never came home and phoned it in at around 3 a.m."

"We can read, Detective. What I'm looking for is the information to determine where to take the case."

"Look, the guy lived by the station and would cross through the wooded area to get to his house. Some cretin must've been watching the late trains, saw this skinny little guy was alone, and took him down."

"Did he need to use the shotgun to rob a small guy? Sure, there isn't something else going on? Any problems with addiction or money?" Cline questioned.

"We have no other reports of shotgun use in the area, or county, for that matter," Sheriff Meril added.

Luca spoke up. "There was a teenager who was robbed as she walked home from the train as well. She said she thought the assailant had a shotgun, but couldn't be sure."

"When was that?"

"I'd have to check, but say two to three months ago."

"Get the case details to Duro. He'll follow up. See if we can get a description of the man from her and take it from there."

Stanley leaned back in his chair.

"That's what I'm talking about. Though I wish these types of exchanges happened at the precinct level, Sergeant. Who's next?"

"Butnick, Igor. You'll remember his body was left in the Holmdel A&P parking lot. The thirty-year-old was a member of the Brooklyn-based Russian ring—"

Luca jumped in. "Look, these Russians are shut tight. No one's talking. A contact of mine tells me it was an inside job—the mob hitting one of their own. This Butnick character was an independent type guy, and who knows? Maybe he stretched things, and the bosses made an example out of him. It happens all the time."

"I don't know if we should spend more time on this. Sounds like we're spinning our wheels, unless it could lead us into one of the top guns in the Russian gang," Cline said.

Stanley stated, "It's isolated to the Russian community. It may make a headline with the mob angle, but it'll do nothing to quell the public fears."

Luca remained silent. He agreed it would be a waste of time to focus on a mob killing. As far as he was concerned, that was one less monster on the street.

Stanley beckoned with his hand and Gesso moved on.

"Tilup, Eileen. Forty-year-old mother of two. Beaten while cooking dinner. Her six-year-old called 911, but Tilup died two days later. Children were traumatized and haven't been able to give us anything to work with. No signs of forced entry. No substantive leads—a real dead end."

"Of all the cases, this one has really hit a chord with the public. I can't tell you how many calls we had on it," Stanley said.

"Who can blame 'em? I mean, geez, if a mother is not safe cooking dinner in her home."

Duro said, "I get it, but we don't have much to go on. By all accounts, Tilup wasn't playing around, so no jilted lover to focus on. Family seems clean. No financial issues. It's a sick society we live in. Maybe it's just a random act of violence—"

Stanley slapped a hand on the table. "Detective, let me remind you that it is random acts of violence, perceived or not, that frighten the citizenry. Our job is not to discount or explain away. We need to bring the perpetrators to justice."

"The Wyatt case had similar circumstances. Could it be the same guy? Are we collaborating?" Cline asked.

Luca fired, "Of course we've collaborated! We've jointly reviewed the crime scene data and evidence, but beyond an assault with a blunt instrument and no apparent signs of intrusion, there doesn't seem to be any connection in the crimes."

Silence held court for a five-second count until Cline broke it. "Well, that seems like a good segue into the Wyatt case."

Gesso shuffled files.

"Wyatt, William. A twenty-eight-year-old Caucasian male, beaten to death inside his home on May fifteenth. No sign of a break-in."

"How close are you to building a case against this Hill fellow?" Cline asked.

Luca shifted in his chair. "He may be in the mix, but I'm not ready to do anything."

Cline said. "What? Unless I'm missing something, we've got quite a bit of incriminating evidence on Hill."

Luca gritted his teeth. "It's all circumstantial at this point."

Stanley said, "Let us be the judge of that, Detective."

"Look, my job is to gather the evidence and present it to you for prosecution. I've been around long enough to know the only good case is one where the evidence holds up in—"

Gesso interrupted. "Why don't we go through it? The suspect, Peter Hill, was seen in front of the Wyatt house on the night of the murder. Hill has a long history of tension with the victim, including finding out earlier that night that Wyatt was going to marry his old girlfriend. Hill doesn't have an alibi, claiming he cannot recall the events of the night in question due to the injury he sustained serving as a Marine."

"Got to be a bit careful with a Marine these days," Weinburg offered.

"Can we prove he was inside the house?"

Luca knew his badge was on the line. "There's another suspect: Jimmy Johns."

"I think circumstantial was the word you used, Detective," Stanley said.

"We need time to focus on Johns. A meth user with an endless need for money. He was at Wyatt's place of work, knew when he was getting paid, in cash, that is. Was seen by a neighbor cutting through yards on Wyatt's street the night of the murder."

"Weak motive. Is that all you have?"

"Some partial prints from the scene match his."

"Nonsense, Luca! That report was inconclusive," Cline said.

"But it didn't exclude Johns. Plus, they came from the same brand of cigarettes he smoked."

"I think we have to focus on Hill. Who knows, maybe we can solve two of these at the same time."

Luca said, "There's nothing that links the cases."

"But I think we'd all agree that on the surface, they seem similar. It's the public's perception I'm concerned about," Stanley said.

Luca said, "With all due respect, sir, I'm concerned with solving homicides, not the public's perception."

Stanley said, "Why not hang a charge on him and bring him in? See what we get out of him?"

Luca stopped grinding his teeth to answer. "Did anyone read the damn medical reports? This kid's fragile. We can't traumatize him. You're so worried about the public? Think about jerking around a wounded veteran and how that'll play."

Stanley steepled his hands. "Did we get anything from the search?"

"Nothing back from the lab. I checked this morning," Weinburg answered.

Stanley looked at Luca. "I'll hold off till the lab results come back, but I don't see any reason not to bring him in. We'll just have to be delicate and consider his service as a Marine."

Luca eyes narrowed. "The reason is we have to be sure. Your office has a history of pressuring us, and that leads to big, damn mistakes."

Stanley straightened in his chair and looked at Gesso, who said, "Barrow case."

Stanley pointed a finger at Luca. "Look here, Detective, that was way before my time, and I resent your insinuation."

"I'm sorry, but that's how it feels from my chair. It feels like we're rushing to pin it on Hill. He may end up being the guy, but I'm not comfortable with it at all."

"Well, get comfortable, before someone else is bludgeoned to death," Weinburg said.

Luca shot out of his chair, and Gesso interceded, saying, "That wasn't necessary, Marc."

"You're right. It was out of line. I'm sorry, Frank."

Gesso steered Luca into his chair and said, "Let's put a halt to the dick measuring contest and move on! We've got more cases to review."

Chapter 27

Luca slammed the door and flopped onto the couch. As he kicked off his shoes, Debra came in from the kitchen.

"What's the matter?"

Luca peeled off his socks. "Nothing."

Debra knelt down. "Don't tell me nothing. You been drinking?"

"Had a couple with JJ. Fucking rough day, that's all."

"What happened? The Wyatt case?"

"I had to turn in some evidence against Hill. Now he's done. The full weight of the system's—"

"But if it's evidence against him, what's the problem?"

"You don't understand."

"Cut the shit, Frank!" Debra got up and started walking away.

"Okay, okay, sorry. It's just this case is getting to me."

"I know you're frustrated, but bringing this home certainly isn't gonna help us."

"You're right. I'm sorry."

She grabbed his hand and pulled him off the couch. "I made you some linguini and clams, but it's probably paste by now."

As Luca tucked into a bowl of pasta, his cell rang. Debra frowned when he pulled it out.

"I gotta take it. It's JJ."

Luca said hello, listened, grunted a protest, and hung up.

"That was fast."

"Yeah, JJ wanted to let me know Stanley is drafting an arrest warrant for Hill." Luca got up from the table.

"Whoa, you're leaving?"

"Nah, getting a bottle of wine."

***

Luca sat at his desk nursing his third cup of java when JJ came in.

"Frank, you know they're bringing in Hill this morning."

Luca snapped his wrist. "Stanley's cracking the whip."

"Cut him a break, Frank. There's a lot of evidence—"

"Get off it, J! You know there's only one way to work a case. We can't have a different script because the press is looking or people are scared. Goddamn it, I'm scared."

Cremora said, "What the fuck, Frank?" as Luca's phone rang.

Luca said hello and then, "Of course, I still want to know."

He jotted down a note. "Thanks, man. I'll be down to pick up the photos."

Luca hung up the phone, shot out of his chair, and punched the sky.

"What's up, Frank?"

"That was the lab! They were able to enhance the video feeds from the 7-Eleven. Got a partial plate number." He handed the note to JJ. "Run these numbers by your guy at DMV. See who owns any possible plate numbers."

Luca grabbed his jacket and said on the way out, "And the best part is, Gianelli's worked his magic and got an image of a forearm tattooed with a scorpion. Sound like anyone we know?"

"You kidding me?"

"Nope, and remind me we owe Gianelli a dinner."

Chapter 28

Luca showed the enhanced photos to Cremora and said, "It's got to be Johns. I can see the bastard sitting in front of me."

"And how. I don't get all these tattoos, man. Geez, even the girls are getting 'em, and some of them are frigging huge."

Luca shook his head as he pinned one of the photos to the case board. "Ain't gonna look pretty when they hit their forties."

"Trashy, if you ask me."

Cremora answered his phone, hanging up quickly. "They got Johns. He's on his way in."

Luca watched his suspect stare at the tabletop as he dragged deeply on a cigarette. Clean shaven, Jimmy Johns wore a nasty scowl as he picked at a fingernail. Cremora sidled up to his partner and said, "You can almost see the chip on this guy's shoulder. How you want to handle this?"

The detectives quickly agreed on a strategy and entered the interview room. Johns didn't raise his head and continued smoking.

"Mr. Johns, I'm sure you remember me. I'm Detective Luca, and this here is my partner, Detective Cremora. We'd like to ask you a few questions."

Johns crushed his cigarette out in the plastic ashtray and coughed. "I got nothing to say."

"Look, we can do this the easy way, or if you'd rather make it hard, we can lock your ass up."

Johns cleaned his glasses with his shirt. "For what? I didn't do nothing."

Cremora said, "I don't know yet, but we'll find something, right Frank?"

Luca narrowed his eyes and nodded.

"You fucking pigs think you can do what you want."

Cremora said, "You know, Frank, this guy's no fool after all."

Luca said, "Look, you answer some questions, and if we're satisfied, you're outta here."

Johns dug out a pack of Newports. His shirtsleeve receded from his wrist, revealing the head of the scorpion. Luca leaned in for a closer look before Johns' arm dropped to his lap. The detective flipped open a file and compared his mental image against the grainy lab photo.

Johns hacked and brought up some phlegm. "Well, you going to ask your fucking questions or not?"

Luca hit the record button and covered the formalities before asking, "Mr. Johns, do you shop at the Keyport 7-Eleven on Broad Street?"

Johns tapped a cigarette on the table. "Sometimes. What's that, a crime these days?"

"When you do go there, how do you get there? Do you walk?"

Johns lit the cigarette. "Walk? You walk across 36 and you're rolling the dice, man."

"So you drive?"

Johns nodded, and Luca stated his affirmation for the record.

"Did you visit that establishment on the morning of May nineteenth?"

"I donno, could've. What's the big deal?"

"The big deal is Billy Wyatt's credit card was used that morning at the 7-Eleven, and he had already been murdered."

Johns took a long drag. "So what's that got to do with me?"

Cremora opened a file and slid a photo across to Johns. "That's a surveillance shot of your car just before the card was used."

Johns picked up the picture, studied it a second, and tossed it Frisbee-like to Cremora. "Maybe it's my car, but I wasn't driving it if it was. I lend it out a lot."

"Yeah? Like to who?"

Johns pulled his collar away from his neck. "A lot of people."

Luca grabbed another photo out of the file. "Well, explain this, then."

Johns' gaze hit the picture and bounced to his arm before going back to the photo. He sat back and said, "And what the fuck is that supposed to be?"

"Why don't you roll up your sleeve, Jimmy boy?" Cremora challenged.

Luca arranged four pictures in front of Johns and said, "This is your car coming in the lot. This guy here"—Luca tapped a photo—"we believe is you walking in, but kudos for trying to keep your identity hidden. Problem is, your scorpion tattoo gave you away, my friend."

Johns puffed incessantly but said nothing.

Luca said, "Now, you going to admit to using Wyatt's credit card?"

Johns swiped a hand across his mouth as he suppressed a cough. "I ain't admitting to nothin'. Even if I did, and I ain't saying I did, I got nothin' to do with his being dead."

"Yeah, sure. You're just an innocent little boy," Cremora said.

Luca asked, "Look, help us out here. We have a witness who said you were seen near the Wyatt house the night of the crime. Now we have you using Wyatt's credit card. How do you explain it?"

Johns crossed his arms and coughed before leaning back in his chair. "I ain't got to explain nothing. I want a lawyer."

"You're sure gonna need one," Cremora said.

Luca stood and said to his partner, "Read him his rights and book him on identity theft and fraud, for the time being."

Chapter 29

"I can't believe that damn Mulberry! Fifteen hundred bucks? Is he fucking kidding?"

"I know it's crazy. Johns has got an arm-long rap sheet."

Luca plopped into his chair. "You gotta wonder whose side these judges are on."

Cremora shook his head. "Yeah, combined with the sleazy lawyers these scumbags hire."

"You're telling me? That Brown is one smug, arrogant bastard. He's too close to Mulberry, if you ask me. He knew he'd spring Johns, otherwise why would his sister be there with the cash to make bail?"

"I know you didn't like this mutt, Johns, from the get-go, and now I'm feeling the same way about him."

"Every frigging turn with this Johns just burns me up. You think I'm fixated, but I'm telling you, this creep is the one who offed Wyatt."

"That's a leap, Luc, so take it easy, pal." Cremora grabbed his jacket. "I'm heading to court, the Sikorsky case."

"Nail the bastard, will you?"

Cremora flashed a thumbs-up and hustled out.

Luca sighed heavily and reached for his in-box. He pawed through a couple of reports and bolted upright when he read about an arrest made by an Officer Sanchez.

***

Luca helped Debra clear the plates and snuck a look at his watch.

Debra said, "That new HBO comedy you like is on tonight."

"Ah, what time?"

"Eight."

"Yeah, well, I've got to do something, but I'll be back before you know it."

"What you got to do at this hour?"

"I gotta run down to the station to speak with an officer named Sanchez. Shouldn't take long."

"Now?"

"He works the overnight shift."

"Can't you get him when he comes off?"

"It's important, Deb, and you never know when something comes up, and then they're in court."

"Is it the Wyatt case again?"

Luca nodded.

***

Luca hung out by the locker room until a rosy-cheeked cop approached him.

"Sarge said you wanted to speak with me."

"Yeah, thanks." Luca extended his hand. "Detective Frank Luca."

"Yeah, I know who you are. I'm Emilio Sanchez. What's up?"

"It's about an arrest you made two nights ago on Main Street in Keyport." Luca unfolded a copy of the arrest record.

Sanchez skimmed it. "Sure, what about it?"

"The license he had belonged to the victim on a homicide I was working."

"Yeah, I remember, but they arrested that kid, right?"

"Yeah, well. Can you tell me who else was in the car?"

"Couple of guys. They were pissed, had to walk when we impounded the car," Sanchez said.

"I didn't see any names on the report. You get their names?"

"Uh, no, they were clean."

Luca pulled out a photo of Johns. "This guy one of them?"

Sanchez examined the picture. "Not sure, don't think so."

"I didn't see an interrogation transcript."

"Yeah, well, it was end of the shift and—"

"The end of the shift? Are you fucking kidding me?"

"Hey, what's this all about?"

Luca stared at him and counted to ten.

"Look, I gotta go on duty. You want anything more, go ask the sarge."

Luca grabbed a cup of coffee and jumped into his car. He checked the address on the arrest report and made a beeline to Keansburg. Luca smacked the steering wheel as he passed the street Johns lived on and counted four blocks to Rosa's residence.

Luca flung the car door open so hard it bounced back at him and bruised his shin. He rubbed the welt and took a few deep breaths before marching up the walkway.

A grizzled man in his seventies pulled open the door.

Luca held out his badge. "Looking for Mike Rosa."

The man nodded slightly, left the door open, and disappeared back into the house. Luca poked his head into the dark house, but all he could see was the light from a TV. Luca stepped back and leaned against a rusty railing when he heard footsteps.

Tee shirted, Mike Rosa looked like a slab of granite. The cigarette dangling from his lip belied the athletic aurora he projected. He stepped onto the small porch and shut the door as Luca showed his credentials.

"What d'ya want?"

"You used a driver's license belonging to one William Wyatt two nights ago."

Rosa nodded as he took a drag.

"Where'd you get the license from?"

"I bought it. You see, I lost mine in a DWI, and I need to get to work and—"

"I don't give a rat's ass about your story except how you came in possession of the Wyatt license."

"What's it mean to you?"

Luca poked his finger into Rosa's concrete chest. "Look, I ask the questions, and you give the answers. You got that?"

Rosa dropped his cigarette to the ground, and Luca's neck hairs rose. Rosa crushed the butt out and spoke. "I bought the fucking thing for twenty bucks. I thought it was a good way to—"

"From who?"

"Guy lives a couple blocks away. He's always fencing shit."

"How about a name?"

"Jimmy. Jimmy Johns."

Luca felt his lips curl. "You sure?"

"Yeah, of course I'm sure, man. Look at all the shit I got from it."

Chapter 30

My lawyer's offices were on the second floor of a low-slung building on Route 35. We sat in the waiting area, declining coffee twice as we leafed through a pile of magazines. After thirty long minutes, Edwards' energetic secretary came out and led us to a small conference room as she chirped away.

Eddie Edwards offered his hand.

"Hello Peter. Vincent. Nice day today, huh?"

I stared at his white hair and said hello as he pulled a chair out for me.

"Sit, sit. You boys want something to drink, coffee, water?"

Vinny said, "Nah, we're good."

Edwards fell into his chair and reached for the phone. "I've asked Johnny Scotto to join us. Is that okay with you, Peter?"

I shifted in my chair and looked at my brother.

Vinny asked, "What's his area of expertise?"

"Primarily white-collar cases, but Johnny's got top-notch instincts to go along with extremely helpful contacts in the prosecutors' offices."

Instincts? If my life is gonna hang on instincts, my instinct is to run. I wondered how fast I could run. Was I fast in high school? Who was the track-and-field coach? I think he was a tall guy. Yeah, I think so. Was it Mr. Chavez?

I spat out, "Vinny, who, who was the gym teacher, nah the, the track coach?"

Vinny leaned in and put his hand on my arm. "Concentrate on the case, man! We'll figure out the other stuff when we get home. Okay?"

The door swung open almost as wide as Edwards' gaping mouth and Scotto strode in. Edwards' eyes shifted from Vinny to me as he closed his mouth and jumped up.

"Boys, you remember my partner, John Scotto."

We said our hellos and Edwards asked, "Peter, you need a bathroom break?"

Vinny grabbed my elbow and said, "Yeah, give us five."

We went into the men's room, and Vinny checked all the stalls. "What the hell's going on?"

"What d'ya mean?"

"Petey, you got to keep it together, man. This is no time to go off on tangents. This is serious shit you're in!"

I nodded and fingered my ringing ear, trying to recall if I had drunk that sandy stuff when Vinny instructed.

"Splash your face with water, man, and concentrate: really concentrate, you hear me?" Vinny turned the faucet on.

"Sure, sure." I cupped some water and washed my face. "I'm okay. Don't worry, Vince."

"Yeah, well I am, and to think you didn't want me to come with you today."

I hung my head. "Thanks, man, you're always looking out for me."

Vinny softened his voice. "I know it's tough for you, but you gotta keep it together. It don't get heavier than this, man."

The lawyers were huddled in a corner when we came back in and took seats across the mahogany table.

"We okay, fellas?"

"Sure, if you're gonna tell me the case is dropped," Vinny said.

"We're doing our best, but frankly that seems out of the question. What do you say we review where we are and explore options?"

I stared at my name on each of the files as Edwards splayed the pile. He drew a red file and opened it.

"The prosecutor's case is based upon a couple of pieces of evidence. You've been placed at the scene at the approximate time of death." Edwards looked up at Peter. "You had an argument with the deceased over your girlfriend. You were seen at the scene with a weapon similar to the type used to kill William Wyatt."

"Weapon? Hey, hold on. That was my cane."

He raised a hand. "The prosecutor will want to know why you went to Wyatt's home."

I sank into my seat as he droned on. I looked at my brother, who had slumped in his chair before I tuned out completely. Sometimes I remembered going to Billy's house, but I couldn't be sure if I really did or if hearing that they knew I was there was why I thought I went there. I couldn't believe I could do what they said. I traced the lines of my palms when the visions of Billy getting hit popped into my head. It couldn't be, could it? They think I did it, so maybe I did? Geez, this was confusing.

"Do you need a break, Peter?"

Vince elbowed me back to reality.

"Uh, uh."

"You want to take a break."

"I don't know, do you?"

"No, I'm okay."

Edwards continued. "All right, so that's the line of attack the DA is likely to take."

Vinny challenged, "But don't we have anything to come back with?"

"Certainly. We'll mount an attack on their evidence. Some of it's very weak, but a jury, and I've seen this happen over and over, could take four pieces of sketchy evidence and pile it up against a defendant."

Scotto jumped in finally. "That's why it's critical that we bolster, strike that, that we present you and your service to the country. Your reputation and service record will help to deny plausibility."

"Will Peter have to take the stand?"

The stand? Like in the movies? I could see Jack Nicholson in that film about a court martial. What was the name of it?

"We don't think that's a good idea at this point," Edwards said.

"But we'd enter into the record, either by stipulation or possibly, dependent on what witnesses the DA proposes, have medical experts testify as to the injuries Peter sustained and how that affects his ability to recall events," Scotto explained.

"You've got to know that putting Peter on the stand could backfire. There's a long record of juries who vote against defendants who simply state they cannot recall events as a defense," Edwards said.

"What do we do?" Vinny asked.

Edwards looked at Scotto, who steepled his fingers. "Eddie and I have debated the merits of the case, vis-à-vis the strategy we should utilize, and we believe the best outcome would emanate from negotiating a plea agreement."

I tried hard to follow things, but by the time I processed what someone said, there were two other exchanges that had passed by.

"Plea? You mean Peter would admit to doing it?"

I caught that! So now Vinny thinks it was me too?

"Well, we'd like to leave specifics in the background at this time and focus—"

"Background? Is that some kinda lawyer gobbledygook for jail?"

Edwards pursed his lips and waved a hand at his clients. "Hold on, Vincent. This is a strategy session. We're here to represent your brother in the best way we can. Johnny is just trying to lay out an option. Any decisions will be made together. Is that clear?"

Vinny nodded.

Edwards asked, "How about you, Peter? You understand?"

I shrugged. "I don't know. I guess so. What do you think, Vin?"

"Let's hear them out."

Edwards stated, "I want to be clear. We need to balance the risks of going to trial versus negotiating an agreement called a plea with the DA."

"Do I have to go, like, to jail?"

"Well, any sentence is difficult to predict at this stage. So why don't we look at the avenues we can pursue and the possible outcomes they offer."

I watched everyone's head bob in agreement. Edwards scooched his chair forward and took a sip of water. "Trials, by their very nature, are difficult to predict and thus carry a large measure of risk for any defendant. Given the circumstances in Peter's case, it may be even more so."

"Why? Why should my brother's case be any different?"

"Well, each case is different, and in his particular situation, possibly being unable to put him on the stand in his own defense . . ."

Situation, I thought. *So that's what all this is called.*

"But I thought lawyers never wanted their clients to go on the stand."

Edwards said, "True, in let's say a majority of cases, but that really depends on the evidence. In this case, the lack of forensic evidence tying a defendant to a crime and victim would present a perfect opportunity to rebut by the defendant."

"So why not put Peter on the stand? You're okay with that, right Petey?"

I shifted my gaze from face to face. "I—I guess so, Vin."

"You have to realize, if he goes on the stand to defend himself, he opens himself up to attack on cross-examination. The prosecution will hit him with a barrage of questions and confuse him. It could likely get ugly, with the result being that it backfires, and Peter looks bad to the jury."

"If the evidence they have is bad, can't we just ask the judge to dismiss the case?"

Scotto sighed. "If only it were that easy. Frankly speaking, the DA has more than he needs to get in the courtroom."

The sound of my brother's hope crashing was almost audible, and the awkwardness prevailed until Edwards said, "A defendant's testimony is just one aspect of risk. We'd have to be on guard for possible developments, such as a new witness or some piece of compromising evidence."

"What about the police finding the real killer? Ain't that a damn possibility?" Vinny asked.

Wow, finding the real killer. It sounded so Hollywood like.

"Sure, of course. I didn't mean to focus on the downside, but it is my responsibility to lay out the risks and outcomes."

"He didn't do it, man. Why doesn't anyone believe us?"

Vinny really believed I didn't do it.

"It's frustrating for all of us. We'll do our own investigation during our preparation that may turn up something helpful. But right now we have to work with what we have."

"So maybe your guys will find somebody who could've done it?" Even to me that didn't sound quite right. So I added, "Like the real killer?"

"Well, it's not our job to find a suspect, but during the discovery process, we'll look at how to discount the prosecution's evidence and look to support and produce evidence of our own."

"You have to keep in mind that the threshold, or bar, for holding a defendant responsible is reasonable doubt. We'd have to convince a jury that there was a reasonable doubt that Peter committed the crime he is accused of."

"But that's possible, no? You said the evidence is sketchy," Vinny said.

"Yes, if it was possible, we'd rule it out. However, I cannot stress this enough, outcomes are very difficult if not impossible to predict, and that translates into risk."

"Okay, okay. I just thought, you know, he'd get off, and that would end this nightmare."

"I understand, but the downside, and I hate to keep being negative, is that we lose the case. And that could be disastrous, with a term handed down of some twenty years or so."

I shut my eyes and couldn't stop myself from mumbling, "I can't do that. I can't. No way. No way."

Vinny put a hand on my shoulder and squeezed it. "Don't worry, we're going to handle this."

Edwards came around the table and pulled a chair out next to me. "I know this is tough, but you have to know that we are working around the clock to get a reasonable resolution to this case. Let's take a short break, and then we'll explore some other ideas we have."

Chapter 31

Eddie Edwards and his partner, Johnny Scotto, shook hands with the Monmouth County prosecutor and his assistant, John Cline.

"Let's sit over there. We'll be more comfortable." Stanley waved toward a couch and two wing chairs around a table. "Would you like something to drink? Coffee? Water?"

"Some water would be great."

Cline grabbed two bottles out of a small fridge and handed them off to the defense attorneys, who had settled on the couch.

Stanley, seated in one of the leather wing chairs, crossed his thin legs and said, "I trust we'll be able to work out a plea on the Wyatt case."

Edwards responded, "As long as your office tones down the rhetoric and considers the circumstantial nature of the evidence you have."

Cline said, "Circumstantial? We have a clear motive. Any jury on the planet gets the jilted lover picture. Hill was seen at the scene. We have his prints inside the house. He refuses to tell us what happened—"

Edwards, who had reached into his briefcase, interjected, "Mr. Hill is unable to recall the events of that night due to the traumatic injury he suffered."

"While serving his country, I might add," Scotto said.

Edwards slid some reports across the table.

"Here are the reports from three neurologists, all experts in brain trauma, who are willing to testify that our client's extensive injury is the source of his inability to recall events."

Cline didn't touch the documents.

"Come on now, gentlemen. You certainly know we'll get rebuttal testimony from our experts."

"And we'll put a string of the Marines he served with, including a general, who'll testify to Mr. Hill's mild manner and—"

Cline asked, "You want to go to trial? We may not get a murder conviction, but manslaughter will be a slam dunk, and your client will be calling Trenton State home for the next twenty years."

"Twenty years? The max for manslaughter is ten years."

"This is a clear case of aggravated manslaughter, and you know it, Counselor."

"A judge would never give an injured vet twenty for this. That is, if you were lucky enough to get a conviction," Scotto said as he scooped up the files.

Stanley finally spoke. "Ten years, medium security, or a psych facility—your call."

"Come on, Bill. Ten years is just way too much," Scotto said.

"Take it or leave it," Cline said.

Edwards said, "There's no way I can recommend a ten-year plea to my client. He'd be better off taking his chances with going to trial."

Stanley sneezed, and a chorus of bless yous broke out. He thanked them and pulled a hanky out of his pocket. After he wiped his nose, he said, "We can strike a deal for seven years."

Edwards leaned forward. "You've got a deal at three years, minimum security facility."

Cline put his hands on his knees. "That's crazy."

Stanley raised a hand. "The state can live with five years, with eligibility for parole after three."

Scotto shook his head. "I don't know, Eddie. That still seems stiff in my book for an injured veteran."

Stanley said, "It's the best you're going to do. I'd recommend you take it while it's still on the table."

"Bill, this kid may not make it three years."

"In minimum security? What's gonna happen to him?" Cline asked.

"This kid has a ton of issues. You may not believe it, but he's got a boatload of problems."

"We don't doubt his medical record, and it's not that we're insensitive, but a man was killed, and the public is demanding justice."

"Yes, but you'll be getting your so-called justice at the potential price of locking up an innocent veteran who can't defend himself."

"All right, all right." Stanley stood and extended his hand to Edwards. "Four years, minimum security, and parole eligibility after two years."

Edwards nodded and enveloped the prosecutor's bony hand. "Thanks Bill. I really think it's a fair deal for both sides, considering the circumstances."

Stanley nodded and said, "One more thing, though. This plea is gonna have to be sealed. I can't have the public knowing all the details. They just won't understand."

The defense lawyers exchanged glances and shook their heads in agreement.

Chapter 32

Vinny was into his second cup of coffee when I came down. The sun was shining, but the house felt ice cold.

"You take your meds?"

I nodded.

"How'd you sleep?" He poured me a mug of java.

"What do you think? You know, it's kinda funny, I struggle to remember all kinds of shit but couldn't shake this last night."

"You sure about this, taking this plea thing?"

I took a mouthful of coffee. "I stopped being sure of anything when Mary dumped me."

Vinny stared at me, then leaned closer. "I'm scared for you, Peter. I don't think this is right. You can fight this."

"I don't know what to believe. You're talking with the lawyers, right? They're saying to take the deal."

"I know, I know, but I don't know if we can trust 'em." Vinny hung his head as his voice trailed off.

"But if I go to trial, it'll cost so much money. We'll have to sell Mom's house, and where you gonna go?"

"Don't worry about me, man. That's the least of it."

"And they, with the evidence, they say I'd probably lose anyway and get twenty to thirty years."

"What evidence? It's fucking bullshit, all circumstantial—shit is what they got!"

"But Mr. Edwards, he said it was a really good deal, Vince. I can be out in two years. It'll go fast."

"I know it may seem fast, but who's gonna watch out for you when you're in there?"

"I'll be all right."

"Yeah, you think so? What about all your meds? They got to be taken when they're supposed to, and the doctor appointments—what about all of them? How about all the exercises?" He shook his head. "Petey, you've come so far, I'd hate to throw it all away."

"I can get visits like three times a week there. You could come and keep an eye on me. I mean, like every now and then."

"Yeah, I know, but I'm telling you it's not the same." He looked right into my eyes. "Don't take this the wrong way or anything, but do you know what I do for you?"

I nodded repeatedly as a tear developed. "I know, and I'm thankful. I really am. You gave up everything to help me, and I'll never forget it. But you did your part, man. It's time I stood on my own now."

"But you're going to jail, Pete! Get it through your fucking head, man. This ain't a walk in the park."

"But Mr. Edwards, he said it's minimum security and all. It can't be that bad, right?"

"What the fuck do I know? I feel like throwing up, thinking about my brother going to jail."

"Mom always said actions have consequences. Remember?"

Vinny's eyes cleared. "What d'ya mean? You talking about Billy?"

"Uh-uh, you know, going with Mary and all."

Vinny sat on the table across from me and locked eyes with me. "Peter, I just got to know. Did you do it?"

"Do what?"

"Stop the bullshit!" Vinny lowered his voice. "Tell me honestly, did you kill Billy?"

I averted my eyes but stayed silent.

"I don't care if you did it or not. I just got to know. It will make this plea shit easier to swallow."

I started to tell him about the dream I'd had two times, where I shot Billy, but he jumped up and got all worked up. I didn't know what to do, so I started crying, knowing it would help.

Vinny took the chair next to me. "It's okay, Peter. Everything's going to be okay."

My sobbing accelerated, and my arms began to tremor slightly. Vinny wrapped an arm around me and tried to stifle the shaking.

"Come on, Pete. Calm down. Take it easy."

Vinny watched my head jerk back suddenly. Then my eyes rolled back, showing their whites. Vinny sprang off the couch, moved the coffee table out of harm's way, and put the cushions on the floor. Then he grabbed the phone and punched in 911.

The seizure lasted longer than the usual minute or two, and I was coming out of it when the EMT workers arrived. Vinny called the neurologist, who pinned the episode on the stress of my legal circumstances and recommended an overnight stay.

As I slept, Vinny contemplated my possible guilt and what toll the stress of imprisonment would take on us.

***

Luca grabbed a cup of coffee and was headed to the interview room when he was told to report to Sergeant Gesso.

The detective poked his head in Gesso's office. "What's up, Sarge?"

"What the hell are you up to?"

"What do you mean?"

Gesso pounded the desk. "You know damn well what I mean! Why the hell is Johns taking up space in the interview room?"

"Identity theft. He had Billy Wyatt's license and sold it."

"Geez, Frank, you're on a wild-goose chase. Hill's agreed to a plea."

"Are we letting ID theft go now?"

Gesso shot out of his chair. "Cut the bullshit, Luca! The Wyatt case is closed, you hear me? Closed!"

"But this scumbag had Wyatt's license. Where do you think he got it?"

"I don't give a rat's ass. I'm telling you to drop it, and that's a direct order. You got that?"

Luca's eyes narrowed. "Loud and clear, Sarge."

"You're a good detective, Frank, but sometimes, I don't know." Gesso shook his head and sat back down. "Look, I'll ask Bernie to follow up on this ID thing with Johns." The sergeant extended a file. "I want you to take over the Spiro case. Kennedy is way too green for something like this."

Luca nodded, grabbed the file, and turned on his heels instead of flinging his java, like he wanted to.

Luca walked by the interview room and peered through the window. Johns looked a bit grayish to the detective but had put on a few pounds and was groomed as if he were making a court appearance. Luca resisted the urge to break a direct order and went to his office. He called the officer Gesso said would interview Johns and got to work on his new assignment.

Right before Luca left for the day, Detective Bernie Kitloff filled him in on the interview. The officer told him that Johns had stuck to a story that he found the license on the street. When Kitloff pressed, he said he was with a guy named Tommy when he found it. Johns couldn't tell him where to find this guy, Tommy, and gave a very vague description. Kitloff knew it smelled like week-old fish, but given the backlog of cases, the DA's office said to release him.

Chapter 33

"Geez, Luc, you look like dog doo."

"Thanks, pal. It's real nice to know you're loved."

"Seriously, Frank. What's going on?"

"Not getting much sleep."

"Everything good with Debra?"

"Yeah, not too bad, actually."

"So what's keeping you up?"

Luca sipped his morning coffee and said, "This Hill case—it's eating at me."

"Shit, Frank, let it go, will ya?"

"I don't know, man. I just can't."

"You think lying in bed ruminating on it is going to help?"

Luca flashed a grin. "Well, actually, I've been keeping an eye on Johns."

"What? You're tailing Johns?"

Luca shrugged.

Cremora shook his head. "You're fucking crazy. You know that? Gesso will have your head when he finds out."

"Can't sleep anyway. What's the big deal with keeping an eye on a repeat offender?"

Cremora pointed his finger at his partner. "You better watch it. I don't know, Luc. You're obsessed with Johns."

"This creep is up to no good. I know it, and I'll nail the bastard."

"Maybe, but how's that gonna help the Hill kid?"

"It may not, but you can't argue the world will be better with that scumbag behind bars."

"Look, bro, all I'm saying is you gotta keep things in perspective. Sure the bastard should be off the streets, like a zillion others, but if you keep on pursuing it, you're . . ."

Luca headed out the door.

"Hey, where you going, Frank?"

"I get nagged at home and don't need any bullshit from you." Luca slammed the door.

Luca cut his lights and rolled to a stop a block away from Johns' apartment. He sipped on a coffee as he waited in the dark. Luca had a gut feeling something would break tonight. It was the fourth day in a row that Johns hadn't worked a menial job to earn the money needed to support his habit.

The detective adjusted his seat for the fifth time as the third hour of observance passed. Luca began to wonder if Johns had slipped out somehow. It was now ten o'clock and no sight of Johns. Could someone have come earlier and they were holed up in his apartment, Luca wondered. Antsy, the detective pawed his cell phone and began punching in Johns' home number when his eye caught a shadowy figure emerging from the basement stairs.

Luca squinted, confirming it was Johns, who'd just lit a cigarette that the detective knew was a Newport. Luca slid down in his seat as Johns, in a hooded sweatshirt, puffed away, bouncing from foot to foot in the dark. Johns crushed out his butt as a car, whose lights were out, came around the corner. Luca's heartbeat picked up as the old sedan pulled up and Johns leapt into the back seat.

Luca slowly pulled out and trailed two blocks behind the car carrying Johns and his cohorts. The detective tried to place the profiles of the two guys in the car with Johns, believing he'd seen them before. The sedan put its lights on as he followed them across Route 36 and back into Keansburg.

As the car headed toward what passed for a boardwalk and beach in Keansburg, Luca figured they were going to cop their drugs from Franklin, and that it would turn out to be another wasted night. The sedan failed to slow down at the notorious intersection where Franklin dealt his goods, and Luca's spirit rose.

Luca stayed a block behind as the sedan shut its lights and rolled to a stop by the run-down arcade. Luca slunk out of his car into a crouch and made his way closer as the three men hopped the amusement park's chain-link fence. The detective knew the struggling amusement park had the day's cash picked up by an armored car each night. So he wondered what their target could be. He watched them as they cut behind the bumper cars and disappeared from view.

Luca picked up the smell of smoke as he scanned the area. He was about to call for reinforcements when he spied them walking down the asphalt path that led to the beach. The detective took cover by the rotting pier and watched them join two figures who were feeding sticks to a small bonfire.

Luca observed the group greet each other and settle on the beach. When they started passing around what he surmised was a drug-filled pipe, he knew he'd wasted yet another night and abandoned the surveillance.

As Luca got back in his car, the realization he couldn't save Peter Hill from going to prison occupied his thoughts. The detective wondered whether he would be able to shake the case, or if it would haunt him like the Barrow case.

The day before Peter was to report to jail, his brother, Vinny, reached out to Luca again. In a near panic that the day of reckoning was upon them, a sympathetic Luca quickly agreed to meet with Vinny at their house after his shift.

Vinny shook hands with Luca while Peter stayed glued to the television.

"Hi Peter." Luca dropped his extended hand when all he received back was a morose stare.

"You remember Detective Luca, don't you?"

Peter nodded slightly.

"It's been a while. You look good, Peter."

Vinny asked, "You want a cup of coffee, Detective?"

"Sounds good."

Vinny made a pot of coffee as the small talk petered out. "I donno. I'm really worried for Peter."

Luca frowned. "It's a tough situation. How's he handling it?"

"Nervous. I mean, who wouldn't be?"

"You know, it's funny and all. I gotta say this is a first for me. Usually, on the cases I work, when the defendant goes to jail, it's kinda like the validation of the investigation: the evidence, the whole thing, and really only then is when we guys in homicide get to move on. But here I, I mean, really, we—nobody really knows what went on here."

"It's like some TV show, you know? You see these people cut deals to get some jail time rather than risk a long sentence, but it always seemed like bullshit in the real world. I mean, who would admit to something if they didn't do it?"

Luca stiffened and picked up his mug silently.

"I'm not saying he did it, but some of the things he says. Shit, I don't know what to believe. Sometimes I think he's not telling everything, and then he does something weird that shows that he's not playing with a full deck."

"What leads you to believe he may not be telling you everything?"

"Uh, I don't know, just kinda like a feeling I'm probably misreading."

Luca lowered his voice. "Look, you might as well get it off your chest. The reality is, nothing is gonna change at this point."

"But I thought you were looking at that Johns guy?"

"You know I am. I've been watching him like a hawk, and on my own time, to boot. Shit, if the sarge found out, he'd run me out of the department." Luca shook his head. "So tell me, what's your gut telling you?"

Vinny silently stared at his mug.

"I just gotta know for my own sake if I'm wrong here, that's all. You've cut your plea, and nothing's gonna change that if he really did it."

"It's hard to explain."

"Try me; give me something."

"I donno, like the time I found out that Billy had been murdered. I was down in Texas, and I called Pete, but he acted all weird about it. Said Billy was a bastard and deserved it. I got pissed. The guy's been my friend my whole life. You know, I didn't really think about Peter's reaction in any other way, since he had the brain injury and all. Then after all the shit happened, I started thinking."

"Well, it seems natural to me. Any other incidents, things?"

"I don't know how to explain it. It's just that . . . I don't know. It seems convenient, if you know what I mean. A lot of times he's good and seems almost one-hundred percent normal, and then when he has to answer questions about all this, he shuts down."

"What do you think it means?"

"I really don't know. Sometimes I think he could be hiding things, but you know, I asked the doctors, and they said when people with TBIs are under pressure they can blank out."

"I wonder if it's the pressure of having to be questioned, or maybe coming to terms with what happened that night."

"That's what I keep rolling around in my head. I just wanna know. Is my brother going to prison for something he did, or not?"

"Anything else?"

"Well, he said he had a dream where he shot Billy."

Peter appeared in back of his brother. "Mom said not to talk about people behind their backs."

"We're not talking about you. I mean, we are, but not in a bad way, just this whole fucking nightmare."

Luca noted that Peter wasn't using a cane. "You look like you're getting around better these days. That's good, a good sign."

Vinny said, "Yeah, yeah, he's really responding to the physical therapy."

"You gotta love it. Now that I can get around, I'll be locked up." Peter shook his head.

"So, can you tell us what this, uh, facility is going to be like for Peter?"

"Well, I've been there a couple of times over the years to interview inmates, and I don't know what it's like when the lights are out, but it's as loose a place as I've seen."

"Hear that, Pete? It's loose there and—"

Peter interrupted. "What do you mean, the lights are out? They shut the lights?"

"Uh, I meant to say, you know, after hours, at night. When I go there during the day, the inmates are doing their jobs, taking classes, you know, doing activities."

"What kinda jobs they have to do?"

"I really don't know, but a couple of times the guys I went to talk to were in the farming program there."

"Farming? Wow, that'd be good for you, Pete. You like gardening."

Peter stayed quiet as Luca went on to describe the place as best he could remember. Then he left the brothers to their last night together for a while.

"What are you doing home at this hour?" Debra asked.

Luca shrugged as he took his tie off.

"You feel all right?"

"Yeah, I'm fine."

"You sure, Frank?"

"Yeah, geez, can't a guy ever win? I stay late, and you get mad. I come home at a normal time and get grilled."

"Lighten up, Frank. You got to be pried away from the job."

"Okay—uncle. You win."

"So what's eating you?"

Luca twisted off the top to a beer. "I don't know, maybe it's 'cause the Hill kid went to Bayside today."

"I know you feel bad about it, Frank, but you worked like the devil to save the kid. Who knows, maybe he did it anyway."

Luca took a long guzzle. "Tell me about it. Last night, even his brother was giving me the vibe he wasn't so sure either."

"So maybe it worked out in the end."

"Maybe, but you know me and my gut feelings."

"Just so happens that I can fix the belly thing. I made turkey meatballs this afternoon."

Luca smiled. "Things are looking up."

"Go grab a bottle of wine while I get dinner started."

"Sounds like a plan."

"And Frank?"

"Yeah?"

"Shut your phone off tonight, okay?"

***

Luca strolled into the office and set down his coffee.

"Where you been, man? I called you a bunch of times."

Luca dug out his phone. "Shit! I shut it off last night. You know, Deb and me . . ."

Cremora raised both palms. "I don't need details."

Luca smiled and took his jacket off.

"So, you don't know?"

"Know what? I'm a detective J, but I don't read minds, bro."

"They got Johns, man! Caught him red-handed in cold-blooded murder."

Luca leaned forward. "What? Don't play with me."

"Last night Johns broke into a house on Foster Street, beat the owner with a bat, I think, killing him. The poor bastard's wife came down screaming, and Johns took off out the front door and ran right into a cop."

"A cop?"

"Seems Cinicola, you know him, he works vice in Middletown, was out walking his dog and heard the woman scream."

"Walking a dog at two in the morning?"

"Crazy, I know, but the dog had some stomach problem and was shitting all over the house."

Luca jumped out of his seat. "We gotta get this case."

"Gesso gave it to Duro already."

"You kidding me? After all the work I, er, we put in?"

"Frank, don't take this the wrong way, but you're obsessed with Johns."

"Obsessed? You still think so, even after last night?"

"You were right, okay? But that don't change the fact that Gesso didn't like the way you were going about it, and if you ask me, he gave it to Duro as a result. From what I know, it's an open-and-shut case."

"They got Johns for sure? On murder?"

"Red-handed. The wife ID'd him, and Cinicola got him dripping in evidence."

"He had the murder weapon on him?"

"Yup, and best of all, Johns was carrying a thirty-eight revolver, to boot."

"Holy shit, man. He's really done."

"You got that right. It's a death penalty case now."

Luca fell back into his seat. "Geez, it's kinda unreal. We've been trailing this guy, and it falls in our laps."

"I wouldn't exactly call it falling into our laps. He beat a man dead in front of his wife."

"Where they holding him?"

"He's being arraigned this morning. Why?"

"Man, I'd love to talk with that arrogant bastard."

"You better stay out of it, Frank!"

***

"Home early again?" Debra asked.

"Yup, let's go out. I feel like celebrating."

"Really? What's up?"

"You're not gonna believe it, but that bastard Jimmy Johns was arrested for murder last night."

"Oh my God. Was he the guy who killed that poor guy on Foster Street?"

"Yeah, that was him, and it's a good thing this creep's finally off the street."

"You and JJ handling the case?"

"Nah, they gave it to Duro."

"Oh? Well, now that this guy's behind bars, I guess you'll be stopping your midnight rambling."

Luca leaned his cheek on his hands. "I'll be sleeping like a baby by ten."

"Yeah, sure, until the next case gets in your craw."

"We going out, or what?"

Chapter 34

Luca bounced into Duro's office. "Yo Matty, how's it going?"

Duro looked up from his monitor. "Nothin' new. Up to my ears in cow shit."

"How you doing with the Johns case?"

"Pretty straightforward, for a change. The mother jumper's gonna fry, Frankie boy."

"Let's hope so. Guess you did a search?"

"Yeah, both the apartment and adjoining areas of the basement."

"Look, I had this guy in my sights for a while. You know the Wyatt case?"

"Who can forget it? Gesso sure was pissed," Duro said.

Luca grinned. "Anyways, I can give you the inside story on him."

"Sure, any help makes my job easier, and Lord knows I'm buried."

"You tell me when you got a half hour."

Duro checked his watch. "Now's as good as any other time. Just give me five. I want to finish this report."

"Okay, I'll hang here. Mind if I browse through Johns' case file?"

Duro pulled a file off the top of his credenza. "Be my guest."

Luca pored over the file as Duro tapped away at his keyboard.

When Luca got to the crime scene evidence list, he asked, "I thought you said a bat was used? It says here it was a tire iron."

"Bat? Who said anything about a bat, blue eyes? It was a tire iron."

"Shit, you know when we searched Johns' car, we didn't find a tire iron. I thought it was weird at the time. But he did have to bring his car in to change a tire, so I kinda dropped it and—"

"Luc, what the fuck are you rambling about?"

"It's a long shot, but I remember thinking at the time that maybe the tire iron was the weapon he used to kill Wyatt."

"Wyatt? That Marine kid pleaded—"

"It's complicated, but when's the lab report due back?"

"Lab report? Fucking blood's not even dry yet."

"Where's the evidence list from the search?"

"Doyle's been out, but Joyce said the inventory list was gonna be ready tomorrow."

Luca got up. "Let me know when you get it, okay?"

Duro watched Luca leave. "I thought you wanted to help me—fill me in?"

***

Luca picked up the phone. "Franco, it's me."

"What now, Luca?"

"I'm fine, and how are you?"

"Come on, Frank. You only call when you want something. What's it this time?"

"The Foster Street murder. I want, uh, I'd like you to check the murder weapon, a tire iron, for blood types."

"It's not my first day on the job."

"Very funny. I know the protocols, but I want to see if there are markers for more than the Foster Street victim's blood."

"Uh, but I thought this was Duro's case. You're working it too?"

"Kind of, just that we have some things pointing to Johns on another case, and I'm running things down."

"Like what other case?"

"Um, the Wyatt case."

"Wyatt again?"

"How fast you think you can run the tests?"

"You know what, Frank? You think I got nothing to do, just waiting for you?"

"Blah, blah, blah. Stop whining, Franco. You know you love me."

After wolfing down a fajita at a Mexican dive for lunch, Luca grabbed a stack of messages from the front desk and headed for his office. Leafing through the pink slips, the detective paused when he came upon a missed call from Vinny Hill.

Luca returned five calls and filed two case reports before dialing Vinny. "Hello Vinny. Frank Luca here."

"Frank! Thanks for calling me back."

"No problem. How's Peter doing?"

"Not sure. It's only been a couple of days. He seems fine on the phone, but I'm heading there Saturday."

"Good. What's up?"

"Well, I saw they arrested that guy Johns for murder. The paper said he beat the guy to death, just like what happened to Billy. I know you had doubts about him, and I was just wondering if this could help Peter."

Luca wanted to say that he was wondering the same thing, but instead replied, "Well, they're going to look at everything and see what, if any, connection this Johns guy has to any other open cases."

"Open cases? But isn't Peter's case considered closed?"

"Yes, but not in my mind." The words tumbled out before he could stuff them back in.

"So, you don't think Peter is guilty."

"I didn't say that."

"But you said not in your mind."

"What I meant was, I look at the entire landscape of cases when any evidence crops up."

"Evidence? You have some evidence?"

"No, no, it's too early yet."

"Oh."

"Look, I don't think it's helpful to get your hopes up here, but if there's anything I think you need to know, I'll clue you in."

Coming home from work, Luca answered his phone as he pulled into his driveway. "Franco, what d'ya got for me?"

"Not much."

"What do you mean?"

"Well, I ran tests on the murder weapon, and we easily tied the blood DNA to the Foster Street victim."

"But what about any other blood on the tire iron?"

"That's just it, while there was a trace of another blood type on it, it's DNA structure was destroyed."

"What do you mean, destroyed? How the fuck could it be destroyed?"

"A couple of ways, but with cleaning solvents or a bleaching agent."

"But you said it was another person's blood. You sure of that?"

"Absolutely, blood type markers are like concrete."

"Good, how can I use it?"

"It's almost useless."

"How the fuck could it be useless?"

"Would you calm down? It's only a blood type, and it's type A, to boot, the most common."

"But that's the same as Wyatt's!"

"And three hundred million others."

"Damn it!"

The call was over by the time Luca slammed the front door.

"Frank?"

"What?"

"You okay?"

"Yeah!"

"Okay, what's up now?"

"Nothing."

"Nothing? You slam the door and come in with a puss on and want to call it nothing?"

Luca headed for the stairs. "It's nothing."

"Look, Frank, I've had enough of this bullshit. You said it'd be different, but the roller coaster of your job has gotta stop. I'm sick of you bringing work crap home to me."

Luca sighed and turned around on the stairs. "You're right. I'm sorry."

"Now tell me what's going on. Get it off your chest."

Luca told Debra that Franco had called to let him know there was other blood on the Foster Street murder weapon, but it wasn't conclusive.

***

Lou Cresi showed his credentials. Then he dropped his briefcase, belt, and suit jacket on a conveyor belt and walked through the metal detector. He collected his belongings and said hello to a guard as a barred door grinded open. Cresi stepped into a small corridor, and as soon as the door behind him slammed shut, the one blocking his path clanged open. Cresi was escorted through two more barred doors before being shown into a windowless room that was outfitted with a simple wooden desk and two plastic chairs straight out of Walmart. Cresi settled into a chair and removed a file from his briefcase.

With an ironclad case against his client looking certain, the court-appointed attorney was about to change tactics. He loosened his tie and cursed the lack of ventilation when a loud buzz rang out. A metal door disengaged and opened, revealing a handcuffed Jimmy Johns accompanied by two beefy guards.

Cresi straightened in his chair. "Good morning, Mr. Johns."

Johns coughed as his cuffs were unlocked, then said, "What's so damn good about it?"

As they retreated, the taller guard said, "You've got a half an hour. He gets out of hand, just hit the buzzer."

"We'll be fine," Cresi said as Johns took a seat.

Johns coughed as he lit a cigarette. "When you springing me outta here?"

"Well, that's going to be very difficult, Mr. Johns, given the circumstances of the case. The judge refused to consider granting bail, which, even if it was granted, would be substantial."

Johns choked as he took a drag. "Look, you need to work something out, you hear me?"

"Maybe you should cut back on the smoking."

"Mind your fucking business! Now when you getting me outta this shithole?"

"I'm going to do the best I can."

"You better watch your fucking ass, Cresi. This don't turn out good for me, it ain't gonna turn out good for you either. You hear me?"

Cresi made a mental note to get the threat on record with the judge and vowed if things deteriorated, he'd ask to be removed from the case.

He had dealt with the worst of the worst, but after ten years in the public defender's office, he was reaching his limits.

The lawyer clasped his hands. "You're facing very serious charges, Mr. Johns."

Johns banged his fist on the table. "You think I don't know that?"

Cresi moved his hands in. "Of course, you do. I'm just attempting to explain where we are."

Johns stifled a cough and stubbed out his smoke. "Cut the lawyer bullshit, and give it to me straight."

Cresi swept his tongue over his teeth and took a short breath through his nose. "Give it to you straight? That's fine with me, Mr. Johns. The most serious charge against you is murder in the first degree. Now, I've already tried to mitigate the charge down to manslaughter, but due to the aggravating factor regarding the brutality of the killing, there is no way the prosecutor or a jury, for that matter, would agree."

Johns averted his eyes and scowled.

"There's a significant amount of evidence against you, Mr. Johns, including an eyewitness and substantial forensic evidence. No two ways around it, they'll have an easy time presenting their case to a jury. Is that straight enough?"

Johns' ears flattened as he nodded.

"Now, before we even get to the felony burglary and home invasion charges, I have to advise you that the fact you were arrested possessing a firearm really complicates things."

Johns pulled out another cigarette. "How so?"

Cresi explained that the prosecutor had already filed a death penalty motion with the court, and word was the judge had agreed. The lawyer then laid out the case for negotiating a plea. When he suggested that Johns plead guilty to manslaughter to avoid the death penalty, Johns shot out of his chair, sending it clamoring to the floor.

"You fucking kidding me? I ain't spending the rest of my life in this shithole!"

Cresi moved his hand closer to the buzzer. "Uh, it was only a suggestion. Let's take it easy now. I'm trying to protect you."

"Protect me, my ass!"

Cresi hit the button. "Look, we've got to maintain our heads here."

The door swung open and two guards rushed in. "Get your ass in the chair, punk!" a guard barked.

Johns' eyes narrowed behind his John Lennon glasses, but he took a seat.

"You through here, Counselor?"

Cresi eyed Johns. "Stay close, but give us another five, okay?"

***

Luca sat, took the file from Duro and flipped to the inventory of items seized during the search of Jimmy Johns' apartment. But a moment after his ass hit the chair, he popped back up. "I gotta see this firsthand!"

"Ain't gonna happen," Duro said, "unless you want to ask Gesso to put you on the case as my assistant."

"Come on, Matty."

"Hey, I don't write the rules."

"I need to see it."

"You know I can't do that, Frank. Gesso will have my ass if he found out, especially if he knew it was you."

"I just want to take a glance, man. Just give me twenty, thirty minutes. Come on, man. It'd really mean a lot to me."

Duro studied Luca and lowered his voice. "Fifteen minutes, max, you hear? Not a second more."

"You da man, Duro."

Duro frowned. "You're gonna owe me, Frank. Just remember when I come to collect."

"Sure, sure, Matty."

Duro checked his watch. "Meet me down in evidence in an hour."

Luca presented his evidence request on an older case and waited in a caged area. Two boxes were brought in for him and placed on the long, metal table. Luca signed for the goods and pretended to examine the contents as the officer left.

Luca was rummaging through the second box when he heard Duro being escorted in. They traded banter while the guard retrieved Duro's request. The officer brought in Duro's evidence and had him sign for it.

When the officer left, Duro slid two boxes toward the middle of the table. He then unloaded some of the contents of one box and whispered, "Your fifteen starts now."

Luca quickly sorted through the assortment of pocketbooks on the table before moving to the box. He pulled out a couple of Hummel figurines before grabbing a beat-up wallet. Luca opened the wallet, but outside of a picture of a little girl in a ballet outfit and a totally faded receipt, it seemed clueless. He opened the center and grabbed a library card, but tossed the wallet aside when he saw it was issued to a Martin Whitney.

Luca moved on to the next box as Duro said, "Tick tock, tick tock."

Luca pulled out a beat-up bracelet that was sitting on a bad knockoff of a Prada bag. When he pulled the fake bag out he saw a wallet that seemed to speak to him. Luca paused before lifting it out. He checked the outside for any markings before opening it up. The top of a frayed white card stuck out of a slot on the right side. He slowly pushed it up with his thumb, like a poker player squeezing out his next card. The Horizon name and the logo of Blue Cross Blue Shield emerged as Luca held his breath and yanked the rest out.

The detective exhaled, shook his head, and whispered, "Damn."

Chapter 35

Lou Cresi waited to see his client in a dimly lit room walled in stone. The old New Jersey State Prison had the distinction of being both the oldest and the only completely maximum security facility the Garden State had.

The attorney shifted in his chair and shook off a chill, lamenting the depressing atmosphere he knew wore away at its occupants. Though the penitentiary, which was originally built in 1798, had expanded and was modernized over the years, the place never failed to give Cresi the creeps.

Cresi checked his watch and shook his head. He flipped open Johns' file to insert his visit receipt when he noticed the receipt said Johns was being held in Block E. That meant Johns was kept deep in the bowels of the structure, next to New Jersey's only death row, and would take time to arrive.

The lawyer shook his head thinking he couldn't wait to get this case behind him. He got up and paced the room to generate some heat and while away the time. He was deep in thought about a disturbing new case when the clanging of an interior door brought him back to the matter at hand.

A red, flashing light over the door lit up, and a buzzer sounded seconds before the door creaked open. Johns, shackled hands to feet, shuffled in as Cresi took his seat before the guards could say anything.

Johns' hands were unshackled from his feet but recuffed to the table. As the guards retreated, the prisoner bent forward and worked a pack of Newports out of his pocket.

"Let me get that for you." Cresi got up, grabbed the matches and lit the cigarette.

Johns nodded an acknowledgment.

"You look, uh . . . you okay, Jimmy?"

Johns nodded, then coughed as he bent forward to take a drag. "I've been in a few joints, but this shithole takes the cake. How's my sis?"

"She's doing fine. I spoke to her yesterday."

"Yeah, what about?"

"She was frustrated that visiting rights are severely limited here."

The prisoner cleared his throat. "Like everything else."

"You getting any time outside the cell?"

"Fucking thirty minutes by myself."

Cresi jotted a note. "Let me see if I can do anything."

"This is bullshit. I'm being treated like I've been convicted already."

Cresi pinched the knot in his tie. "You've got to understand, as I mentioned in our last meeting, the state has a strong case, an exceedingly strong case against you."

Johns' ears flattened. "Ain't it your fucking job to get me out of here?"

Cresi shook his head. "Miracle worker I'm not, Jimmy." Cresi clasped his hands. "I've been through all the evidence the prosecutor has put together at this point, and it's compelling." Cresi unhooked his hands and laid them on the table. "The fact that they have you where you are, in Block E, speaks directly of it." Cresi rapped his thumbs on the table. "Now, the last time we talked about a plea, you were upset, and I understand that, but you've got to trust me on this. I truly think it is the best course of action."

Johns pulled a hard drag on the cigarette. "What kinda deal can we make?"

Cresi couldn't believe Johns was talking like he held some ace in the hole. Cresi gathered his thoughts before saying, "It's hard to tell, but it's early yet, and if we approach them before they spend any resources on the case, well, that's a big plus."

Johns pulled an earlobe and spit out some phlegm but said nothing.

"Now, we've got to lean hard on the substance-abuse angle. You were under the influence, etcetera, etcetera."

Johns slowly nodded and grimaced as he reached for his back.

"Now, you've got to be willing to go into rehab. You're okay with that, no?"

"Yeah." Johns flipped his burning butt into an aluminum tray and immediately reached for his pack.

Cresi helped him with another smoke, hoping Johns would choke to death before he had to explain the process of pleading. Cresi continually stressed the part about saving his life, which had worked like an elixir in prior cases.

"But I ain't agreeing to nothing that don't give me a shot at parole. You hear?"

"I don't know, Jimmy. They'll resist the idea, but let me work on it."

Secretly hoping his client would rot in prison, Cresi worked out a deal with prosecutors to get the case off his desk. However, despite Cresi's sense that Johns finally realized he was in deep trouble, he knew it would be a tough sell. The lawyer had a strategy to convince Johns it was a good deal and put his idea in motion.

***

"Hello Jessica, it's Lou Cresi."

"Oh, hi Mr. Cresi. Is everything all right?"

"Yes, fine, fine. There's no need for formalities, Jessica. Please, call me Lou."

"You sure?"

"Of course. Listen, I've got great news regarding Jimmy's case."

"Really?"

"It wasn't easy, but I was able to negotiate a plea to a reduced charge."

"Does Jimmy have to go to prison?"

"I'm afraid so, Jessica. Jimmy is facing very serious charges, and as you know, the death penalty. I don't mean to bring bad tidings, but my contacts tell me he would be fast-tracked on the death penalty phase. I'm afraid it would be a certainty."

"Oh my God."

"I know, but that's what makes this deal so attractive. Instead of first-degree murder, Jimmy would plead to manslaughter and only receive a twenty-year term."

"Twenty years!"

"It may seem like a long time, but it's much better than death row, Jessica. Besides, he'll be eligible for parole."

"How long would that take?"

"It'd be some years before eligibility, but let's not get ahead of ourselves. The important thing is he would avoid being put to death."

"I know you're right. We can't let that happen. It's just that twenty years—I don't know how Jimmy'll make it."

"Exactly. Now, I was able to get a couple of excellent concessions, and I'll tell you, it wasn't easy."

"What do you mean?"

"Well, first off, he'd be moved from that, and excuse my language here, hellhole called Block E. That place is just terrible, inhuman, if you ask me. I've got half a mind to file a lawsuit to prevent any poor soul from being put in that dungeon."

"Jimmy'd like that."

"And the best part is it would enable you to visit him much more frequently."

"Oh, that's great. It's been hard on both of us."

"I can imagine. Family is all you got, you know."

"Nothing truer than that, Mr. Cresi."

"Lou, please, it's Lou. Now, I don't know if Jimmy mentioned this to you or not, but he's been restricted, really isolated, but if he accepts the deal, he'd be in the regular population, and that'd mean daily time in the general pen. He'd be able to be outside every day, socializing with the other inmates."

"That'd make things easier for Jimmy, for sure. He's gonna like that, Mr., ah, Lou."

"There you go, Jess. Now, I don't want to be seen as talking out of school, but Jimmy, he can be stubborn at times, not that we all can't be. It's just that I don't want this special deal to be pulled by the prosecutors."

"They can do that?"

"Unfortunately, they can. That's why we've got to move quickly on this, and if need be, you know, kinda help show Jimmy what a good deal this is."

"He's just got to take it."

"That's how I feel, Jessica. I just think it's important for you to convey your feelings to him on this."

***

I watched Vinny and his escort get buzzed through the door to the visitor hall. It was a Saturday, and the place was packed with families visiting their imprisoned family members. Vinny saw me waiting by myself at a table and waved to me.

I stood, waved, and smiled as Vinny approached. "Hey, good to see you, Vin." I hugged my brother. It *was* great to see him.

"You okay?"

"I'm good."

"You sure?"

"Yeah, I think I'm good. I really am."

Vinny noticed that one of the arms of my eyeglasses was missing, causing my glasses to tilt. "What happened to your glasses?"

"Uh, yeah, I was working the seeder, and when I bent down, they came off, and I kinda fell trying to get them and snapped an arm off."

"You've got to use your cane, Peter. How many times do I gotta tell you?"

"I know, I know. They're gonna get me new ones, though." I pursed my lips. "But we gotta pay for them."

Vinny dug out his J deposit form receipt and handed it to me. "It's okay. I just put in a hundred for you. That should cover it."

I hated taking money from him all the time. "Thanks."

"You been taking your meds?"

"Yep."

"All of them?"

He still thought I couldn't remember anything. "Of course."

Vinny was visibly relieved that I didn't exhibit signs that I was going off the rails, which I thought was amusing. He smiled and asked, "So what you been doing all week?"

"Been busy. I know it's a jail and all, but you know I like gardening, and here I get to work on a farm, and it's fun. The day goes by in a flash."

We spent the rest of the hour talking and making plans for when I'd get out.

***

Johns lifted his head off the cot when he heard the buzzer echo through the cell block. His interest piqued when he identified two sets of footsteps making their way down the corridor. Johns lay back down and reached for a pack of Newports but was taken by surprise when the hatch on his door was unlocked.

"Stick 'em through, Johns!"

Johns grabbed his glasses and swung his legs off the cot. He stood at the door and put his hands through the opening to be cuffed.

"Step back!"

The prisoner stepped back, and the heavy door creaked open.

"Where you taking me?"

"You got a visitor."

Johns checked the date in his head, knowing he wasn't eligible for a visit. "What, you having an open house?"

"Shut up and march!"

Johns was ushered into a windowless room and cuffed to a steel table that was bolted to the floor. As the guards retreated, Johns asked, "Hey, you got a smoke? I left mine in the cell."

The guards smiled at each other. "Guess you're shit out of luck, then."

"Fuck you too!"

Johns mulled over the last visit with his lawyer and the plea agreement, figuring it was Cresi who wanted his answer. When the door opened and his sister was escorted into the room, Johns tried to jump out of his seat but was restrained by the handcuffs. "Jess! How'd you get in?"

Johns' sister smiled as he coughed. "Mr. Cresi pulled some strings." She kissed her brother and sat down. "You don't look so good, Jimmy."

"You got any smokes?"

"You know I don't smoke, Jimmy, and listen to you, coughing all the time. Why don't you try and quit? It'd be good for you."

"Come on, sis. Get off my back, will you?"

"Okay, okay, it's just that I get worried about you, that's all. I'm sorry, but I care." Jessica took a seat. "Oh, here's the J receipt." She stuffed the receipt in his pocket.

Johns studied his sister. "Are you okay, sis? You look, I don't know, real pale."

Jessica's eyes welled up. "I'm okay, Jimmy. I'm just worried about you, that's all."

"Don't worry about me, you hear? You take care of yourself."

She sniffled and wiped a tear from her face. When her lips started to quiver, Johns tried to change the subject. "So, how'd you get in here, what, two and a half weeks early?"

"I know. I was surprised when Mr. Cresi called me and said I could come to see you. He said I'd be able to visit regularly when you take the plea 'cause you'll be moved to the regular population."

Johns had a coughing fit. "Ain't made no decision on no damn plea."

"But Jimmy, Mr. Cresi said if you plea, then you won't have to, you know, go through a horrible trial and all. And he says the prosecutor is pushing for the death penalty." Jessica leaned forward. "Oh Jimmy, we can't take a chance. You'll be able to save your life. If something happens to you, I don't know what I'd—"

"If I can get me a chance at parole, I'm thinking I'd take it."

"Oh good, Jimmy. Mr. Cresi, he said it's possible, and I think if you can get help and get clean, for good this time." She studied her brother "You're not using in here, are you?"

"Shit, Jess, they got me locked up by myself all the time."

"Poor thing. It must be real tough on you, Jimmy, but Mr. Cresi said you'd be getting regular visits with the plea, and I'd be here as much as I could."

***

I shifted my glance between the door and the clock. Where the heck was he? Vinny was never late. I hoped he was okay. Finally, the door swung open, and Vinny rushed into the visitor's room. I stood and waved.

We embraced, and when we broke, Vinny checked his watch. "These motherfuckers!"

"What's the matter?"

"Can't you see what I'm wearing? They gave me a frigging hassle over my shirt."

"Shirt? What do you mean?"

"I was wearing my FedEx shirt. I'm going to work the night shift after this, but they got some cockamamy rule about delivery uniforms— said it was against rules. What bullshit. What do they think, I'm gonna sneak you out or something?"

"It's okay, relax."

"I know. I'm sorry. It's just that—ah, forget it. How you doing?"

"I'm okay. What's going on with you?"

"Well, remember last Wednesday, I told you I had to tell you something?"

What I remembered was him telling me not to forget to do things, and I nodded to pacify him.

"Well, look, I spoke to Luca, Detective Luca. You remember him?"

I nodded. Like I could forget the guy who interrogated me.

"Well, he told me about the guy he always thought might've been involved in Billy's murder. You remember that guy, Jimmy Johns."

"What about him?"

"Well, they got him red-handed in a murder case right after you came in here. Luca said he was going to push him to see what he could get out of him on Billy's case."

"Sounds like a long shot."

"I don't know, maybe he was the one who did it, and you can get the hell out of this shithole."

"Yeah, maybe, but it really ain't too bad here, Vin. Don't worry. I'm fine with everything." I smiled as wide as I could. "You know I like the farmwork we do here. Who knows, maybe when I get out we can move and get us a farm and work it together."

"Yeah, maybe."

Chapter 36

Luca watched as Monmouth County Prosecutor Stanley read a statement to the reporters assembled outside his office. The detective smirked when Stanley touted the plea arrangement he reached with Jimmy Johns as a win both for crime solving and for the taxpayers. Luca acknowledged how smooth an operator Stanley was as he watched him bat away concerns about a possible parole for Johns with both the cost-saving benefits and the certainty that the plea brought.

When a question came up about foregoing the death penalty, Stanley spat out statistics to support the position that capital punishment was ineffective in reducing murder rates. Luca considered the position questionable, at best, and it certainly disappointed those who clamored for an eye for an eye. Luca enjoyed it when the prosecutor was challenged about the costs to keep a prisoner incarcerated for life, but Luca was sorely disappointed when Stanley dismissed the cost-benefit claims of capital punishment when he cited the costs of endless appeals. On that, he ended the press gathering.

Luca headed back to his office. He was filling in his partner on Stanley's performance when his phone rang.

"What you got for me, Matt?" Luca listened and protested. "Ah, come on, man. You gotta lean on him." Luca rolled his eyes, shook his head, and said, "Yeah, sure. Thanks anyway." Luca hung up the phone.

Cremora asked, "Duro get anything?"

"Zippo. Said Johns got the wallet from somebody else, blah blah blah. Same old bullshit."

"It doesn't jibe."

"Tell me about it. When we nailed Johns with Wyatt's credit card, he said he bought it. Now we know he had the wallet."

A uniformed officer poked his head in the detective's office. "Sarge said they're ready to get started."

Luca nodded at the officer and said to his partner as he grabbed his jacket, "How's a cop gonna get anything done around here when all we do is pat ourselves on the back?"

Luca entered the pressroom behind Sergeant Gesso, Prosecutor Stanley, and Captain Fusco. The detective stood to the right of the podium and shifted his weight from foot to foot as Stanley droned on. Luca wasn't one for attention, but he couldn't help realizing that Stanley always spoke in the "I" vernacular and never mentioned anyone else by name when doling out credit.

The prosecutor finally turned the mic over to Captain Fusco. Luca cringed when his superior began with, "The department is grateful to Prosecutor Stanley. It is his office's vigorous enforcement of the forfeiture statutes that provide much-needed resources to our department. The additional funding we receive through the seizure of assets involved in the commission of crimes enhances our ability to protect our citizens, not to mention, the loss of these assets exacts a toll on those engaged in crime," Fusco said.

Fusco surveyed the room and got serious. "Over the last five years, police departments throughout Monmouth County have been the recipients of over fifteen million dollars. This extra money allows us to increase patrols, surveillance, and to invest in upgraded equipment. I know there are some out there who believe the seizure program is controversial."

Suddenly, all eyes shifted to Luca, who had spat out, "That could work."

Luca covered his outburst by coughing and stood at attention as Fusco finished his statement. The detective's mind raced as he was called up to the podium by Fusco.

"And now we'd like to call Detective Luca up to receive his citation."

Luca shook hands with Fusco and forced himself to focus on the matters at hand as Sergeant Gesso handed a framed award to Fusco.

"We are proud to honor Detective Luca for the critical role he played in the largest forfeiture in the county's history."

Though distracted as he accepted the accolade, Luca made sure to give a special thanks to Gesso before retreating from the podium.

***

"You're doing what?"

"Going to see Johns."

"Frank, have you lost it? I thought Sergeant Gesso warned you about this witch hunt."

"It ain't no witch hunt, Deb. And besides, Gesso owes me one. He won't mind."

"Nobody owes anyone anything, least of all your boss. So, don't throw me the bull dinky, Frank."

"No, really, Deb. After that big seizure I brought in, the precinct got a nice chunk of change, and Gesso's like a pig in shit."

"You told him you were going to see Johns?"

"Not exactly, but you know, I said I had a new lead on Johns and was gonna follow it up."

"You like playing with fire, don't you?"

"It's gonna be all right. This is the last time, I swear. If nothing pans out, I'm wiping him and the whole frigging thing out of my mind."

"Yeah, sure, just like Barrow."

***

On his way out of the station, Luca popped his head into Matt Duro's office. "Yo, Matty."

"Hey, Luc, I know you ain't got much, but how's it hanging?"

"At least I don't need tweezers to take a whiz."

Duro laughed. "What's up?"

"Just want to let you know I ran into Johns' sister."

Duro cocked his head. "Yeah, and where was that?"

"Uh, her house."

Detective Duro pushed away from his desk. "That's my damn case, Luca, and it's a closed one! What the fuck are you up to now?"

"Take it easy, Duro. Just trying to clear up a thing or two."

"Bullshit. You tell me what the fuck is going on, or I'm gonna let Sarge know your sticking your big nose where it shouldn't be."

"It's no big deal, Matt. Don't go making a federal case out of it, okay?"

Duro stood up. "Look, you gonna open up, or am I going to Gesso?"

Luca sat down. "Okay, okay. Look, I was thinking this over, and you know me, sometimes I get anal."

"You're telling me."

"So anyway, I went to see Jessica Johns, okay? I thought since you guys recovered Billy Wyatt's wallet from her house, that she could shed some light on how it and other stolen goods ended up in her house."

"How the fuck you think? Her brother's a damn thief."

Luca put up his hands. "I know, I know, but I mean, damn, she lives there, and she must know something."

"Don't you think we talked to her? What d'ya think, this is our first case?"

"Come on, Matty. We're on the same side."

"Yeah, sure, that's why you go sneaking behind my back."

"It's not like that."

"Yeah? What's it like, then?"

"Look, we talked to her too. Didn't get much outta her. She was playing the good sister and all, but now we got something to work with, that's all."

Duro stared at Luca for a moment. "You're a piece of work, Luca. You know what? I don't give a rat's ass what you do with this or anything else. You're on another fucking crusade, but I'm telling you, you get in over your head, don't come running to me, you hear? When Gesso gets wind, I'm not covering, you hear?"

Luca nodded.

"Now get the fuck out of here, Frank."

***

"So how did it go with Duro?"

"Piece of cake."

"Wow, I'd thought he'd be pissed," Cremora told Luca.

"Ya gotta know how to talk to folks, J," Luca said. "It comes in handy from time to time."

"So how you wanna play this?"

"Get on the horn with Jessica Johns. Make it like you're with the, let's say the New Jersey, ah, Forfeiture Division, or something. You know, nothing formal, just windmill her. Use your cell, but don't worry, I already checked. She ain't got caller ID."

Cremora took her number from Luca. "Okay, what's the angle?"

Luca sketched out the way he envisioned things, and Cremora picked up the phone. Luca sat on the edge of his partner's desk, silently coaching with his hands as Cremora played his role. JJ finished the four-minute call by promising to call her before the paperwork was going to be filed with the courts.

Luca leapt up. "How'd she sound?"

"I don't like this shit, Frank."

"Necessary evil. Besides, she's gonna be fine. What'd she say?"

"Shit her pants, is what. When I told her we were filing to take the house, she started begging. Said she couldn't understand how it could happen. Anyway, you better get moving before she gets a lawyer involved. She was freaked out."

Chapter 37

Jimmy Johns was sitting on a picnic bench smoking a cigarette with another inmate when a guard approached. "Let's go, Johns. Someone's here to see you."

Johns coughed. "Now?"

"Yep. Stick 'em out."

The guard cuffed his hands and escorted him to an area where prisoners met with their lawyers. When Johns spied Luca waiting, he said, "Geez, not this guy."

The guard started to cuff him to the table, but Luca waved him off. "It's okay."

"You sure?"

Luca nodded as the guard left, wondering if it was just the orange jumpsuit that made Johns look worse than he'd ever seen him.

"So how's it going, Jimmy?"

"Look, I ain't got to fucking talk with you."

"Whatever you say, my friend, but if you don't, it's not gonna be good for your sister."

"You keep her the fuck out of this. She ain't got nothing to do with this or anything."

"Just a couple of questions, that's all, and if everything's good, she's off the hook."

Johns coughed. "What fucking hook? You're full of shit, Luca."

Luca got up. "Have it your way."

"Hold on now. What the fuck you want, anyway?"

"It's real simple, Jimmy boy. I wanna know what happened to William Wyatt."

"I told you, I had nothing to do with that."

Luca leaned forward. "Yeah, you can say what you want, but I don't believe you. You got a problem with the truth, but you know what? Funny thing is, the truth always seeps out."

Johns silently lit a smoke and had a coughing fit.

"You better lay off the butts before you cough up a lung."

Johns laid the butt on the ash tray.

"Let's see, Jimmy. You said you got Wyatt's credit card, the one you used at 7-Eleven, from some guy."

The prisoner picked up the butt again. "Yeah, that's right. I bought it—happens all the time."

"But you don't know who you bought it from?"

Johns took a deep drag and blew the smoke at Luca. "I don't remember. I was probably jacked up."

"Then the guy we picked up with Wyatt's license fingers you as the supplier."

"I told you, I don't remember. He's gotta be wrong."

"Maybe, but here's the thing, Jimmy. Guess what we found at your sister's house?"

Johns suppressed a cough, licked his lips, and took a drag. "How the fuck should I know?"

Luca slammed his palm on the table. "William Wyatt's wallet, that's what!"

"So fucking what?"

"I'll tell you what I think. I think you went to break into Wyatt's house. Maybe you thought it was empty, or maybe you just didn't give a damn. He surprised you, and you beat him to death. That's what I think."

Johns clenched his teeth and reached for the back of his shoulder. As he massaged it, he said, "Look, man, I took the wallet, okay? But that's all. I didn't do nothing to that guy."

"That's good, Jimmy, coming clean." Luca beckoned with his hand. "So, tell me how it went down."

"It was nothin'. I was out back and saw the door open. So I went in. Saw a wallet, snatched it, and took off."

"Come on, Jimmy. You expect me to believe that?"

"You believe whatever the hell you want. That's the truth."

"Yeah? Well up until a few minutes ago, the truth was you bought it."

"Look, I'm telling you the way it went down."

"Except you left out the part where you bashed his head."

Johns shook his head and cleared his throat. "No, man. I had nothin' to do with that."

"You really expect me to believe that?"

"It's the truth."

"Look, we know you did it. Now, you may not have meant to kill Wyatt, pal, but that's exactly what happened."

"You ain't got nothing on me," Johns said.

"Maybe, but we got something on Jessica."

Johns' face ticked as he pushed his glasses up. "What? What the fuck you got? You think my little sister offed this guy?" Then he smiled. "You know what? You're fucking crazy." Johns laughed. "Yeah, Jess is some badassed killer."

"Close enough for hand grenades, pal, but not quite it. You see, Jessica's obstructed a case, a homicide case."

"You're fucking nuts."

"See how nuts I am when your sister's sitting in the next cell."

Johns' eyes went wild, and he jumped out of his seat.

"Sit the fuck down and listen to me!"

Johns glared at Luca.

"I said sit down. Now!"

Johns rolled a shoulder, winced, and complied.

Luca pointed at Johns. "Your sister is gonna be indicted for obstruction for hiding vital evidence in her home."

"Come on. She didn't even know it was there." Johns stubbed out his butt.

"That's what she'd like us to believe, but we believe she hid it to protect you. She's been protecting you her whole life, ain't she?"

"This is bullshit, and you know it."

Luca shook his head. "It's as serious as it gets, James." Luca leaned back and fingered his tie. "Now there is something you can do. You know, we can make a deal, like what you did on your other case."

Johns tapped another cigarette out. "What the fuck you want from me?"

"The truth, nothing but the truth. You confess to the Wyatt murder, and we drop any charges against your sister."

Johns nearly spit out his cigarette. "What? That's fucking blackmail, man. I didn't do nothing to that guy."

Luca paused to digest Johns' adamancy. "Come on, Jimmy. You don't want Jessica to go to jail, do you?"

"I told you to leave her the fuck out of this."

"Nothing would make me happier. You tell me what happened with Wyatt, and she's free as a bird."

"How many fucking times I gotta tell you, I didn't do nothing to him."

Luca was surprised that Johns wouldn't crack. "So, I guess you're sticking to your story and sending your sister to the slammer for a year or two?"

"Look man, I ain't saying nothing. I feel for Jess, but you're bluffing. She's lily white, man. No judge is gonna give her time for this trumped-up shit you're pushing."

"Guess with all your time in front of judges you've become an expert."

"You're trying to scam me, bitch."

"So, you're gonna keep your mouth shut?"

"Damn right I am."

"So you're comfortable letting this play out and taking the chance she goes away?"

Johns jutted his jaw and nodded.

Luca pushed away from the table. "Okay, if that's your call." Luca started to get up but sat back down. "Oh, there's one other thing."

Johns coughed, flopping his hands onto his lap.

"Your sister has another problem, and this one, well, there's no doubt about it."

Johns leaned forward. "What kinda bullshit you throwin' now?"

"You see, since we found all of your, how do I say it, stuff, in her house, you know, the wallets, the pocketbooks, the drug paraphernalia, and so forth, and well, in the State of New Jersey we have ourselves a forfeiture law. And what that means, my friend, is that your sister's house is going to be seized."

Johns shot of his seat again. "That's total bullshit, man! You fucking cops are jerking us around! You can't do that."

"Sit down before it gets even worse, Jimmy!"

Johns' eyes narrowed behind his granny glasses, and for a second, Luca thought he was going to attack, but Johns sat back down.

"Look here. It may not seem fair, but get over it. The law's the law. And you know what, Jimmy boy? The seizures bring us money to keep punks like you off the street."

Johns' hands were trembling as he lit a cigarette. He inhaled deeply, choking as he exhaled. "This is fucked up, man—really fucked up. You can't do this to her. The house is all she's got. Where the fuck she gonna go?"

Luca softened his voice. "Look, Jimmy, I agree it seems crazy, but that's what's going to happen. Even though Jessica didn't do anything, the law's the law, and the fact is this program brings in money, and the system wants to get its hands on the assets. I don't have to tell you there's no sympathy when money's involved."

"Shit's stacked against the little guy. We're fucking powerless."

"Most of the time, Jimmy, but here, right now, you have a chance to change things. Make a stand for your sister. Turn the tables and help her out for a change. All you got to do is tell me what happened, and she's safe as a baby."

"I didn't do nothing. I swear, man. I wanna talk to my fuckin' lawyer!"

Luca got up. "Talk to anyone you want, but you better move your ass. I'll be back in two, three days max if you feel like talking. Otherwise it'll be too late to stop the process, and Jess's house is a goner."

Chapter 38

Johns waited in line for his turn to use one of the two pay phones. He'd stewed the two days since Luca's visit waiting for his eligibility to make a call. He joined the chorus of inmates telling callers to hurry up as he moved to the front of the line.

Johns grabbed the phone and dug out a quarter from his jumpsuit. He jammed it into the slot and dialed. Jessica quickly accepted the collect call.

"Jess, what's going on?"

"What'd ya mean, Jimmy?"

Johns hacked away.

"Jimmy, you okay? You sound terrible."

"Some detective came around and said you was in trouble. Said you could lose the house."

"I know. I'm really scared, Jimmy."

"Did you talk to Cresi?"

"No, should I?"

"I'll handle this. No fucking way they're gonna drag you into this."

"What'll I do if they take the house, Jimmy? I don't have anywhere to go."

"I said I'll fucking handle it. Now I gotta go."

Johns put his finger on the clicker and scooped out his quarter and stuck it back in. As he started dialing, the next guy in line put his hand on his shoulder. "Hey, it's my turn."

Johns threw an elbow. "Fuck you! I gotta call my lawyer."

"I don't give a shit who you gotta call!"

"Hey man, my sister's ass is on the line. I gotta make the call. I'll give you five smokes."

"Make it ten and you got a deal."

Johns barked at Cresi's secretary to accept the collect call, and she transferred the call to her boss.

"Cresi here."

"Yeah, well it's Johns here, and I got a big fucking problem."

Cresi liked the way that sounded. "Well, I guess so, being in prison."

"Don't be a fucking wise guy."

"What's the problem?"

Johns cleared his throat. "Well, that detective, Luca, came around saying some bullshit that my sister was in trouble and all."

"What kinda trouble?"

"Well, for one, they said she obstructed things, which is bullshit, and then they said they was gonna take her house under the forfeiture laws. That sounds like bullshit."

"Well, I'd have to get more information on the obstruction charge, but it's entirely possible she could have her house seized. The contraband in your apartment gives them grounds."

"What the fuck you talking about? She had nothing to do with it."

"Well, you dragged her in, Jimmy, and New Jersey is desperate for money, and you can be sure they'll be aggressive."

"What can you do?"

"Me? Nothing."

"What d'ya mean—nothing?"

"Once the state starts proceedings, it's a steamroller. You'll never stop it. Nothing anybody can do. It's hopeless."

"Well, this Detective Luca, he said if I told him some things he wanted to know, he could help."

"Look, if you got something they really want, you never know, maybe they could do something. It's worth the attempt to keep your sister in her house."

Johns coughed. "You think so?"

"I've seen it all. Look, I gotta run."

Chapter 39

After showing his credentials, Luca waited to be escorted to see Johns. The detective wondered if Johns was going to take the bait when the guard behind the window called him over. "Hey, Detective, the prisoner's in the infirmary."

"What? What for?"

"How the hell would I know? Half the time they fake it to get out of working."

Luca nodded as he processed the news. "As long as it's nothing contagious, I still gotta see him. It's an important case I'm following. Time is of the essence."

"Your call, Detective. I'll get someone to take you down."

The prison's dingy medical ward was something they hadn't upgraded. A drab beige color added to the hopeless feel the place had. Johns was moaning as he lay on a thin, black pad set on a steel bed. Luca studied him as he approached. Johns looked different, but Luca noticed it was the first time he saw him without his granny glasses and left it at that.

"What's going on, Jimmy?"

Johns winced. "Fucking pain in the back of my shoulder."

"They giving you something for it?"

Johns coughed meekly. "Fucking aspirin, man. It ain't doing shit."

"I guess they gotta be careful what they dish out."

"They'll give me somethin' harder after the X-rays."

"Look, I know you ain't feeling too good right now, but like I told you, if we're gonna stop—"

Johns raised the arm that wasn't cuffed to the bed. "I'll give you what you want, but nothin' better happen to Jessy. You hear?"

"Don't worry, Jimmy. Her house will be safe."

"And none of this obstruction bullshit, either."

"Sure. She'll be in the clear."

"I'm telling you, man. You better keep your word."

Luca yanked out a pocket recorder. "I'll put it all on tape."

Chapter 40

A sky that had turned to dishwater couldn't put a damper on Luca as he breezed into the precinct. He patted the lump in his breast pocket and smiled as he turned the corner into his office.

"Guess what I got us for Christmas?"

Cremora peered over his reading glasses. "Not underwear again?"

Luca whipped out the recorder, placed it on his partner's desk, and rolled over his chair. Luca smiled. "Nope, my boy. I got us Jimmy Johns confessing to the Wyatt murder."

"What?"

"The plan worked, bro. Ole Luca's a genius. Johns sang like Sinatra to get his sister off the hook." Luca looked both ways and lowered his voice. "Not that she was in—anyway, that's between us girls."

Cremora grabbed the recorder. "I gotta hear this."

When Luca clicked the recorder off, he said, "Pretty sweet, huh?"

"I donno, Luc. It kinda seemed like you were leading him a bit."

"What d'ya mean? You heard him. He said he beat Wyatt over the head."

"I know, but—"

"But what? It's the same way we always do. Weren't you listening?"

"Yeah, I guess you're right. It's just hard to believe it after all this time."

"I can't believe it either. We finally got him!" Luca high-fived his partner.

"It was all you, bro. But I gotta admit, I thought you were going off the deep end again."

"Well, you weren't alone."

"So, what's next? I mean, Hill's been put away for this."

"School me. Stanley's going to freak out," Luca said. "Man, I'm gonna enjoy playing this for him."

"You gotta play your cards right here. You make a lot of noise and embarrass him or that egomaniac Weinburg, and—"

"Yeah, I know. Much as I'd like to jam it up his—

Sgt. Gesso blew into the room like a tropical storm. "I told you to keep away from Johns. Now we've got some mess on our hands."

"Come on, Sarge. The Hill kid didn't do it. I wouldn't call that a mess."

Gesso shook his head. "You're right, Luca."

"You mean again?"

Gesso's eyes flashed fire. "Don't push it!"

Luca put a hand up and spun the recorder with the other.

"Okay, let's hear what you got."

Gesso took his hands off the desk when the tape ended and nodded slowly.

"Good work, Frank. Damn good work. Now we've got to do this right with Stanley. We've got to handle this internally. Keep it quiet. For God's sake, don't be running to the press."

Luca said, "Nobody knows but us."

"Good, good. Let me go to Stanley—alone—okay?"

"It's your call, Sarge. Whatever you say."

Gesso turned to Cremora. "Boy, how many times have I heard him say that?"

Gesso picked up the recorder and turned to leave.

"Hey Sarge, what about the Hills?"

"What about 'em?"

"It'd be nice if they knew what has happened."

Gesso wagged his head. "Didn't I just hear you say, 'Whatever you say'? I'm telling you to keep this wrapped up. If word gets out, trust me, this thing will blow up."

***

Luca closed the front door and headed for the stairs.

Debra came out of the kitchen. "So how did it go today?"

Luca undid his tie. "Johns confessed."

"To the Wyatt murder?"

"Yup."

"Well you don't seem happy about it."

"What do want me to do, cartwheels?"

Debra put her hands on her hips. "Every day it's something new with you, Frank. You obsess over this guy, and when you finally . . . oh, oh, I get it now. Now that you don't have something to focus on, some wrong to right—"

"Come on, Deb. It's not like that."

"Yeah, what's it like?"

"Let's just forget this and start over."

Luca backpedaled to the door. He quickly opened and closed it and flashed a smile. "I'm home."

***

Luca straightened his tie as he stepped into Sergeant Gesso's office. "How's it going, Sarge?"

Gesso tightened his lips and nodded to a chair.

Luca gingerly lowered himself into the chair. "How'd it go with Stanley?"

Gesso scratched his neck. "I ain't got to tell you, he wasn't too pleased with what he called"—Gesso fingered quotation marks—"a development."

"Ever the politician."

"Let's keep it to the case for once, okay?"

Luca nodded. "What did he say?"

"Well, I played the confession for him, and then he brought in Weinburg to hear it. They had some concerns about you leading him and also what the motivation was."

"Could be his conscience."

"I threw that out as well."

"Great minds think alike."

"Yeah, but they shot holes in it. Last time he pleaded out but insisted on a chance at parole."

"Like he's got a shot at parole?"

"I know, but what don't jibe is, why he'd risk any chance at parole with a new charge?"

"You know, Johns was in the infirmary. Could be he's really sick and maybe just wants to unload. Maybe it's eating him up."

"I don't know, but they got questions."

Luca threw his hands up. "Lawyers, don't they always?"

"Hey, can't say I blame 'em. They gotta be careful how this goes. Their mitts are all over it."

"What're they going to do?"

Gesso explained that the prosecutor's office was first going to ask a judge for a gag order to prevent any news about the confession—and its repercussions—from leaking out.

"This shit gets out, and the press is gonna be all over Stanley. Not gonna help his campaign."

"Yeah, but it shouldn't be a problem. He's got plenty of friends in the court."

Gesso nodded. "Anyway, after they get the gag in place, they're gonna want to verify the confession. Shouldn't be any issues with that, right, Frank?"

"Yeah, sure. Why should there be?"

Gesso paused, looking straight into Luca's eyes. "Just checking. Well, then they'd take Johns' guilty plea to the judge who took the original plea from Hill and ask him to allow Hill to withdraw the plea."

"And Hill will walk?"

"Yup, but Stanley said he'd have to get a suppression order for that as well. He doesn't want the Hills to run to the press."

"I can't believe Stanley's really gonna play ball here."

"It looks that way, Frank. I know. It kinda caught me by surprise."

Luca nodded. "Not that I'm complaining or anything, but it seems like they just pulled this plan outta their desk drawer."

Gesso cocked his head. "How long you been around, anyway? You think this is the first time anything like this has happened?"

Chapter 41

I couldn't believe the news. Now I knew how people felt when they won the lottery. Nah, this was frigging bigger than winning Powerball. When Vinny told me that Jimmy Johns had confessed to killing Billy Wyatt, I was confused as all hell, just blown away. I mean, why would he do that? I know he was in jail and all for murder, but helping me out? I didn't even know the guy. Did I?

Anyway, we agreed to keep quiet about it all. I mean, I felt so lucky, I wouldn't be saying anything to anyone. In fact I wanted to disappear before I woke up and realized it was a dream. Maybe I should go down to Texas with Vinny. Last thing I wanted was another reversal. I wanted to get away from it all, away from Mary, Billy, and fucking New Jersey before it slipped away.

I just can't really believe it—this guy, Jimmy Johns, confesses, and I'm off the hook? Maybe things are evening out for me. First my mom getting sick and all her suffering. Man, that sucked. And Dad—shit. He doesn't deserve that title. He splits when we needed him most. Then to top it off, Mary dumps me for that tyrant Billy? I'd say I was due, man— way overdue. Damn right I was. Who knows, maybe he paid it forward.

***

"Hey Luc, you hear that Johns is dying from lung cancer?"

Luca's gaze shifted from his monitor. "You shitting me?"

Cremora shook his head. "That's what Weinburg told me. Said he received a petition for some mercy release bullshit into hospice."

Luca fell back into his chair. "You know, J; I had a feeling."

Cremora frowned.

"No, I really did. You know, when I went to see him, in the infirmary, he was sick and something he said stuck with me. He said they would give him something stronger for the pain once they saw the X-ray. It was like he knew that he was real sick."

"Think that's what made him fess up and bail out his sister?"

"I donno; could be." Luca lowered his voice. "You know, all along he really denied doing it, even when we cooked up the scheme with his sister. I gotta see him."

"You better hurry. Weinburg said he's in rough shape."

"They gonna let him out?"

"No way, man. Weinburg said Stanley would never allow it. Guess he's not taking any chances the press gets their mitts on the Wyatt debacle."

Luca nodded.

"He's banking the details die with Johns. Can't say I blame him—the case turned into one royal fuckup."

"And how."

Luca checked his watch and picked up the phone. "I'm gonna call, see if I can run down and see Johns. I don't gotta be in court till two."

Luca put the phone gently in its cradle. "Guess that's it. We'll never know."

"What happened?"

"Johns is in a coma. They induced a coma. It's the only way to control the pain. Cancer spread to the bones, and this guy said he's only got a few days, max. Pain meds affect the breathing, and with his lung cancer . . ."

"I know it's hard to believe, but I kinda feel sorry for the bastard."

Luca's voice trailed off. "I know what you mean. He got what he deserved, but . . ."

The partners remained silent for a minute until Luca said, "You know, this really puts one of my tenets on its head: Sometimes you solve a case but never know what actually happened." Luca shook his head. "Forget about understanding what happened. Now I'm starting to wonder if we really got the right guy."

"I donno, Luc. You ever meet anyone who sucked up a charge unless they really did it?"

"Man, let's just hope it was a real deathbed confession."

Chapter 42

The next morning, as the partners had their coffee, Luca brought up the Wyatt case.

"Come on, Frank. How many frigging times we gonna go over this?"

"I know, it's just—"

"The guy's dead. Hill's out. Geez, get over it." Cremora threw his hands up. "We got cases up the wazoo, so let's move on."

"Okay, okay, but can I walk it through one more time?"

Cremora sighed. "If it'll make you happy, partner."

"So, last night I couldn't sleep, again, and went over the transcript of Johns' confession."

"What? You took a transcript home?"

Luca shrugged.

"Geez, get a life, Frank."

"Excuse me for caring."

"That's what you call it?"

"Anyway, something's bothering me."

"Here we go again."

"Johns said he was out back of Wyatt's."

"Yeah, we know, Frank. We have witnesses."

Luca thrust a palm forward. "Saw the back door open and went in. What's bothering me is he said he saw the wallet on the kitchen counter and took it."

"So? Mary said Wyatt didn't like to carry a wallet."

"Right, but the thing is, Johns was a first-class thief. He could've snatched the wallet and been outta there clean."

"Maybe he was looking for more stuff to steal."

"That fits, and it's what's gnawing at me. Johns was a junkie who stole to support his habit. He needed money for a fix, and he got it with Wyatt's wallet. He should've been hightailing it outta there to get his hit. It just doesn't fit with reality."

"What the fuck don't fit, Frank? The guy was a junkie. By definition, that made him unpredictable."

Luca rolled his chair over. "I've been thinking a lot about how we got him to confess with his sister and all. And now, knowing the guy was sick as hell, I mean, the guy was a scumbag, no doubt, but I don't know, maybe I was too anxious to nail him."

"Look, Frank, I know I'm talking to the wall, but you gotta put this behind you. You gotta find a way to move on."

Luca nodded.

Cremora stood. "Let's get moving. We've got a full plate to deal with."

Luca and Cremora entered the precinct after a day of running down leads on a second double homicide in the county—this time in Neptune. Luca stopped at a secretary's desk and grabbed a fistful of message slips. As the partners headed to their office, Luca stopped to chat with a curvaceous policewoman who had transferred in from Ocean Township.

Cremora had to pry his partner away, and Luca lamented, "Damn shame to hide such fine china in a uniform."

"You're a piece of work."

Luca smiled and flipped through the messages before he handed them off. "I ain't hanging around. Nothing here seems to be boiling."

"Maybe you can catch her in the parking lot."

Luca shut his computer down. "Very funny, wise guy."

Cremora thumbed the messages. "There's two from Franco. You're not calling your buddy back?"

"I promised him I'd help him at St. Mark's soup kitchen this weekend."

Cremora reached for his ringing phone. "Ever the saint, ain't you?"

"Look, I gotta go. I'm meeting Deb at Zoes. If I'm late again she'll have my head."

Luca grabbed his jacket as Cremora spoke into the phone. "Hey, Franco, how you doing?"

Luca waved at his partner, who told the caller, "No, he just left. Anything I can help you with?"

Cremora nodded and held up a forefinger to Luca. "Okay, okay, maybe I can catch him in the parking lot. You know how he likes to chat up the girls on the way out."

"Ha ha. What did he want?"

"Wants you to head straight down to Freehold."

"What? Now?"

"Yup, *sobito*. You're not gonna believe it, but it's about Johns."

Luca checked his watch. "He's dead, and I ain't got the time. Deb will skin me alive." He reached for the phone. "I'll call him instead."

Cremora watched his partner's face break out into a huge smile as he spoke to Franco. When Luca hung up, he threw up his hands. "Man, what a frigging roller coaster."

"What's up?"

"You're not gonna believe it, but it really was Johns who killed Wyatt."

"How did he know that?"

"Franco confirmed the blood on the shirt was Wyatt's."

"What shirt?"

"The tee shirt we got from Johns' car."

"But they said it wasn't a match."

"Yeah, school me. But thank God for the Jordan case. After that one, the department mandated all crime scene blood samples to be checked for matches in the database; you know, looking for links to other cases."

"Yeah, I heard about that."

"Anyway, they ran the blood, and bingo, they got a hit on the Wyatt case."

"You're losing me."

"When the lab results from that double homicide in Cliffwood Beach produced a match with the Wyatt case, they told Franco."

Cremora nodded as Luca continued. "When Franco saw it was Wyatt's, he pulled the evidence out. He questioned it, probably because of all the fuss I'd been making. He reran the test on the shirt. The results confirmed it was Wyatt's blood all the time."

"You shitting me? How the hell did this happen?"

"Said the lab might've switched samples, or maybe they could've tested the same one twice or something."

"Geez, what frigging clowns. That could've saved us a whole lot of heartache."

"Man, I can't believe it, but at least we know it was Johns."

"Yeah, but I just wish we knew what really happened that night."

"It doesn't matter, Luc."

"It does to me."

"You know what you say: 'You can solve a crime and not know what really happened.'"

"Guess you got me there, partner."

Cremora smiled. "Make it a real celebration tonight."

Luca nodded as he reached for his jacket. "Oh yeah, I'd better get going."

The End

Thank you for taking the time to read *Am I the Killer?* If you enjoyed it, please consider telling a friend or posting a short review. Word of mouth is an author's best friend.—Thank you, Dan

Dan has a monthly newsletter that features his writing, articles on Self Esteem & Confidence building, as well as educational pieces on wine. He also spotlights other author's books that are on sale.

Visit Dan's Website: http://danpetrosini.com/

Other Books by Dan

Luca Mystery Series

Am I the Killer—Book 1

Vanished—Book 2

The Serenity Murder—Book 3

Third Chances—Book 4

A Cold, Hard Case—Book 5

Cop or Killer?—Book 6

Silencing Salter—Book 7

A Killer Missteps—Book 8

Uncertain Stakes—Book 9

The Grandpa Killer—Book 10

Dangerous Revenge—Book 11

Where Are They—Book 12

Burried at the Lake—Book 13

Suspenseful Secrets

Cory's Dilemma—Book 1

Cory's Flight—Book 2\

Cory's Shift—Book 3

Other works by Dan Petrosini

The Final Enemy

Complicit Witness

Push Back

Ambition Cliff